The 'old woman' didn't restrict her attentions to Gertrude. Still displaying the rapidity which had replaced her earlier slow and doddering movements, she advanced further into the car. So swiftly was she acting that none of the men were prepared for her. Before any of them could move her right foot went to the seat of Basnett's trousers and shoved sharply to propel him forward. Losing his hat and with the revolver flying from his grasp, he landed in a helpless sprawl face down across the table. A strong hand dug on either side of his head into his black hair, raising and slamming his features against the top of the table. On being released he toppled backwards to land on the floor.

Letting out startled and profane exclamations, the other two men began to turn around. Of the two, Fisher came off worst. Even as he was trying to turn his weapon upon the transformed 'old' woman, he saw the handle of her umbrella being swung horizontally in his direction. For just a moment he thought he was beyond its reach. He was wrong, but by then he was unable to fight back . . .

J.T. EDSON

J.T.'S LADIES

CORGI BOOKS
A DIVISION OF TRANSWORLD PUBLISHERS LTD

J.T.'S LADIES
A CORGI BOOK 0 552 11223 2

First publication in Great Britain

PRINTING HISTORY
Corgi edition published 1980

Copyright © J. T. Edson 1980

This book is set in 10/10½pt Baskerville

Corgi Books are published by Transworld Publishers Ltd.,
Century House, 61–63 Uxbridge Road,
Ealing, London, W5 5SA.
Made and printed in Great Britain by
Hunt Barnard Printing Ltd., Aylesbury, Bucks.

For Glenys Gibbon, Leslie North and Margaret White, the three most important ladies in the author's life at his 'spiritual' home, the White Lion Hotel, Melton Mowbray.

AUTHOR'S NOTE:

For the benefit of new readers, but to save our 'Old Hands' from repetition, we have given details of the backgrounds and special qualifications of Dawn Drummond-Clayton, Woman Deputy Alice Fayde, Belle 'the Rebel Spy' Boyd and Martha 'Calamity Jane' Canary in the form of Appendices. We also realise that, in our present 'permissive' society, we could employ the actual profanities used by various people who appear in this volume, but we do not concede that a spurious desire to create 'realism' is a valid reason for doing so.

J. T. EDSON,
Active Member, Western Writers of America,
MELTON MOWBRAY,
Leics., England.

CONTENTS

INTRODUCTION

Being an avid reader of the wonderful action-escapism-adventure fiction which had its vintage years from the mid-1930s to the late 1950s, I could not help noticing how small a part was allocated to what my generation could refer respectfully to as the 'gentle sex' without arousing screams of 'male chauvinist pig' from over-reacting supporters of 'Women's Lib'. In fact, with very few exceptions,[1] action-escapism-adventure fiction in books and movies tended to be a masculine domain.[2] Heroines were expected to be beautiful, shapely and virtuous – this being in the days before sexual promiscuity was turned into an apparently essential virtue – but meek, mild and dependent upon the hero for protection when danger threatened. So, on embarking upon my career as a writer,[3] I decided to try to remedy the situation.

[1] Dr Clark 'Doc' Savage Jr and Richard 'The Avenger' Benson, whose biographies are recorded by the exceptionally prolific Kenneth Robeson — which it has been suggested, is actually a 'house name' for a group of writers led by Lester Dent; see *DOC SAVAGE, His Apocolyptic Life* by Philip José Farmer – had respectively Patricia Savage and Nellie Gray among their coterie of 'sidekicks'. However, competent as each lady undoubtedly was, she was never called upon to quell a villainess. In fact, their main function appeared to be falling into straits of dire peril from which either 'Doc' or 'The Avenger' was obliged to rescue them.

[2] Ladies fared somewhat better in Hollywood's action-adventure-escapism movies than in books. As the author pointed out in the Introduction to Calamity Jane's section of *J.T.'s HUNDREDTH*, they were especially useful in 'Westerns' for dealing with a villainess as her sex precluded the hero from being able to handle her as he did with her male associates.

[3] How the author embarked upon his career is told in the main Introduction to: *J.T.'s HUNDREDTH*.

My heroines would be beautiful, shapely, even virtuous.

However, they would not need to be dependent upon *anybody*, except themselves, when in a perilous situation!

Martha 'Calamity Jane' Canary was the first of my 'Ladies' to take a 'starring' role and, so far, is the only one to have attained the status of a series of her own.[4] However, the lady outlaw, Belle Starr,[5] had preceded her into print by making a 'guest' appearance in my second published work, *Part Four, Mark Counter In 'A Lady Known As Belle'*, THE HARD RIDERS. She had also made another 'guest' appearance in *Case One, 'The Set-Up'*, SAGEBRUSH SLEUTH and paved the way for Calamity to appear by there being a reference to a scar on her hand which was acquired when they had fought with one another on their first meeting.

As my editor and secretary can tell you, writers do not function in the same way as normal human beings. Or, at least, I don't. This is proved by the fact that Calamity's first appearance in print, which took place in *Part One, 'Better Than Calamity'*, THE WILDCATS, came before the episode in which her first meeting with Belle Starr and Mark Counter was published in *Part One, 'The Bounty On Belle Starr's Scalp'*, TROUBLED RANGE. So, as both books are

---

[4] For the benefit of new readers, details of Martha 'Calamity Jane' Canary's background and special qualifications are given in *APPENDIX ONE*.

[5] How Belle Starr met Mark Counter and the progress of their association is told in: *Part One, 'The Bounty On Belle Starr's Scalp, TROUBLED RANGE; RANGELAND HERCULES; THE BAD BUNCH; THE GENTLE GIANT; Part Two, The Floating Outfit Series, Mark Counter in 'We Hang Horse Thieves High, J.T.'s HUNDREDTH; Part Four, Mark Counter in 'A Lady Known As Belle', THE HARD RIDERS* and how it ended is recorded in: *GUNS IN THE NIGHT*. Belle also makes 'guest' appearances in *HELL IN THE PALO DURO, GO BACK TO HELL, THE QUEST FOR BOWIE'S BLADE* and *Case One, 'The Set-Up', SAGEBRUSH SLEUTH*. We have occasionally been asked why it is that the Belle Starr we describe is so different from the photographs which appear in various books. The researches of fictionist genealogist Philip José Farmer, q.v., have established that the 'Belle Starr' in our works is not the same person as another equally famous bearer of the same name. However, the Hardin, Fog and Blaze clan have asked that we and Mr Farmer keep her true identity a secret and we intend to do so.

in the Floating Outfit series and 'star' Mark Counter, we have the somewhat peculiar state of affairs wherein Calamity had already had her first printed meeting with him before she had met him chronologically.

I have already described how Calamity developed the status of having her own series in the Introduction to her section of J.T.'s HUNDREDTH. I also explained in the same volume how I brought Belle 'the Rebel Spy' Boyd's adventures into print.[6] Although Belle has not yet attained her own series, she has played a major role in several volumes. In fact, she was the 'star' in her own right in TO ARMS! TO ARMS! IN DIXIE! and THE REMITTANCE KID, with the respective heroes supporting her. However, these titles are listed for convenience in the Floating Outfit and Calamity Jane series.

In spite of having been mentioned several times since the first of my books, TRAIL BOSS, appeared in 1961, Betty Hardin did not come on the scene in person until 1963. Her appearance is another example of how the mind of this particular writer functions. Although Betty is married to Johnny Raybold in GUNSMOKE THUNDER,[7] her original meeting with him was not described until THE RIO HONDO WAR was published in 1964. Nor were her talents at *ju-jitsu* and *karate*, learned from Tommy Okasi,[8] the Japanese 'valet' of her 'grandfather', General Jackson Baines

---

[6] Details of the background and special qualifications of Belle 'the Rebel Spy' Boyd are given in *APPENDIX TWO*.

[7] The author wishes to state that *GUNSMOKE THUNDER* was not our title. Our choice was *COMANCHE BLAKE'S GIRL*. However, our publishers at the time of its first printing, Brown Watson, Ltd., made this substitution, without informing us, on the grounds that readers would be put off by the mention of a female name in a Western's title. A similar situation arose when Corgi Books replaced Belle Boyd with a male figure on the cover of *THE WHIP AND THE WAR LANCE* because a wholesaler said a 'cowboy' book had to have a 'cowboy' on the cover or it would not sell. The author considers some form of snobbery is responsible for such reasoning.

[8] The name, 'Tommy Okasi' is an Americanized corruption of the one given by the man in question, a fully qualified *samurai* warrior who had had to leave Japan for reasons which the author is not permitted to disclose, when rescued from a derelict vessel in the China Sea.

13

'Ole Devil' Hardin,[9] exploited to any great extent until THE BAD BUNCH in 1968. What is more, considering her status as a leading member of the Hardin, Fog and Blaze clan, I confess that I have neglected her somewhat. Her section in this volume will, I hope, make amends for my having been so remiss in the past.

Woman Deputy Alice Fayde fared far better than Betty Hardin. Except for in THE SIXTEEN DOLLAR SHOOTER and THE SHERIFF OF ROCKABYE COUNTY, numbers one and two in chronological sequence, although both were written *after* the other titles in the series, Alice has had full 'staring' status ever since THE PROFESSIONAL KILLERS ushered her, her partner Deputy Sheriff Bradford Counter and the other members of the Rockabye County Sheriff's Office on to the printed page in 1968.[10] While she and Brad are not yet partners at the period of the incident, she plays an active role in the Rockabye County series' section, 'Preventive Law Enforcement', J.T.'s HUNDREDTH. She is, in fact, the senior partner in their investigation team and is involved in a greater share of the action than any other female peace officer with whom I have come into contact via books, movies, or television series.

Hollywood in particular seems to have a mental block where the employment of their lady detectives in physical action is concerned. To me, this reached its highest point in one episode of POLICEWOMAN. Having been pushed and locked in a closet by a professional killer, who then set fire to the room, 'Sergeant Pepper Anderson' (Angie Dickinson) the policewoman of the title, did nothing more constructive than bang on the door and shout for the man to let her out. As Alice demonstrated in the past and will continue to do, she is fully capable of protecting herself and would have

[9] Details of General Jackson Baines 'Ole Devil' Hardin's early career and background are given in the author's *Ole Devil Hardin* series. He also appears in the *Civil War* and *Floating Outfit* series. His death is reported in *DOC LEROY, M.D.* His sobriquet, 'Ole Devil' was caused by his Mephistophelian features and because his contemporaries said he was a 'lil ole devil in a fight'.

[10] Details of Woman Deputy Alice Fayde's background and special qualifications, also of the organization of the Rockabye County Sheriff's Office are given in *APPENDIX THREE*.

14

taken much more positive action for her salvation if she had been in 'Sergeant Anderson's' position.

I have covered the background of the creation of the Bunduki series in my Introduction to its section in J.T.'s HUNDREDTH and there is no point in repeating it verbatim.[11] However, although I regard Edgar Rice Burroughs as the greatest action-escapism-adventure writer of all time, I must confess I feel he never exploited his heroines to their full potential. This is especially true of Tarzan of the Apes' wife, Jane. Except in TARZAN'S QUEST, when she made a bow and arrows with which to hunt for food after she and several friends were stranded by a plane crash in the jungle, she rarely demonstrated whatever survival techniques she had learned from her husband.

On being granted permission by Edgar Rice Burroughs Inc. to introduce Dawn Drummond-Clayton[12] and James Allenvale 'Bunduki' Gunn, adoptive great-granddaughter and adopted son of Tarzan of the Apes, I followed my usual habit of allowing the former to be as self-reliant as any of my other Ladies. I considered that, with her background – based upon Philip José Farmer's magnificent TARZAN ALIVE, *A Definitive Biography Of Lord Greystoke* and the family tree he supplies therein – Dawn would be able to cope without needing to scream for help the moment any danger threatened; although, particularly in every 'Tarzan' movie I have seen, this appeared to be all Jane was capable of doing.[13]

---

[11] As the present management of Edgar Rice Burroughs Inc. have rescinded the permission to quote the connection between Dawn Drummond-Clayton, James Allenvale 'Bunduki' Gunn and Tarzan Of The Apes, despite the author offering to share the profits of all future earnings of the *Bunduki* series – including *BUNDUKI, BUNDUKI AND DAWN* and *SACRIFICE FOR THE QUAGGA GOD*, which were in the original agreement – we will be continuing the series without mentioning it, starting with *FEARLESS MASTER OF THE JUNGLE*. We wish to point out, however, that Dawn's parents Sir Armond John and Lady Hazel Drummond-Clayton are the creations of Philip José Farmer, q.v., and he has kindly given us permission to refer to them.

[12] Details of the background and special qualifications of Dawn Drummond-Clayton are given in *APPENDIX FOUR*.

[13] Although in *TARZAN AND THE SLAVE GIRL*, Jane (Vanessa

Amanda 'the School Swot' Tweedle came into being after I saw BLUE MURDER AT ST TRINIANS. In this film, the well endowed actress Sabrina was shown sitting in bed and reading a very thick book despite various distractions going on about her, being referred to as 'the school swot'. That was all she was required to do, but I could see how she could be put to far greater use. On writing to the production company and outlining my idea, I was informed that no more St Trinians' movies would be made. Two more have been, but my plot was never used. Nor, considering the format adopted by the producers, would I have wanted it to be.

However, I *never* forget a good idea for a story.

A few years later, when my name as a successful writer of 'Westerns' was established, hearing various people connected with the British film making business complaining they could not obtain suitable plots for family movies, I unearthed my basic plot and, in collaboration with Peter Clawson, turned out a screen play. To avoid this being a waste of time, as my agent had informed me that — despite the claims we had heard — selling it to the British film producers would be exceedingly difficult if not impossible, I also worked upon the manuscript of what became BLONDE GENIUS. I had altered the basic idea a little and Amanda also was subjected to a change. She was still to be the beautiful, curvaceous kind of 'Mr Belvedere' character as portrayed by the actor, Clifton Webb, in the movies, SITTING PRETTY, MR BELVEDERE GOES TO COLLEGE and MR BELVEDERE RINGS THE BELL, apparently knowing and being able to do practically everything exceptionally well. However, Sabrina had been supplanted as the model for Amanda by the delectable and, I considered, far more suitable Aimi Macdonald.

BLONDE GENIUS was one of the few books I have written to receive the attention of a literary critic. L. F. Lampitt commented most favourably on it in the EVENING

Brown) demonstrated some skill at unarmed combat by defeating the 'slave girl' (Denise Darcel) in a brief tussle, she reverted to type on being captured by the 'baddies' and did nothing except wait to be rescued by Tarzan (Lex Barker).

NEWS, suggesting it would make a suitable movie for the family market.[14] So I hoped this might induce somebody to turn it into a film, but the hope did not materialize. Apparently one has to have a certain social and political background, which I am pleased to say I lack, before one's work is regarded as acceptable by the British film industry. Although disappointed at the time, I am now pleased it was refused as I doubt whether the story would have been adhered to. I would have refused to allow it to be changed to contain the kind of one-sided iconoclastic socio-political diatribe, filled with specious irony and glorifying promiscuity, infidelity, or sexual deviation, which forms the content of most entertainment put out by British film and television production companies. While these are always filled with a 'message', or 'social significance', they rarely offer a single character in whom the audience can take any interest as a person, or feel any concern over what happens to him or her.

While Amanda has previously only appeared in one volume, I have an idea for a second and, as I mentioned

[14] The review, quoted by kind permission of *EVENING NEWS*, *Associated Newspapers Group, Ltd.*, appeared on April the 16th, 1973 and said:
Paperbacks Of The Week
When Lolita Packs A Luger
ST TRINIANS was never like this! Even the most accomplished arsonist in the third form at St T's could not measure up to the least promising junior at Benkinsop's Academy For The Daughters Of Gentlefolk.
Nor could any principal at St T's hope to vie with the headmistress of the Academy — Miss A. P. D. Benkinsop, M.A., B.Sc. (Oxon), etc. etc.
For Miss B., flawlessly beautiful and, in spite of her Bond Street tweed two-piece, as shapely as they come, ran a very special school indeed. Her Folk Dancing classes included the subtle art of fan dancing and strip-tease (and Miss B. was ever ready to show the girls how it *should* be done). The Wise Shopping Course was dedicated to successful shop-lifting, and Home Economics embraced the technical skills of safe-breaking.
As for Amanda, the busty 'School Swot' — could she not, with twin Lugers steadied against her luscious hips, put the contents of two magazines through the same two holes in the window of the gym?
BLONDE GENIUS, by J. T. Edson and Peter Clawson (Corgi 30p), is a rollicking bit of nonsense which cries out for translation into a sort of junior James Bond film. L. F. LAMPITT.

elsewhere, I *never* forget a plot. However, as I explained in the Introduction to Waco's section of J.T.'s HUNDREDTH, my experiences with the DOC LEROY, M.D. syndrome have taught me *never* to refer to a proposed book by its title until work upon the manuscript has at least been commenced.

Anyway, enough of the explanation.
Let's meet J.T.'s LADIES.

PART ONE

Amanda 'The School Swot' Tweedle

In

FIFTEEN, THE HARD WAY

'It's good of you to see us, Amelia,' Maxwell Spender declared, taking the seat he had been offered at the well polished, magnificent antique, yet still functional, desk and hoping the companion he had been compelled to bring would remember the warning he had given with respect to refraining from inserting profanities into every sentence.

Tall, burly, distinguished looking, with dark hair turning grey at the temples, the man who was known to Scotland Yard as the current 'managing director' of the South London and Southern England Crime Consortium, was dressed excellently and in perfect taste. He had the carriage and bearing indicative of military training such as was acquired only in the days when the British Army was still a force to be reckoned with throughout the world. However, his demeanour at that moment was redolent of frustrated annoyance. Yet, while he could – and, on occasion, did – express himself with all the breadth of forceful profanity of the drill sergeant in the Brigade of Guards which he had been, that background – untainted by the 'liberalism' of the so-called 'permissive society' – had also instilled an appreciation of when and where such language was or was not permissible, no matter how justifiable the circumstances were.

The room of the magnificent Georgian mansion to which Spender had fetched his companion definitely came into his category of being a place where even the mildest profanity

19

was out of the question. Particularly when they were in the presence of the revered headmistress of Benkinsop's Academy For The Daughters Of Gentlefolk and one of her pupils.

Decorated and furnished to the height of refinement, so as to express luxury and utility, but devoid of ostentation, the room contrived in a subtle way to combine the atmosphere of all its functions. It was, as the situation warranted, sitting-room, study, or business office. On the walls hung portraits, each by the most celebrated artist of the day, of Miss Amelia Penelope Diana Benkinsop's predecessors as owners of the mansion. From the Regency, through Victorian, Edwardian and World War I to the present incumbent, whose likeness was included, there was a strong family resemblance which was understandable. Every one bore the same name and they were all her ancestors.[1] Each was illustrated wearing the height of her period's fashion and all, even the one posed against the background of what – to a connoisseur of such matters – was clearly a hunting camp in the range country of the United States of America during the mid-1870s,[2] had on a splendid diamond, sapphire and emerald necklace.

[1] The researches of fictionist genealogist Philip José Farmer, q.v., with whom the author consulted have established that the eldest daughter of each successive generation retained the name, 'Amelia Penelope Diana Benkinsop' no matter who her father might be. The current Miss Benkinsop is not only a Master of Arts and Bachelor of Science (Oxon), but was awarded the George Cross – the highest award for valour given to civilians – for her service in British Military Intelligence's little known 'Group Thirteen'; other members being Beryl Snowhill (some of whose career is told in: *'CAP' FOG, TEXAS RANGER, MEET MR J. G. REEDER* and *SACRIFICE FOR THE QUAGGA GOD*) and the parents of Dawn Drummond-Clayton and James Allenvale 'Bunduki' Gunn, q.v. She was also made a Honorary Member of the Holloway Old Girls Association during a period of voluntary incarceration in that prison while obtaining the evidence which helped to break up a combined Nazi and Communist spy ring early in 1940, before Russia went to war with it's former ally, Germany. J.T.E.

[2] The scene represents part of the visit made by that generation's Miss Amelia P. D. Benkinsop to the United States, details of which are *given in: BEGUINAGE IS DEAD!* and *Part Five, 'The "Butcher's" Fiery End'* of this volume. J.T.E.

'It is always a pleasure to receive you, Max,' replied the woman to whom the gratitude had been directed. 'I know your business is urgent, but can I offer you tea?'

While the particular piece of jewellery common to all the portraits had been recovered, along with the rest of Miss Benkinsop's property which was stolen at the misguided instigation of a now defunct leading member of the Mediterranean Syndicate,[3] she was not wearing it at that moment. Her appearance lost nothing because of its omission, for it would not have gone with her attire.

Neither too tall nor too short in height, the headmistress had golden blonde hair treated with the kind of ultra-elegance which a very prominent *coiffeur* in London's West End specialized in creating. It set off her flawless beauty and emphasized the regal distinction of her patrician features perfectly. She was dressed, as was *always* the case when attending to the School's affairs – even if it was granting an interview to a perturbed parent seeking advice on a matter not directly concerning the welfare of any of his three daughters who were her pupils – in the appropriate fashion. The white silk blouse, as crisp as when it was donned that morning, Harris tweed two-piece costume, silk stockings and walking shoes had come from the best establishments in Bond Street specializing in such wares. The garments neither sought to detract from, nor draw attention to, her extremely curvaceous figure. Her age was indeterminate, but she was certainly somewhat older than appearances suggested.[4]

'We'd be pleased to have some,' Spender assented, darting a scowl as the man sitting at his side moved restlessly and displayed other signs of impatience.

'Now,' Miss Benkinsop said, after having passed over the intercom on the desk a request for tea and cakes to be brought in. 'What can we do for you?'

'We've got trouble at the Puppydog Club,' Spender replied, taking two transparent celluloid dice – each with an insignia in the form of an attractive young dog of indeterminate breed on its 'one' surface – and laying them in front

[3] Told in: *BLONDE GENIUS*. J.T.E.
[4] How this came about is explained in the second paragraph of *APPENDIX FOUR*. J.T.E.

21

of the headmistress while continuing with his explanation. 'If it isn't bad enough having those left wingers picketing outside, these have turned up at the big stakes craps table.'

'Hum, most interesting,' Miss Benkinsop declared, showing not the slightest surprise as she picked up the dice. However, after having given them what appeared to be only a very cursory inspection considering they were the reason for the visit, she handed them to the fourth person in the room. 'What do *you* make of them, Amanda?'

The person to whom the question had been directed was a girl of perhaps eighteen. As the light blue collar of her navy blue blazer signified, she was not only a Sixth Former, but one of the Prefects and responsible for helping to maintain the School's discipline. In spite of her youth and appearance, and for all his appreciation of the situation's gravity, Spender did not show the surprise his companion was registering over her being consulted any more than the headmistress had when he produced the dice.

As the only child of a brilliant scientist, albeit one in the classic 'absented-minded professor' mould, Amanda Tweedle did not possess the requisite family background for admission to the School.[5] However, having delivered her there in the erroneous belief that he had arrived at Roedean, her father went away and was killed whilst conducting an experiment before the mistake could be rectified. Not even Miss Benkinsop's vast, if far from conventional, resources had been able to locate a single relation who might have assumed guardianship and responsibility. So, with her usual compassion, she had waived the usually strict conditions of entrance and allowed the little orphan to stay.

The decision had proved remarkably beneficial all round!

Amanda had soon acquired the sobriquet, 'the School Swot', by virtue of her extraordinary ability to absorb all

[5] Benkinsop's Academy For The Daughters Of Gentlefolk accepted pupils from only the very best criminal families. The offspring of ponces, grasses (informers), drug pushers, Socialist millionaires, Communist trade union officials and left wing entertainers – many of whom sought admission in spite of publicly expressing views opposing privilege in schooling for the children of others – were *never* accepted. J.T.E.

kind of knowledge and through a rigid attendance to her studies. Not that she looked anything like the way in which tradition suggested the bearer of such a nickname should be. Convention expected a person imbued with such proclivities to be tall, lanky, plain of features, possibly pimpled, peering owlishly through thick-lensed spectacles and with shoulders rounded by long hours spent poring over books.

Surrounded by a halo of perfectly coiffured blonde hair, Amanda's exceptionally beautiful face bore an expression of demure, almost elfin innocence which could bring out all the protective instincts of even a confirmed misogynist. The School's uniform – a blazer, white blouse, red, white and blue striped tie, navy gymslip reaching to just above the knees, black stockings and matching well polished shoes with heels of moderate height, as prescribed by the headmistress – could not hide the fact that inside the garments was a body with superlative feminine contours.

Although the School Swot was five foot seven in height, she conveyed the impression of being very small and helpless. It was a case, as Spender knew and his companion clearly did not, of appearances being deceptive. She had attained an almost omniscient erudition, to which she was continually adding, and was capable of putting much of what she had learned to practical use. Spender was aware that she could handle a powerful car as well as any top driver on the international racing circuits, or the best 'wheel-man' employed by the Consortium to ensure a safe get-away from a robbery. What was more, not only did she have a knowledge and ability at unarmed combat which put to shame the toughest of his organization's 'minders', but she had also proved herself equally adept in the use of every type of hand-held weapon.

A slight hint of a frown came to Amanda's face as she looked at the six surfaces, then held up and peered through each dice in turn. Watching her, Spender was reminded of a perplexed pixie. Yet he, if not his companion, had no doubt she knew exactly what she was doing. Furthermore, he felt sure she would not only confirm his suspicions, but could in all probability also supply the solution to the problem with which he was faced.

23

An unashamed imitation of the more celebrated inter-national Playboy Club, although catering for a somewhat less wealthy clientele, the Puppydog Club owned by the South London and Southern England Crime Consortium relied upon the proclivity of its members for gambling to provide its main source of revenue. Nor were the profits acquired by cheating. As in every honest casino's games of chance, the odds were so adjusted that the operators were assured a percentage of every wager that was placed came to them – no matter whether the result was for or against the 'house' – and, in the long run they must be the winner.

However, from time immemorial, unscrupulous players had sought for means to nullify the 'house's' advantages. Experience had taught them that the only successful way to achieve this was to reduce the all important percentages. Much thought and ingenuity had been devoted to attaining this desired state of affairs.

The pair of dice which had caused Spender to seek the advice of Miss Benkinsop and the almost omniscient School Swot, despite the opposition and thinly disguised disapproval of his companion, were the end products of such devious experimentation. A fast action game such as 'craps',[6] which was played with only two dice – thereby limiting the various combinations of numbers upon which the decision of each 'throw' and wager depended – was particularly susceptible to such manipulations.

So, having put the matter into the most competent hands he knew, the Consortium's managing director sat back to await the results.

*   *   *   *   *

On seeing the dice and listening to Maxwell Spender's com-ment, Amanda Tweedle had suspected they might be what had once been called 'Dispatchers' and were now generally

[6] The definitive work on the game of 'craps' and most other games of chance using dice is: *SCARNE ON DICE*, by John Scarne with Clayton Rawson. It is a companion volume to that author's equally authoritative work: *SCARNE ON CARDS*. J.T.E.

known as 'Tops'.[7] Her preliminary examination had established this was not the case. As was traditional with honest dice, each was numbered correctly from one to six around the cube and the total of the opposing pairs of surfaces added to seven.

Discovering her original premise was incorrect, the School Swot concluded she was holding a pair of 'loaded' dice. While there was no visible evidence of tampering, she knew a means by which she could ascertain whether this had been carried out. Laying down one of the dice, she gave the other her full attention. Taking it between her right thumb and forefinger as gently as if it was fragile, she held it by two diagonally opposite corners so that its 'one' surface was uppermost. When the cube rotated of its own volition, she repeated the method of holding it with each set of opposite corners in turn and found that only the original pair produced the movement.

'I've never got the hang of doing the "pivot test",' Spender remarked quietly, deducing from the cessation of restless movements that his companion had a similar lack of manual dexterity, as the girl was exchanging the dice and commencing a similar experiment.

'I confess I don't find it easy myself,' Miss Benkinsop replied, but the second man refrained from making any comment. 'In fact, should the need arise and circumstances permit, I prefer to use the "water test".'[8]

---

[7] 'Tops' are also known as 'T's', or 'Mis-spots'. The archaic name, 'Dispatchers' arose from the suggestion that they would send any victim of their use 'to the cleaners' with dispatch. Based upon the inability of the human eye to see unaided around corners, which prevents more than three of the cube's surface being visible to the player at one time – even when a transparent material is used – without picking it up and turning it around, 'Tops' have the numbers of the exposed surface duplicated on the opposing sides, or substituted with different denominations. 'Tops' are made in various combinations – including the rarely used 'Door Pops', on which one dice bears only the numbers six and two, the other having nothing but fives — but their employment in games of chance does not come within the province of this volume. J.T.E.

[8] 'Water test': the suspect dice is lowered into a tall tumbler filled with water and released with each surface uppermost in turn. If it sinks evenly every time, it is not loaded. However, the weights which have been

25

Repeating the 'pivot test' with an equal dexterity, Amanda satisfied herself that her assumption was correct. Gravity had caused the weighted surface of the dice to turn downwards when suspended lightly between the thumb and forefinger. Each dice was designed so that the three higher numbers and the 'six' in particular would finish on top at the end of a 'throw' more frequently than would otherwise have been the case, thereby ruining the long term percentages upon which the 'house's' advantages were based and its profits depended. For all that, she still felt puzzled at the conclusion of the experiment. However, being a well bred young lady, she did not offer to interrupt her elders' conversation.

'All right, Amanda,' Spender said, noticing that the girl had put down the second dice and was looking at him. 'How about it?'

'I must confess I'm puzzled, sir,' the School Swot replied, tapping one of the dice gently with her right forefinger. As in the headmistress's case, her accent was that of an upper class English 'county' gentlewoman; but less authoritative. Rather it sounded properly respectful in the presence of older people and had a slightly lisping intonation which made her seem almost mouse-like. 'They *are* *l*oaded – !'

'Huh!' Spender's companion snorted. 'We didn't need to come all this f – this way to be told *that*!'

The abrupt termination of the profanity the second visitor had been about to utter was caused by a kick on the ankle, accompanied with a prohibitive frown, from the managing director.

Slightly shorter than his superior in the hierarchy of the Consortium, Leonard 'Lenny-Boy' Hotchkiss was burly and powerfully built. If it had not been for a broken nose, a couple of pits and scars on his face – giving it the appearance of having been stepped on, which had happened on two occasions – he would have been passably handsome. Although just as expensively dressed as his companion, his clothing was more garishly 'trendy' and his longish black hair had drawn a brief glance of disapproval from the head-mistress when they were introduced despite having been

inserted cause a loaded dice to turn over when it is placed in water facing upwards. J.T.E.

styled by a fashionable 'gay' hairdresser who catered to all the leading pop stars and television performers.

Acknowledged as the leading junior executive of the Consortium, Hotchkiss had ambitions to rise higher. He was suspected of being disinclined to wait until the voluntary retirement of those above him, as a result of old age, brought his ascension in the natural and orderly fashion. When the Board of Directors had decided that the situation caused by the appearance of the loaded dice was sufficiently serious to warrant calling in outside aid, as the operation of the Puppydog Club was his responsibility, Spender had not been able to refuse when Hotchkiss had asked to be present at the meeting with the experts who were to be employed.

Despite Hotchkiss's present status, he belonged to a family which had not previously ascended from the lower echelons of criminal society and therefore his sisters had not gained acceptance to the school, so he had tended to discount the stories he had heard concerning Miss Benkinsop's establishment and the School Swot's abilities. What was more, he had not cared for being compelled to accept Spender's choice of the way to deal with the predicament. So he was torn between a desire to have the mystery solved before it caused an adverse affect to his aspirations and a hope that it would not happen as a result of the help which the managing director had insisted upon using.

'The fact that they are loaded isn't what I find puzzling – sir,' Amanda corrected and, in spite of her apparently gentle tone of apology, there was something about how she looked at Hotchkiss while employing the honorific which made him feel very uncomfortable.

'I always thought transparent dice couldn't be loaded,' Spender commented, not displeased by noticing signs of his companion's discomfiture. 'At least, not strongly enough for them to work as well as *these* do.'

'That isn't what I find puzzling, sir,' Amanda replied, but there was a subtle difference in the way she addressed the older man. 'I'm afraid it has been made comparatively easy for a sufficiently heavy loading to be carried out.'

'How do you mean?' Spender asked.

'Normally with transparent dice, sir, only the painted spots of the numbers are opaque,' the School Swot explained. 'This means the areas which can be weighted are limited. But the Club's insignia on these dice allows a filling of – I would assume platinum or gold, rather than tungsten or amalgam – to be applied beneath it and so attain a greater weight.'

'How the f – How could it be done?' Hotchkiss challenged, once again accepting the warning of a kick to his ankle and expunging the intended profanity, being genuinely interested as it had been at his instigation that the insignia was employed, to prevent the possibility of unscrupulous players introducing their own suitably prepared dice.

'I wouldn't have thought it could be,' Spender supplemented, realising that such a task would be far more complicated than merely drilling the cavities of the spots slightly deeper and fixing the weights – suitably painted to match the untreated numbers – in position, as was done with most types of loaded dice with which he was acquainted. 'But, if *you* say so, it obviously has been done. The thing is, how?'

'The technique is new to me, sir,' Amanda answered, having thought up her own method of producing the desired result while in the Fourth Form.

'But that isn't what is puzzling you either, is it, dear?' Miss Benkinsop suggested, remembering her pupil's experiments, but deciding they had nothing to do with the matter under discussion.

'No, ma'am,' Amanda agreed and tapped each dice in turn, continuing, 'You did say they *both* appeared on the high stakes craps table, sir?'

'They did!' Hotchkiss confirmed bitterly, although the question had been directed at Spender. 'And the others!'

'*Others*, sir?' the School Swot inquired.

'We didn't bring all of them,' Spender elaborated. 'But we've had *five* more put into the big game over the past fortnight.'

'*Five*,' Amanda said, nodding her head in the fashion of one who sees where she had been in error. 'That accounts for it, sir.'

'How do you mean?' Hotchkiss challenged.

'I thought they were *both* put into play at once – !'

Amanda began, but was not allowed to continue her explanation.

'Do leave off, darling!' Hotchkiss requested indignantly. 'They might not have been to a bloody toffee-nosed public school, but our dealers and stickmen[9] were sent over and trained in Las Vegas. There's *no* way anybody could rip in a bad 'n', much less two at once, at the big table. Particularly *after* the first time it happened and I'd warned them what I'd do if it was done again.'

'But it *did* happen again,' Miss Benkinsop pointed out, her demeanour such that an iceberg might have considered it decidedly chilly.

'Yes – Well – I – !' Hotchkiss spluttered, more disconcerted by the headmistress's obvious disapproval than he would have believed possible; especially a woman. 'That is – !'

'It happened even when *you* were watching,' Spender reminded, as his companion relapsed into sulky silence.

'*You* didn't see whoever's doing it last time, neither!' the junior executive countered and, although he refrained from adding, 'So there!' the words were implied in his tone.

'I didn't,' Spender conceded.

'Then we are up against somebody who is *exceptionally* proficient,' the headmistress declared. 'I would have thought that *you* would be able to spot him, Max, or at least work out who is doing it and how it is being done.'

'I've tried and I'll be da – blowed if I can,' Spender asserted, but he was so pleased by the tribute to his ability that he felt sufficiently forgiving towards his companion to lead him to continue, 'No more than Lenny-Boy here has – And it's not for the want of trying on *his* part. In fact, before it happened, I'd have sworn nobody was good enough to rip

---

[9] For the 'open' variety of 'craps' played in a casino, the 'dealer' acts as cashier and general supervisor, being responsible for collecting in and paying out of the bets, as well as acting as mediator in all points pertaining to the play. 'Stickmen' are the croupiers, performing the task of retrieving and passing the dice to the 'shooter', announcing the decisions and generally assisting the 'dealer'. Ideally, they are tall men with a long reach. Like 'dealers', they possess a sound knowledge of how the various crooked moves are performed and keep watch for the would-be per-pertrators. J.T.E.

"work"[10] into a game he was casing without him sussing out what was going on before the dice stopped rolling.'

'Then something unusual is amiss,' Miss Benkinsop said, in a voice which neither confirmed nor denied whether she believed what she had been told. 'Give Mr Hotchkiss the dice back, please, Amanda.'

'Yes, ma'am,' the School Swot assented promptly and, as the two men looked at her, reached out what appeared to them to be an empty right hand and did as she was told.

Instead of merely handing back the dice after she had picked them up, Amanda shook them in the fashion of the 'shooter' at a game of craps and the men could hear them clicking together in her clenched fist. Then her right arm moved with a whip-like snapping motion of the wrist and her hand opened.

However, the objects which landed on the desk and bounced towards Hotchkiss were two five pence pieces!

'What – !' the junior executive gasped, raising his gaze from what should have been a pair of dice and staring at the School Swot's open and displayed palm as if unable to believe the evidence of his eyes. 'How – ?'

'Just a harmless prank, Mr Hotchkiss,' Miss Benkinsop understated, behaving as if nothing out of the ordinary had taken place. Nor, where the angelic-faced girl standing so demurely at her side was concerned, did she consider it had. Swinging her gaze to where the study door opened and her maid entered with a small trolley, she went on, 'Ah, tea. You may stay, Amanda, if these gentlemen don't object.'

'We *don't*!' Spender stated, appreciating that he had just witnessed a remarkable feat of legerdemain and, impressed more than he would have cared to admit, the junior executive nodded a vehement concurrence.

* * * * *

'We've taken all the precautions we could think of, Amelia,' Maxwell Spender declared, after tea and cakes had been consumed, returning to the subject which had brought his

[10] 'Work' : a colloquial term for dice which have been made for cheating purposes. J.T.E.

companion and himself from London. 'And those you suggested. We've had every member photographed as he came in and covered the table with closed circuit television cameras, but we still haven't a clue who's ripping in those "loads".'

'I *know* it won't be *this* simple,' Miss Benkinsop admitted. 'But have you checked upon which players consistently win by betting on the high numbers?'

'We've *tried*,' Lenny-Boy Hotchkiss replied, the question having been put to him. 'But it's never the same blokes and, even them we've clocked didn't "shoot" all night. There's something else I can't suss out. How does the f – bloke who's doing it know when his dice comes back into play after a box up?'

'Well, Amanda?' the headmistress requested, noticing that the avoidance of the profanity had not been caused by Spender's intervention on this occasion and aware of the convention in crap games whereby the two dice in play were frequently returned to a box with others so a fresh pair could be selected.

'It's the way they are numbered, sir,' the School Swot obliged. 'If you hold a fair dice so the "six" is on top, a line drawn through the spots of the "three" extends upwards to the right. This is the convention followed by *all* legitimate manufacturers. These, put to the same test, have the "three" rising to the *left*. It may only seem a small thing, but it is quite noticeable when one is aware of what to look for.'

'Well I'll be f – b – *blowed*!' Hotchkiss spat out as he glared at the two cubes, still just contriving to refrain from employing the obscenities which usually speckled his conversation no matter in whose company he might find himself. It never occurred to him to question the explanation, as he felt sure it would prove correct. 'I never noticed *that*!'

'Neither did I,' the managing director confessed, being equally willing to accept what he had been told. 'The thing is, Amelia, what can we do to stop whoever it is coming back and hitting us again?'

'There's only one thing,' Miss Benkinsop replied. 'Catch him at it. But, before you ask, I haven't the faintest idea how to go about it. Have you any suggestions, Amanda?'

'Well, ma'am,' the School Swot answered hesitantly. 'I have a vague idea of *how* it was done, but would prefer not to say without seeing for myself.'

'We've got all the video tapes from the nights when the dice were ripped in,' Spender offered. 'Between them and the photos that have been taken of *everybody* as they came in, you might be able to pick out somebody *we've* never seen or heard about, but who'd be able to pull it off.'

'Possibly, sir,' Amanda replied dubiously. 'But, if I don't, merely looking at the tapes and photographs might not be enough to supply the information I need.'

'What else do you want?' Hotchkiss said and the words were more of a request than the kind of demand he normally made when posing a similar question to others.

'It would help, sir, if I could be present in person to watch the play,' Amanda explained, giving the honorific a more respectful timbre than previously.

'*You?*' Hotchkiss asked. 'As a *member?*'

'I thought as one of the "Puppydog-girls", sir,' the School Swot corrected. 'If that would be permissible, ma'am?'

'Well – !' Miss Benkinsop commenced dubiously, gazing at the girl for a moment. Then she turned her eyes towards Spender. 'I believe you said something about the Club being picketed, Max. Are you involved in some kind of industrial dispute with a trade union?'

'We don't have any unions in the club,' Hotchkiss put in, before the managing director could answer. 'It's all about that black bird the floor manager hired –'

'You objected to a coloured girl being hired?' Miss Benkinsop challenged frostily.

'Hell, no!' the junior executive corrected vehemently. 'We've had coloured girls ever since we opened and they've always been good, reliable workers.'

'This one *wasn't*,' Spender elaborated. 'She was bone idle, called in sick at least once a week and was late on the days when she came in. But she was also a "professional black". If she was told off for being late, or a member complained about the service he was getting, it was never because she was at fault, but always because she was coloured. Anyway, she walked out early one night when we were short staffed and

32

Lenny-Boy gave her the elbow. Next thing we know, she was claiming it was racial discrimination and because she'd been trying to get union recognition for herself and the rest of the staff. And now we'd got a bunch of greasy, unwashed, long-hair left-wing layabouts picketing the premises.'

'I'd half a "something"[11] mind to send some of the boys to see 'em off!' Hotchkiss stated, letting slip one of the words he had up to that point been prevented or voluntarily refrained from using.

'It only takes *half* a mind to do such a thing,' the head-mistress replied, as if rebuking an unruly pupil. 'You must remember, in our present society, it is quite all right for pickets to indulge in intimidation and violence, but the height of fascism should reprisals be taken against them.'

'That's what Maxie said,' Hotchkiss admitted. 'But it's a bleeding liberty. We've been paying dropsy to half a dozen Labour councillors and have a couple of Left Wing M.P.'s on our books to cut down police harassment and make sure the screws don't ill treat any of our lads who're doing porridge.[12] But none of them will lift a finger with a Union involved.'

'That's only to be expected,' Miss Benkinsop stated. 'Are the pickets threatening the girls, Max?'

'Just let the bastards try it!' Hotchkiss growled.

'We're not giving them a chance,' Spender answered, ignoring his companion's heated comment. 'They come by taxi and go in through the front entrance, instead of around the back like they used to, and there's always a couple of our "minders" standing by.'

'But you mentioned picketing,' the headmistress objected.

'It's being done at the back,' Spender explained. 'Some of the delivery blokes said they wouldn't cross a picket line, but we've got around that.'

'What about the girl?' Miss Benkinsop wanted to know.

'She shows up now and then,' the managing director re-

[11] See second paragraph of Author's Note. J.T.E.

[12] For the benefit of readers unacquainted with the term, 'doing porridge' is a colloquialism meaning to be seving a period of imprisonment. It was derived from porridge once having been the only food served to prisoners for breakfast. J.T.E.

plied. 'Some of the Board said we should offer to buy her off, but I wouldn't have a precedent like that set. Anyway, it's not the pickets I'm worried about. I'd be obliged if you'd let Amanda come for a few days, Amelia.'

'I'll look after her like she was my own sister,' Hotchkiss promised.

'Thank you,' Miss Benkinsop said and meant it. She knew the junior executive had a reputation, in spite of his faults, for loyalty and devotion to his family, but was confident her star pupil did not require *anybody's* protection, particularly in such a well run establishment as the Puppydog Club. 'But I'm not sure –'

'Perhaps I might be allowed to take a friend to act as chaperon, ma'am?' Amanda suggested, with an air of mingled hope and helpfulness.

'And just *who* do you have in mind, young lady?' the headmistress challenged, eyeing the girl with what was close to suspicion.

'Well, ma'am,' the School Swot replied, exuding an aura or artlessness which deceived the two men, but was less successful where it was being directed. 'I thought Penny would be most suitable. She *is* the School Captain –'

'I'm fully aware of Penelope Parkerhouse's status,' Miss Benkinsop warned, hard put to retain her unsmiling demeanour. '*Fully.* Very well, Max. Amanda can go with you.' Catching the School Swot's pleading glance, she continued, 'And Penelope, too.'

* * * * *

Although Alexander Kitson, Raymond Buxton, Jack Thompson and Andrew Bends had apparently been coal miners, bakers, hospital porters and dustmen, not one of them had done a day's work in any of those capacities – or anything more strenuous than drawing unemployment and Social Security benefits – since their respective State-supported periods of university education had ended. They augmented their far from hard earned incomes by payments which came, surreptitiously and tax free, from an unspecified donor for their attendance at political demonstrations or on various Unions' picket lines. Currently, due to the proximity of the 'summer holidays', it was a slack time for the kind of large scale and well publicized 'industrial action' which was most lucrative. So they had not been averse to accepting when offered honorary membership, with exemption from subscriptions, in the Non-Specialized and Associated Unskilled Workers' Union and being sent to lend support to another member who was being victimized by the capitalist management of the Puppydog Club.

After two weeks' performance of their noble and self-sacrificing mission, the quartet were beginning to regard it as a mixed blessing. It was not attracting the coverage by press and television news' services which brought an added revenue to those on the spot, particularly if required to take part in some specific action. On the other hand, despite some fears, it was less dangerous than they had anticipated. Since their one attempt to form a picket line across the Club's front entrance had been discouraged by the presence of several large and muscular men, who they suspected would not be constrained by the regulations affecting the conduct of the police, they had confined their activities to the rear of the building. This had the dual advantage of removing them from the blast of wind which blew from the Thames Embankment on to the front and also prevented their subsidizers discovering who was present or absent at any given time. It also removed the burdensome business of having to wash, shave and wear cleaner – less 'with it' – garments than their usual attire so as to appear as passersby would expect of striking employees from such an establishment.

One of the four's chief bone of contention, which was growing more acute, had been the number of times their victimized 'brother' failed to put in an appearance. After the first few days, particularly as it had become obvious the anticipated television coverage would not materialize, the girl had repeatedly found excuses to leave early, or stay away completely.

'Hey!' said the tall, bulky, bearded Bends, having looked out of the alley in which he and his companions were sitting in the van which had brought them to the picket line.

'There's a couple of the Club's birds coming.'

'So what?' asked shorter, thickset and heavily moustached Thompson.

'So they don't have any minders with them,' Bends replied. 'And there's been some hints that this picket's not worthwhile keeping going.'

'We'd better make sure they stop thinking like that,' tall, lean, sallow-faced Buxton declared. 'You sure there's none of the "minders" around, Andy?'

'No!' Bends confirmed, after taking another look.

'Great!' Buxton said, picking up the thermos flask which had been left capped to keep its contents hot. 'Let's go and put the frighteners on them.'

*　　*　　*　　*　　*

'Cor, you ain't 'alf clever, "Mand",' Penelope Parkerhouse praised, as she and the School Swot walked side by side along the pavement towards the rear entrance of the Puppydog Club. 'I wouldn't *never* 'ave thought of getting us off classes for a bit like you did.'

Despite her exalted status in Miss Benkinsop's exclusive establishment, the School Captain spoke with a pronounced accent indicative of having been born well within the sound of Bow Bells. Not more than five foot in height, she had bubblecut blonde hair and a pretty face with a merry, perky expression. She had a well-developed, curvaceous buxom figure which was firm fleshed with no superfluous fat. Nor did the extreme décolleté of her green sleeveless silk blouse, ending just below an imposing bosom and exposing a waist requiring no aids to make it slender, figure hugging jeans which had had the legs cut off to the limits of decorum and low-heeled Grecian sandals with cross-straps extending to just below knee-level, seek to conceal it.

'I hoped Benkers would agree,' Amanda Tweedle replied, being clad in the same general fashion as the girl who was her best friend and presenting an equally fetching appearance. 'But I don't know what she will say when she hears about *this*.'

'*You'll* talk her 'round, luv, same as always,' Penelope

declared with complete confidence. The faith inspired in all who knew the School Swot was equally apparent as she went on, 'But don't you go copping that bloke *tonight*. This's our chance to have a few days in the Old Smoke.'

'I don't believe I will be that fortunate,' Amanda answered gently. 'After all, Mr Spender and several gentlemen whose livelihoods depend upon their ability to detect dishonest practices have failed to do so for the past few weeks.'

'They're not *you*, luv!' the School Captain pointed out. 'And I bet you know how it's being done already.'

It was three o'clock on the afternoon of the day after the conversation in the headmistress's study.

Having been driven to London that morning by the School's music teacher and accompanied without Miss Benkinsop's knowledge by another Sixth Former, the girls had been accommodated in the headmistress's luxurious flat in Park Lane. Once there, they had set about making arrangements for taking up their temporary employment. They had been successful in acquiring the one item which it had not been possible for them to bring with them, but was indispensable if they wanted the visit to be a success. With all their preparations completed, they had made their way to the Puppydog Club.

However, despite having brought clothing more suitable for travelling to and from their temporary place of employment, neither Amanda nor Penelope was carrying as much as a handbag. Nor were they arriving as they had been informed was currently expected of the Club's female employees, but were approaching along a narrow and apparently deserted street towards the rear entrance.

Before Amanda could respond to her friend's suggestion, four scruffily dressed and unprepossessing looking young men ambled from an alley to halt across the pavement in front of them.

'Well well, brothers,' Andrew Bends said, with all the majesty of one who had aspirations to be an actor although lacking in histrionic talent. 'What do we have here?'

'They look like scabs going to work for the capitalist scum who are discriminating against our black sister, Andy,' replied Alexander Kitson, who was tall, skinny and, if possible, even less pleasant looking than Raymond Buxton, parroting off the jargon which amounted to almost all he remembered from the period he had spent at the taxpayers' expense receiving education intended to make him a doctor. 'How about you, Ray?'

'Right on, man, right on,' Buxton confirmed, teetering on his heels and grasping the top of the thermos flask.

'Excuse me, *gentlemen*,' Amanda said mildly, as she and Penelope came to a stop, but neither they nor the four young men paid any attention to a Ford delivery van bearing the insignia of a prominent London store halting across the inter-section of a street joining the one they were on. 'But we would like to come by.'

'Oh you would, would you?' Bends scoffed. 'And just who the "something" to you "something" think you "something-well" are, you "something' little Roedean snob?'

'Excuse me,' the School Swot put in, seeming almost on the point of breaking into tears. 'What was that you said last?'

'I said who the "something" do — !' Bends commenced, possessing the belief that using profanities in mixed company was proof of his sterling 'liberal' ideals.

'I'm afraid you are under a misapprehension,' Amanda interrupted, apologetically if her demeanour was to be believed. 'I asked what you said *last*.'

'*Last?*' Bends repeated, frowning, then understanding struck him. 'I said, you "something" Roedean snob.'

'I *thought* that was what you said,' the School Swot admitted. 'And I hope that you are not implying my friend also comes from *Roedean*?'

'What the "something" if Andy is?' Buxton demanded, gesturing with the partially opened flask, as he and his companions formed a menacing half circle around the girls. 'If you and her get what's in here thrown in your faces, you'll not be able to scab.'

'Would you do *that*?' Amanda challenged, if such a mouse-like intonation could qualify for so vigorous a description.

'Of course we would!' Bends assured, although puzzled by a response far different from that of other recipients to the threat. 'What do you think we are, full of the honour of the old school tie and all that sort of capitalist crap, you "something" Roedean whores?'

'Oh dear. He called us that *again*, Penny,' the School Swot informed her friend, in tones of horror, then went on although she was not looking at the man to whom the words were directed, 'I really must ask you to refrain from –'

'You're asking for some of this – !' Buxton spat out, removing the cap from the flask.

Estimating the distance as accurately as with a tape measure, despite employing only her eyes, Amanda suddenly brought up her right leg. While the movement was performed with a grace the *premiere danseuse* of a top class ballet company might have envied, the kick she launched arrived at a force closer to that of a mule. What was more, the change from what had seemed to be timid passivity to aggression took all four young men completely unawares.

Of all the quartet, Buxton was most discommoded. Because of the means by which it was constructed, the thermos flask was ill-equipped to receive such a sudden and powerful impact. As it was propelled from his grasp, its interior shattered and he had cause to wish he had not removed its cover. Flying out, very hot tea and slivers of glass from the double inner lining of flask sprayed over his hands and features. Letting forth a wail of pain, he staggered backwards with his fingers scrabbling at his face.

Giving no more indication of her intentions than was shown by the School Swot, Penelope bent forward at the waist and lunged into the attack. Her head rammed against Thompson's bulging paunch, impelled by all the exceptionally puissant muscles of her curvaceous little body. The effect was impressive. Spitting out a *marihuana* cigarette which formed part of the quartet's payment for picketing, he blundered away from his assailant until falling on to his rump hard enough to drive what little breath remained from his lungs.

Startled exclamations burst from the remaining pair of young men. Then, displaying not the slightest qualms over being in contention against two girls, considering rather that such was far safer than tackling members of their own sex, they set about implementing hostile action.

And quickly came to wish such a thought had never been envisaged!

Swinging a punch towards Amanda's head, although he would have preferred to tackle the smaller girl, Bends found his advancing wrist caught by two hands which seemed to have the grip of a steel clamp. Jerked forward, he had a vague impression of his intended victim weaving out of his way. Then her knee rose to catch his *solar plexus* and, his arm being released, he was flung into an involuntary retreat. However, in one respect anyway, he might have counted himself fortunate. Due to her avoidance of a collision and the speed required to deliver the knee thrust, Amanda was unable to develop the full force of which she was capable. So the effort was painful, but not incapacitating.

Nor did Kitson fare any better, despite certain measures he had taken in preparation for similar eventualities. Having come under the 'liberally' acceptable influence of the television series, *Kung Fu* and believing such knowledge would make him as invincible as the hero, he had expended some of his bounty from the State and clandestine earnings to learn the esoteric form of Oriental unarmed combat. So he was confident in his chances, no matter how the little blonde had treated Thompson.

What Kitson did not know was that, in addition to being School Captain, Penelope was the leading light of the Debating Society; whose 'discussions' took the form of free-style wrestling. What was more, with the exception of Amanda, she was capable of defeating the largest and heaviest girls who 'debated' with her. With such a background and the thorough training she had received during her years under Miss Benkinsop's care, she was neither impressed nor frightened by the young man's apparent command of *kung fu*.

Adopting the readiness position he had been taught, Kitson saw the buxom little blonde dart towards him. Before he realized what was happening, much less thought out a way to counter it, she had sprung into the air and caught him with a drop kick to the chest which pitched him in a pinning arc to trip over Thompson.

Despite the girls' successes, they had failed to render any

of their assailants *hors de combat* during the brief opening
exchange of hostilities. However, when they came under
attack once more, they set about remedying the omission
with considerable gusto. For a short while, anybody who had
chanced to be watching would have been treated to a superlative display of unarmed self-defence. Good as Penelope
was, she would have been the first to admit that her efforts
were minor compared with those of the School Swot. In fact,
such was her friend's command of various fighting arts that
she could have stood aside if she had not wished to share the
fun. As a result of their combined efforts, the brief fracas
ended with a badly bruised, battered and unconscious quartet
sprawled on the street, while those responsible for their
conditions were unmarked and barely out of breath.

Although none of the four men had any clear recollection
of what happened, they later attributed their defeat to
having been caught unawares and attacked by at least a
dozen strike-breaking members of the National Front.

While Amanda was examining the quartet to ensure none
of them had need of medical attention, the doors of the
delivery van opened and two members of her sex emerged.
The elder, a ravishingly beautiful and voluptuous platinum
blonde in her late twenties, was clad in an ensemble similar
to that worn by Miss Benkinsop during the daytime at the
School. She was, in fact, Miss Peaches Pedlar, the music
teacher. About eight years younger, the other had exchanged
the attire of a Prefect for a stylish blue cat suit which she
filled not inadequately and had a Canon AE-1 camera with a
telephoto lens attached suspended around her neck. She was
Dora Haverstock and, apart from Amanda – who actually
instructed it – was the most competent member of the
School's Photographic Club.

'Did you get all that?' Penelope asked.

'Everything,' Miss Pedlar replied. 'That microphone you
made works a treat, Amanda. I played the tape back and it's
so clear you might have had them speaking right into it.'

'You were absolutely right about the time and aperture
settings I'd have to use, too, Amanda,' Dora went on, having
been focusing the camera through one hole in the side of the
van – loaned by Penelope's father and modified, with his

41

permission, by the School Swot – while the music teacher operated the special microphone and tape recorder. 'If there's *one* exposure that doesn't come out, I'll come and have a "Debating" work out with you in the gym, Penny.'

'I'll keep you to that, luv,' the School Captain warned, but with a grin, being equally confident there would be no error as Amanda's suggestions for setting up the camera had been followed. 'Let's get these yobbos shifted, shall we? Then you can go back to develop the "pickies" so Benkers will have something to look at while she's listening to the tape.'

* * * * *

'Let me understand what you're telling me,' Miss Benkinsop ordered into the mouthpiece of her study's telephone. 'You both felt the need for fresh air and exercise, so you decided to *walk* to the Puppydog Club and, on the way to the *rear* entrance, you were set upon by four ruffians?'

'Yes, ma'am,' Amanda Tweedle replied, her tone neutral, speaking from the dining-room of the headmistress's flat in Park Lane.

Some two and a half hours had elapsed since the defeat of the picketers. The arrival of Miss Pedlar, requesting an interview, had been timed to coincide with the telephone call Miss Benkinsop was in the process of answering. Sitting nursing the tape, listening to and watching her employer, the music teacher felt much as she had on those not infrequent occasions when, as a Third Former, she had been called to 'Benkers's Drum' – as the *sanctum sanctorum* of the School was irreverently, yet lovingly, termed by the pupils – to answer for some misdemeanour. What was more, she did not doubt her perturbation was noticed by the eagle-eyed headmistress.

'And,' Miss Benkinsop went on, 'just by a pure coincidence, Dora Haverstock – about whose *fortuitous* presence I may wish to ask questions later – was there with her camera to take photographs while Miss Pedlar recorded what was said with equipment she had, by *chance*, brought with her?'

'Yes, ma'am,' Amanda confirmed. 'The men's attitude was

42

so hostile, we considered it advisable to have some record of what took place.'

'Putting aside the matter of why you elected to use the Club's *rear* entrance for the moment,' the headmistress continued, although she knew Amanda and Penelope Parkerhouse were quite capable of defending themselves without needing to adopt the course she was about to suggest and was convinced there was a satisfactory explanation for their behaviour, 'Why, may I ask, did you not turn and hurry away when you saw them, or call for assistance from the staff of the Club?'

'We *thought* of doing one or the other, ma'am,' Amanda admitted, having instructed Penelope to consider the possibility and avoid the necessity to lie if the point was raised. 'But I'm afraid I lost my temper when one of them insulted us.'

'In what way?' Miss Benkinsop inquired, genuinely interested.

'He accused us of being from *Roedean*, ma'am!' the School Swot explained, in a voice redolent of acute distaste. 'Not just *once*, which I *might* have excused, but no less than *three* times.'

'Did he, by Georgina!' Miss Benkinsop ejaculated, turning her head to prevent the music teacher from seeing the smile she was unable to withhold and pleased it was beyond her pupil's range of vision. 'What happened after that?'

'I made sure none of them were *too* badly hurt, then we put them in their van and took them somewhere we thought they might feel at home,' Amanda answered, hoping she would not be asked for the location as she had yielded to the School Captain's selection of a particularly wet and malodorous Council refuse tip.

'Most considerate of you, I'm sure!' Miss Benkinsop said dryly, having detected the timbre of evasiveness in the reply. 'And who, may I ask, decided where *that* would be?'

'Me, ma'am,' Penelope confessed, the call being made over telephones which Amanda had converted to allow more than one person to listen and speak simultaneously when necessary.

'Then, knowing your *distressing* sense of humour, I think I would rather *not* ask where it was,' Miss Benkinsop decided.

'However, Amanda, while I can't *really* blame you for taking exception to suggestions that you are domiciled at a *lesser* school, I feel your conduct was ill-advised.'

'I told them they hadn't got to go through with it if there was more than *ten* picketers there, Miss Benkinsop,' the music teacher intervened. 'But there were only *four*, although I got just a little worried when one of them threatened to throw hot tea over them and –'

'I've heard such a threat has been made on other occasions,' the headmistress admitted, having no doubt that Amanda had been equally well informed. 'But I was referring to how this incident could cause Mr Spender and his associates a great deal of extra inconvenience by leading to an escalation of the picketing.'

'Yes, ma'am,' the School Swot conceded, sounding contrite. 'And I appreciate how our participation could reflect adversely upon the good name of the School. Perhaps *you* can suggest how this might be avoided?'

'I suppose, as you are all my pupils – or a member of my teaching staff, I'll have to try,' Miss Benkinsop declared, with what might have been resignation. She refrained from glancing at the discomforted music teacher in case she disclosed her true feelings. 'Now, my girls, unless you have any other *trivial* little problems to plague me with, I would suggest you start getting ready to carry out the task for which you were allowed to visit London.'

In spite of an awareness of how difficult a task she would be undertaking, the smile was still on the headmistress's face as she hung up the receiver. It was caused by an appreciation of the way in which her star pupil had manoeuvred her into being able to take action upon a matter which up to then she had considered could not be classed as her concern, no matter how much she would have liked to intercede. Knowing that the rules by which she lived would not allow her to intervene so long as the dispute remained confined to the Consortium's Club and the Union, Amanda had caused the School to become involved. She realized that, particularly after the chances the two girls had taken to permit her participation, she must do everything possible to justify their faith in her and was grateful for having studied the newspapers to learn the identities of the people most concerned with the industrial action.

'I suppose I should have asked *you* before letting them go through with it, ma'am,' Miss Pedlar said, more in the fashion of an errant pupil than a valued member of the teaching staff, as her employer looked at her with a face that no longer bore a smile.

'I suppose you *should*,' Miss Benkinsop agreed, showing no sign of her true feelings. 'But it's too late now.'

'This is the tape – !' the music teacher said hurriedly, seeking a diversion.

'Leave it on the desk, please,' the headmistress requested. 'Then would you go and see if the photographs are ready?'

'Of course,' Miss Pedlar assented, only too pleased to have an opportunity to leave.

'I suppose I've one thing to be grateful for,' Miss Benkinsop remarked, as the younger woman rose hurriedly. '*You* aren't the same age as Amanda and Penelope. From what I remember of you as a pupil, Miss Peaches Pedlar, I think the combination of the three of you would have turned my hair grey.'

*   *   *   *   *

'Mr *Buckingham*?' inquired an impersonal feminine voice, as the receiver of the unlisted telephone was lifted by the owner of a luxurious West End flat shortly after eight o'clock in the evening. 'What does B–14321–GEH–280 mean to you?'

'What – How?' Morris Lichenhell gasped, the number being that of an account he had under the *nom de plume*, 'George Edward Henry Buckingham', at a bank in Zürich.

However, neither the information nor the number of the telephone were available to the general public. Nor, out of consideration for his position as President of the Non-Specialized and Assorted Unskilled Workers' Union, could he regard with equanimity the realization that his caller was aware of both.

'Don't hang up!' ordered the voice so peremptorily that it brought the action it was intended to prohibit to an abrupt stop and caused the receiver of the call to glance around nervously, if involuntarily, to find out whether he was being observed. 'If you *do*, I will have to call you at your headquarters tomorrow and you never know who might hear what I have to say should you be "unavailable".'

'Wh – Who are you?' Lichenhell croaked, his porcine features registering alarm. His speech had lost all the unctuous, yet bullying, timbre it held at less fraught moments.

'That's none of your affair,' Miss Benkinsop replied, confident the man she was addressing would not recognize her voice in the unlikely event of them meeting socially.

'I – I don't know wha – !' Lichenhell commenced.

'Don't waste my time!' the headmistress ordered. 'I can quote your exact balance, including the date you deposited the fifteen hundred pounds you drew from your Union's funds when you flew to Yugoslavia to, how did you put it, "bring back our brother who fled there to escape the persecution of the neo-fascist British police"?'

After the music teacher had taken her departure that afternoon, the headmistress had made a telephone call to a colleague in Zürich and made a request. While waiting for it to be carried out, she had listened to the tape recording of the conversation in the street behind the Puppydog Club. What she had heard did nothing to lessen her intention of bringing the picketing to a halt, as she knew the next time something similar happened the intended victims might be less capable of defending themselves. When her contact had returned the call, she discovered that he had justified his claim to be the most competent of the people who made a living by supplying information regarding what should have been secret depositors in his homeland's banks. Making use of the fund of clandestine knowledge he had available, he was able to supply her with details which she had felt sure would let her attain her ends.

'I – It's a "something" lie put out by the capit – !' Lichenhell protested shrilly.

'Then you will have no objections to my sending photostat copies of my information to the press, television and – ' Miss Benkinsop suggested, continuing after a slight pause, 'your colleagues on the Trade Unions' General Council?'

'For God's sake don't send it to *them*!' Lichenhell begged, collapsing on to the easy chair by the telephone's table and, as he hated the thought of having to part with money, a shudder ran through him as he went on, 'How *much* do you want?'

'Not a penny,' Miss Benkinsop declared truthfully, being aware that Maxwell Spender would have the Consortium recompense her for her expenditure should she be successful.

'Then *what* do you want?' Lichenhell challenged, knowing *he* never did *anything* for nothing and assuming everybody was equally mercenary.

'The picketing of the Puppydog Club brought to an end,' the headmistress replied.

'Are you in with those "something" National Front bastards who attacked our "brothers" this afternoon?' Lichenhell demanded, having been informed of the incident without so far taking any action on it.

'No,' Miss Benkinsop declared and her voice became charged with menace. 'And I'll thank you to moderate your language. I'm not some Left Wing "trendy" who regards profanity as a symbol of oneness with the "little people".'

'Then why – ?' Lichenhell asked.

'Your so-called "brothers" were threatening two girls for whom I am responsible,' Miss Benkinsop explained. 'They intended to go *beyond* threatening, too, not knowing the girls were experts in martial arts. I have a tape recording of what they said and photographs of what happened to them. The media, especially that portion which favours the Right, would be delighted to receive copies.' Again there was a pause pregnant with warning, before she finished, 'And, *if* I am compelled to send them, they will not go alone. The information about your Swiss bank account –'

'How *can* I call it off?' Lichenhell requested, filled with consternation and apprehension as he knew there were many within his Union and the T.U.C.'s higher hierarchy who would be delighted to possess such details as a means of ending his career.

'If the girl who has caused the dispute was to find lucrative employment elsewhere – say in television – ' Miss Benkinsop supplied, having given thought to the matter, 'there would

47

be no further need for the picketing and that would save your genuine "brothers'" funds being expended on the picketers' wages.'

'I'll see what I can do,' Lichenhell promised, knowing he had an associate employed by B.B.C. Television who was in no position to refuse him a favour. He also saw how the latter point would be an even greater inducement to call off the far from productive picketing than the 'victim' being found gainful employment. Then another thought struck him and he continued, 'Hey though, can you get this kind of information about other folk?'

'I can,' Miss Benkinsop admitted, making an accurate guess at what would come next.

'Then how about doing it on the other members of the General Council?' Lichenhell hinted. 'I'd make it worth your while.'

'I'll give the matter my consideration,' the headmistress promised, although knowing the answer would be in the negative. 'And will inform you of my decision *after* the picketing is finished.'

*   *   *   *   *

'Good evening, sir,' Amanda Tweedle greeted the Japanese businessman who had just entered the Puppydog Club, speaking his native tongue as fluently as she had when addressing members from five other overseas' countries each in his own language. Nor had she restricted herself to just the salutation, but carried out a conversation in the same fashion on every occasion.

'Blimey, Penny!' gasped one of the regular "Puppydog girls", standing by the School Captain and watching in fascination as the clearly delighted Oriental visitor entered the main gaming room. 'How many languages does she speak?'

'Every one,' Penelope Parkerhouse replied, loyal as always to her best friend. 'And *all* of them perfect.'

'Really, Penny, you do *exaggerate*!' the School Swot protested. 'I still have several languages to learn and my Jivaro

48

Indian and Menangkabau[13] leave much to be desired.'

Four days had elapsed since Amanda commenced her investigation.

Apart from the pickets having been withdrawn following the management agreeing to make a 'redundancy' payment to the discharged girl – a face-saving device suggested by Miss Benkinsop, although the sum was considerably less than had originally been demanded – who was now employed as a bit-player by B.B.C. Television at Morris Lichenhell's instigation, nothing of note had taken place. The School Swot and Penelope had quickly become popular with the Club's employees and members. Certainly nobody could have claimed they were physically or technically unsuitable for the role they were playing. Each had a figure which enhanced the decidedly skimpy costume of a 'Puppydog-girl' and they had from the start demonstrated complete competence in all aspects of their duties. What was more, although the story of how they had handled the four picketers was not made public, it had taken only one exhibition of each's ability in the martial arts – backed by a warning from Leonard Hotchkiss, although this had been superfluous where the recipients of the demonstrations were concerned – to prevent them from being subjected to the male members of the staff's unwanted attentions.

Despite having made an extensive study of the photographs and video tapes supplied by Hotchkiss, Amanda had had to admit she was unable to pick out the player responsible for introducing the dishonest dice. Nor had any of those she selected as possible candidates proved to be the guilty party and she had been no more successful while greeting the new arrivals at the Club's entrance. However, she had had the consolation of knowing no further substitutions had been made since her arrival. On the other hand, the fact that several other clubs reported being subjected to similar impositions suggested the perpetrator was merely changing venues and had not retired to enjoy his substantial ill-gotten gains. So, much to Penelope's obvious delight and Amanda's

[13] The Jivaro Indians are natives of the Andes' foothills in South America and the Menandkabau a warrior race famous throughout the Indonesian Archipelago. J.T.E.

less obvious satisfaction, Miss Benkinsop had given permission for the surveillance to be continued.

The arrival of a tall, heavily bearded man clad in the traditional attire of a wealthy Arab brought the debate concerning the School Swot's linguistic prowess to an end. In spite of displaying surprise similar to that of other overseas members on being addressed so fluently in their native tongues, the man duplicated Amanda's action by placing together his hands – each decorated by rings of varying values – and responding in the accepted fashion to her Islamic welcome. However, he employed heavily accented English to inquire what games of chance were available. On receiving his answer in Arabic, he nodded gravely and walked into the main gaming room.

'Would you take over for a while, please, Alma,' Amanda requested, a few seconds later, as she had done on other occasions during the previous evenings. 'I want to have a word with Lenny-Boy.'

'All right,' the girl assented, although she had drawn the wrong conclusions over the reason for Hotchkiss having given orders that the beautiful blonde should be allowed access to him any time it was requested.

Crossing the gaming room accompanied by Penelope, who had been afforded the same privilege, the School Swot made her way to where the Arab was joining the crowd at the big stakes craps' table. As she drew nearer, she listened to the stickman carrying out one of his duties by chanting what had become an accepted litany.

'Get it down, men! Send it in to the book! Double up and *beat* the book! If you don't bet, you can't win! Them as don't speculate never accumulate! Watch it now! Here they come! Coming out – now! And he's made it! Eight, the hard way!'

Having attended the School's American Customs' Class, which offered instruction in *all* aspects of gambling, Penelope had as little difficulty as her friend in following the meaning of the chant. She was aware that the number 'eight' had been the 'shooter's point' and he had won his wager by 'making' it via a score of four from each dice, this being referred to as the 'hard way'.

'And here's a new "shooter"! A gentleman from the

Middle East!' the croupier announced, retrieving the dice in the ring on the end of the wooden stick which created his alternative title and thrusting them across the table towards an outstretched brown hand. 'Let's see if you're as lucky as you are at finding oil at home, sir!'

Gathering up the two cubes, the bearded Arab raised them to his mouth in the way other players did when intending to blow on them for luck. Just as the clench fist reached his lips, Amanda slapped him hard between the shoulders. As when she had kicked the thermos out of Raymond Buxton's hand, the unexpected and far from gentle blow produced a spectacular effect. Not only did its recipient give vent to a gasping profanity in English, with a pronounced *American* accent, he unclenched his fist involuntarily.

And *three*, not *two*, dice flew forward to bounce on the green baize top of the table!

The fact that the spots on the 'three face' of the one in the centre pointed in the opposite direction to those of the other two indicated it did not belong to the casino!

Snarling further obscenities in his New York accent, the 'Arab' spun around and launched a blow at the person he realised must have been his assailant. A moment later, although unable to decide exactly how everything happened, he felt his wrist caught and receive a twisting wrench which not only dislocated his shoulder, but caused his feet to leave the floor. Executing a somersault, which was not of his own doing, he crashed down again and, following a brief eruption of bright lights before his eyes, lost all interest in the proceedings for a short while.

'Ooer!' Penelope gurgled, irrepressible as always, staring at the three 'five' faces which were uppermost, in the silence which had followed the brief flurry of action. 'Fifteen, the hard way!'

* * * * *

'How the "someth – " How did you get on to me?' demanded the 'Arab', his headdress and well-made false beard having been removed to display the deeply tanned features of a Caucasian in his mid-thirties. He was slumped on a chair in

51

the manager's office, surrounded by a far from friendly crowd, about half an hour after his exposure. The amendment to his question had been created by the receipt of a sharp blow on the back of the head, accompanied by an order to keep his mouth clean in the presence of ladies, from an indignant Leonard Hotchkiss. 'My clothes are genuine and the beard's made of real hair. And I got that Arab greeting off so perfect the feller who taught me said he'd have thought I was one.'

'Well, sir,' Amanda Tweedle replied, being too well bred to contradict an older person by pointing out his delivery of the greeting – while good – was far from as fautless as he had been led to assume. 'I must admit your attire and false beard were flawless, but I wondered why one who dressed and behaved after the fashion of a Moslem should be wearing a Christian *crucifix* ring.'

'So *that* was it!' Henry 'the Actor' Steffens growled, glaring at the incriminating item of jewellery on his right little finger which he had believed was so insignificant it would be overlooked among the other, more imposing rings he was wearing. Proud of his ability in following a family tradition of employing disguises as an aid to committing crimes,[14] he drew what little consolation he could from believing he had only made the one mistake. 'By god, kid, you're *good*.'

There was little else the 'Arab' could regard as a bright spot. Having lost their heads when he was apprehended, the three men who were his associates were also in the hands of the casino's staff.

'Thank you, sir,' Amanda replied, polite as always. 'May I congratulate you upon how very efficiently you have been operating? You always arrived in a different disguise and only acted as "shooter" on the occasion when you substituted the dice in your mouth for one belonging to the club, having slipped yours there after entering the gaming room and carrying the other in it until you were safely away from the table and could put it in your pocket. On the other hand, your three associates never touched the dice, but concen-

[14] Details of a visit paid to England by another member of the family, Joseph 'Joe the Actor' Steffens, are given in: *'CAP' FOG, TEXAS RANGER, MEET MR J. G. REEDER*. J.T.E.

52

trated upon betting on the high numbers.'

'When did you guess how it was being done, Amanda?' Hotchkiss inquired, his original misgivings having been replaced by something close to reverence.

'I suspected a "mouth switch" as soon as you told us only one dice was being introduced at a time,' the School Swot replied. 'My problem was detecting who was responsible. Which is why I asked to be allowed to come and keep watch. Will you be needing Penny and me any more, sir?'

'Not unless you want to stay on as chief floorwalker,[15] with a piece of the action,' Hotchkiss suggested hopefully.

'Good heavens, *no*!' Amanda gasped, sounding aghast at the thought. 'Miss Benkinsop would *never* allow it.'

[15] 'Floorwalker': the supervisor of the gaming room, with authority over all the other employees. J.T.E.

PART TWO

Dawn Drummond-Clayton

In

DEATH TO SIMBA NYEUSE

Although only one was aware of the other's presence in the vicinity, there were two exceptionally fine examples of different major predatory species prowling through the night-darkened woodland which fringed a smallish clearing about three miles from a Gasali village and close to the boundary of the Ambagasali Wild Life Reserve. Both were hunting, but only the more competent of the two could achieve its purpose. As had always been nature's pattern and way, the other would pay the price of failure.

The lion had been hungry since the disappearance of its consort during what should have been a temporary separation two days earlier and catching prey was difficult.[1] The lion approaching the clearing, attracted there by the bleating of a goat. Since they had been driven from the pride of their birth by the dominant male, the lion and his mate had discovered that such creatures and, occasionally, the villagers' stunted cattle offered a more easily obtained source of sustenance than the wary wild creatures upon which they had fed in the area they had been compelled to vacate.

Standing close to forty inches at the shoulder and measuring close to nine foot,[2] inclusive of its fairly long, black-tufted

[1] What happened to the second lion is told in: *Part Twelve, BUNDUKI series, 'The Mchawi's Powers', J.T.'s HUNDREDTH.* J.T.E.
[2] With the exception of calibres appropriate to certain weapons – i.e., Luger 9mm automatic pistol – the author has no intention of following

tail, the lion was approaching the prime of life. Aided by the easy pickings derived from the villagers' incautious way of allowing domestic stock to graze without adequate supervision and protection, its tawny and powerfully muscled body – backed by the long fangs, teeth and the sharply pointed claws at present sheathed in the pads of its feet – had produced a weight in the region of four hundred and fifty pounds. This would stand it in good stead when the opportunity arrived for it to make a challenge for the right to mate and support the continued existence of its species. Tawny in body colour, the magnificent hirsute appendage flowing from its head, neck and forming a fringe along its stomach, served as a symbol of its virile masculinity.

Such a splendid adornment was not uncommon in the region. The lions of Ambagasali had long been famous for the exceptional quality of their manes. However, while the vast majority were yellow in colour – ranging from a blondish tinge to almost golden – the young male's decorative hair was the rarely seen black which, in the past, had caused its kind to be classed as 'royal' game. Hunting them had been the prerogative of the kings of the country, their male heirs, or very privileged important guests.

Arriving at the edge of the clearing, the lion did not allow the pangs of hunger to cause it to act hastily. Instead, flattening on its stomach while still in the concealment of the bushes, it surveyed the situation. There was sufficient light for it to be able to study its prey without difficulty. Tethered in the centre of the open ground, some thirty yards away, the half grown goat was ideal for its purposes. Not only were its movements restricted by the short rope attaching it to a stake, it was neither large enough nor had its horns grown sufficiently for it to be able to put up a dangerous struggle when attacked alone and unsupported by a consort.

Such considerations were of vital importance to a predatory animal which depended upon agility as much as strength to catch and pull down creatures capable of rapid movements. Any injury sustained could reduce its powers to a

---

the current 'trendy' pandering to the exponents of the metric system and will continue to employ miles, yards, feet, pounds and ounces when referring to distances or weights. J.T.E.

point where making a kill became impossible. In that event, lack of nourishment would eventually cause death by starvation; or from a mass attack by scavengers it would have been able to put to flight if in good condition.

Despite being able to attain a speed in excess of fifty miles per hour, bitter experience already had taught the lion that a charge from a distance could prove futile and unproductive. It had learned that a careful stalk as close as possible to the prey was more likely to produce satisfactory results. So, keeping its eyes upon its intended prey, it began to approach with the belly-scraping gait which all members of the *Felidae* could perform with great grace, skill and effectiveness. Unfortunately, due to its hunger and comparative inexperience, it forgot the essential aid to survival of remaining alert for signs of possible danger to itself.

Not that the second predator, which was stalking the lion as eagerly as the tethered goat was being sought, was giving any unnecessary indications of being so close. Rather the opposite in fact. Being aware of how formidable an antagonist its intended prey could be, granted an opportunity, it was applying all the skill it possessed to avoiding detection.

Bipedal, feminine in gender, also approaching the full blossom of maturity, the other was an even finer representative of its species, *Homo Sapiens*, than the lion was of *Panthera*, or *Felis* – depending upon one's scientific proclivities – *Leo*.

Five foot eight inches tall, with 'vital statistics' measuring: bust, 38 inches; waist, 20 inches; hips, 36 inches; Dawn Drummond-Clayton – without any form of artificial aid – had a figure many a 'sex symbol' movie actress strove to attain. Kept cut short for convenience, her curly tawny hair set off almost clasically beautiful features whose lines denoted breeding, strength of will and intelligence. Sleek, power-packed, yet not unfeminine muscles played under skin tanned to a gorgeous golden bronze by the elements, indicating the possession of perfect physical condition and health.

In spite of being clad in an open necked nylon khaki bush shirt, with matching trousers tucked into the calf-high legs of brown, rubber-soled hunting boots, Dawn Drummond-

Clayton conveyed an impression of timeless and savage feminine pulchritude. This was enhanced by the expression on her face, the Randall Model 1 'All Purpose Fighting' knife – having an eight inch long clip point blade[3] and a 'finger-grip' handle made from the horn of sambur stag – hanging in its sheath from the left side of the two and a quarter inch wide Bianchi 'Border Patrol' belt around her waist, and a quiver suspended upon her back so the flights of the arrows it contained rose above her right shoulder to facilitate an unrestricted and hurried removal when necessary. In a competent manner she carried her seventy pound pull Ben Pearson Maurauder 'Take-Down' hunting bow. There was a second quiver, holding eight arrows, attached to its recurved limbs and she had a ninth, fitted with an unconventioned type of head, nocked to its string ready for use. Nor was the primitive aura diminished by her having a powerful Smith & Wesson .41 Magnum revolver in a Bianchi Model 104R swivel holster with a 'snap-lock' retaining strap at the right side of the belt and twenty-four spare cartridges in its loops.

Being aware of the possible dangers of the task she was performing, Dawn did not regard her armament as either ostentatious or excessive. Furthermore, she was sufficiently skilled in the use of her weapons to feel confident that she could protect herself with any of them should the need arise, as well as carrying out the task she had set herself by employing the bow and its specialised arrow.

That the girl was stalking the lion did not imply she was urged by blood lust, or a desire to prove some point by killing a creature so much more powerful than herself. Her participation was the product of necessity. Along with its consort, the lion had acquired the habit of preying upon the livestock of the nearby Gasali village. Such a proclivity could develop into making the villagers themselves the object of its attentions as it lost its inherent fear of human beings through increased familiarity. So it had to be prevented from con-

[3] For the benefit of new readers: a 'clip point' blade has the otherwise unsharpened back swooping to join and form an extension of the main cutting surface in a concave arc. This is the kind of point employed upon the legendary 'Bowie' knife. J.T.E.

tinuing its depredations.

Despite her love of nature and living creatures, Dawn was no over-reacting 'bleeding heart' conservationist. She accepted there was a limit to how much tolerance could be permitted where any animal was concerned. No carnivore could be allowed to prey upon domesticated beasts, with the possibility of human beings being added to its menu, particularly when there was an abundance of natural food available not too far away. What was more, in the present case, continued depredations would offer fuel for the vote-seeking political opportunists in the country who were campaigning to have the Reserve thrown open for human habitation. Should that happen, all the animals which at present found sanctuary within its bounds would face extinction.

At the request of Ambagasali's well liked and respected ruler, Prince Simba Nyeuse, Dawn's adoptive cousin, James Allenvale 'Bunduki' Gunn, had recently become the Reserve's Chief Warden. Being on vacation from her post as head of Physical Education at the University of Ambagasali, she had joined him to help with the organization entailed in the appointment. Knowing the importance of winning the support of the population nearest to the Reserve, he had wanted to dispose of the stock killing lions with the minimum of delay. However, after he had taken care of the first lion, another matter of a similar nature had come to his attention. So Dawn had offered to deal with the second lion while he attended to the newer problem. Aware that, like himself, she had received a thorough education in all aspects of natural history from her family – than whom there were no greater *practical* authorities in the world – he had had no hesitation over accepting her suggestion.

Travelling to the village near which the remaining lion had been reported, accompanied by two young Ambaga men who were being trained as game scouts, Dawn had put her extensive knowledge of the species *Panthera Leo* to good use. Deducing from the lack of complaints, or signs to the contrary, that her quarry had not been successful in its hunting since the loss of its consort, she had decided how she might be able to bring it to her instead of spending time searching for it.

58

Obtaining a young goat from the village, although there had been some reluctance on the part of its owner to allowing her to use it, Dawn had taken it to the nearby woodland and staked it out as a decoy in the clearing. With the preparations made, she had sent her companions to wait within hailing distance as she believed that she could best handle the task alone. Her decision had not arisen from a sense of 'white supremacy', but because she knew neither of them had had any practical experience in such matters. Although in the past the Ambaga nation had been lion hunters second only to the Masai in Kenya, the pair were city born and mission educated, so they had never found the need to acquire the traditional masculine attainments of their ancestors.

Separated from the rest of the flock and alarmed at finding its movements restricted by the picket-rope, the goat had begun to bleat when left alone in the darkness. While the girl's hope that the lion would hear and be attracted had materialized, she was annoyed to discover it was not coming from the direction she had anticipated, despite having heard faint sounds of movement suggesting it would. However, employing the skill she had acquired where such a task was concerned, she had contrived to pass through the undergrowth surrounding the clearing until she had attained a position from which she could use the bow without betraying her presence.

Adopting a shooting posture, still without alerting her quarry to the danger, Dawn performed a bow-hunter's 'cheek' draw with deft ease.[4] As she was taking aim, she was pleased to see the lion was behaving as she had envisaged by making a slow stalk instead of dashing to the attack. This made her task easier, although she still did not consider it a sinecure. As she did not want to kill the lion, but hoped to render it unconscious so it could be taken somewhere sufficiently far removed from human habitation to end its stock raiding, she was using an arrow tipped with a specially

[4] Descriptions of how to perform the 'cheek', or 'high', draw and other modern archery techniques are given in the *BUNDUKI* series. For a comparison with the methods used by Japanese *samaurai* bowmen, see the various volumes of the *OLE DEVIL HARDIN* series. J.T.E.

designed hypodermic syringe. While the drug it carried would achieve her purpose, aiming it was more difficult than when using more conventional hunting or target points.

Watching the lion's slow advance, Dawn released the string when satisfied she could not improve her aim. Propelled forward as the limbs which had been held under tension returned to the unflexed position, the arrow sped towards its intended mark. Although the sound of its liberation and flight across the clearing was heard by the carnivore, the warning came too late. Passing through the hairs of the mane and striking the less yielding tawny hide of the neck, the thin protective head of the syringe crumpled, allowing the needle to be pushed into the flesh below and the immobilizing drug to be expelled to do its work.

Letting out a pained and startled squall, the lion bounded into the air. Twisting its body while still rising, it tried to see what had attacked it. Having failed to do so, the moment it landed, it forgot the goat and took flight across the clearing. Before it had taken four bounds, so potent was the drug, its legs buckled and it went down. Struggling briefly to rise, it subsided and became motionless.

'Thank heavens for *that*!' Dawn breathed, refraining from extracting the second arrow equipped with a hypodermic syringe which was attacked to the bow-quiver, as she had not been enamoured of the prospect of trying to send it into a rapidly moving target. Then she raised her voice to a shout and continued, speaking Ambaga as fluently as she could the half a dozen other African tribal languages in which she was conversant, and the variety of Swahili that is the *lingua franca* throughout much of the continent.[5] 'Abu, Kioti, I've got the lion. Bring the truck.'

'Very good,' came the answer from Abu, the elder of the scouts.

Even as Dawn heard the engine of the party's specially adapted Land-Rover being started, her attention was

[5] Derived from *Ki-Swahili*, a very complicated language native to Zanzibar and the coastal belt of East Africa, to which corruptions of English and Hindustani words were added, the *lingua franca* was referred to as, 'Up Country Swahili', or, derisively if spoken badly, as 'Ki-Settler'. J.T.E.

attracted by movements amongst the trees on the side of the clearing from which she had expected the lion to come. A glance in that direction informed her she had not imagined the slight sounds which led to the drawing of the erroneous conclusion. As she had feared might happen, the lion was not the only creature to have been attracted by the goat's bleating. First one, then four more fully grown spotted hyenas emerged from the undergrowth. Despite their physical conformation causing them to move with what appeared to be a slinking, furtive gait, which made some people consider them to be cowardly, they showed no hesitation before making for what their instincts informed them was a victim sufficiently restricted in its movements to offer an easily obtained meal.

Remembering she had promised the owner of the goat that she would do her best to ensure its return unharmed, the girl knew she must protect it from the scavengers. What was more, the fact that they had ignored her shout warned there was only one way this could be accomplished.

Lowering the bow swiftly to the ground, as she knew it would not serve her purpose at that moment, Dawn sent her right hand to the butt of the Smith & Wesson. While her thumb and the other three digits were taking hold, her forefinger flipped apart the press-stud of the 'snap-lock' retaining strap. On being liberated from the security device, the revolver left the holster smoothly. However, not until its muzzle was pointing away from her did she insert the finger through the triggerguard.[6] Bringing her left hand to join its mate and help support the heavy revolver, she raised and extended them to arms' length in a continuation of the draw. As an aid to aiming in poor light, there was a round, luminescent insert on the foresight blade. Making use of this, she aligned the six inch barrel and squeezed the trigger.

Struck in the head by a .41 Magnum calibre bullet delivered at high velocity, the leading hyena went down as if it had suddenly been boned. Swinging the revolver, as the double handed hold allowed her to control its not inconsider-

[6] For the benefit of new readers: a description of how dangerous the failure to take such a precaution could be is given in: *THE FAST GUN.* J.T.E.

able recoil, the girl aimed and fired again. The foremost of the other scavengers gave a yelp of agony and collapsed, kicking spasmodically, in its tracks. Although her third shot missed, in spite of her shout having failed to deter them, the others decided discretion was the better part of valour and, uttering the weird cackling, whooping sounds which had given the species its alternative name, 'laughing hyena', fled into the undergrowth. Nor, if the noise of their departure was any indication, did they intend to return.

'That's right, *fisi*,' Dawn said, lowering the Smith & Wesson but, although she took her left hand from the butt, making no attempt to return it to its holster, as she employed the more generally used of the two Swahili names for the hyena.[7] 'Keep going and I hope for your sakes you've learned some respect for human beings, or somebody will have to shoot some more of you until the idea sinks in.'

With the sentiment uttered, the girl walked cautiously and with the revolver ready for instant use across the clearing. Reaching the lion, she ensured it would be unlikely to recover before her companions arrived and it could be secured in the powerful lightweight travelling cage on the back of their vehicle.

*   *   *   *   *

'This must be them,' remarked Abu, the older of the Ambaga trainee game scouts, as he drove the Land-Rover around a corner of the narrow dirt road through the woodland fringing the Fisi Maji River.[8]

'Yes,' Dawn Drummond-Clayton replied and glanced over her shoulder to where the black maned lion was lying passively in the travelling cage. 'I hope they've got something larger than that to keep him in.'

Three days had elapsed since the capture of the stock killer.

[7] The second Swahili name for the spotted hyena, *Crocuta Crocuta*, is '*nyangau*'. J.T.E.

[8] '*Fisi Maji*': 'water hyena', literally, 'hyena water', the Swahili name for any kind of otter. The sub species indigenous to Ambagasali is the 'Cape clawless otter', *Aonyx Capensis (Schinz)*. J.T.E.

On returning to the base camp Bunduki had established in another Gasali village, the girl had participated in the final stages of the bizarre events which followed the capture of several Ambagasali baboons.[9] Before the lion could be transferred to the interior of the Wild Life Reserve, where it would be compelled to live by hunting non-domestic animals, they had discovered another fate was in store for it. A junior official of the Government had arrived with instructions that it was to be delivered to a party of Russians who were collecting specimens of the local fauna. As the letter had been signed by the Secretary of State For Overseas Relations, there was nothing to be done except obey. However, as Bunduki, his chief game scout, M'Bili and Kioti were required for an inquest that had arose out of the incident, it had fallen upon Dawn and Abu to make the delivery. Having left the lion in the cage on the Land-Rover, instead of placing it in more commodious accommodation, they had set out at dawn that morning. By about three o'clock in the afternoon, they were almost at their destination.

Turning her head to the front, Dawn studied the camp of the people to whom she was transporting the lion. Set in a large clearing on the banks of the river, it was comprised of a marquee with dimensions suitable for the 'big top' of a moderately sized circus, two smaller tents, a combined kitchen-mess hall with mud walls and a thatched roof, an improvised shower and an equally makeshift toilet capable of holding only one person at a time. The three latter structures were of local manufacture, but the rest looked new and showed signs of having had attention devoted to their erection and maintenance. Transport was provided by a Ford Bronco and four large lorries, one like a horsebox and a second equipped to supply electric power.

Only Africans were in sight when the Land-Rover turned the corner. The majority were of the dusty black pigmentation, medium height, thickset physique which differentiated between the Bantu-descended[10] Gasalis and the generally

9 See *Footnote One, Page 54* of this episode. J.T.E.
10 Bantu: pertaining to one of the many Negroid tribes such as the Zulu, Bechuana, Xhosa, Damara, Swahili, Kikuyu, Wa-Kamba, etc., of Central and Southern Africa. J.T.E.

taller, invariably more slender, reddish brown, delicate featured Ambasa, who were of Nilotic origins.[11] One of the former glanced at the approaching vehicle, then turned and strode hurriedly through the closed entrance to the marquee. All the rest began to gather in a group, talking and pointing in an excited fashion at the newcomers.

Apart from a solitary elephant standing at the far side of the clearing, with a small and elderly man who appeared to be a Gasali sitting near it, there was no sign of whether the party had been successful in their attempts to catch specimens of the local wild life. Looking at it, Dawn decided the pachyderm had not been a result of their efforts. As it was a fully grown female representative of the species *Loxodonta Africanus*, the fact that it was standing at liberty suggested it was not a recent capture. On the other hand, the proximity of the man and the wide brass rings about its forelegs indicated it was not wild and had merely strayed into the camp by accident. Knowing that Prince Simba Nyeuse's grandfather had duplicated the efforts being made in what was then the Belgian Congo to domesticate the African elephant after the fashion of its Asian cousin, *Elphas Maximus*, the girl deduced the animal was one which had been subjected to the treatment.

Noticing the flap of the marquee opening, Dawn turned her attention and thoughts from the elephant. She looked with considerable interest at the two women who emerged, followed by a pair of white men and the Gasali who had entered to notify them that the vehicle bringing the lion was coming. Being aware that many of the 'technicians' and 'agricultural advisers' sent by Russia were in reality members of the armed forces with different educational intentions in mind, she wondered if the pretence at animal collecting was a cover for similar activities. If that was the case, it raised the point of why they should have requested the lion be delivered. At that moment, however, she was more concerned with studying them than trying to solve the possible puzzle.

[11] Nilotic: possessing the physical characteristics of people native to the Nile Basin. The Masai are probably the best known examples of this group. J.T.E.

Clad in a tight-fitting, high-necked, but sleeveless white satin blouse, a wide black leather belt, form hugging white riding breeches and well polished brown boots, the shorter of the women was about Dawn's height, almost as curvaceous, but several years older. She had black hair, taken back in a severe bun and a bronzed, sultrily beautiful face. Her female companion was nowhere near as shapely or attractive. Almost three inches taller, although somewhat younger, she was so bulky that she showed barely any feminine contours. Cropped boyishly short, yet without charm, her black hair did nothing to improve a massive, surly, somewhat Mongoloid set of sallow features. Her long sleeved, baggy blouse, masculine trousers and the heavy, blunt-toed jackboots into which they were tucked were all black and showed signs of long wear.

One of the men was young, tall, lean, swarthily handsome, clean shaven, but with longish brown hair. Older, shorter, thickset and completely bald, the other nevertheless sported a bushy black beard which had the advantage of hiding much of his unprepossessing, scarred and scowling features. Both were bare-headed and wore khaki bush jackets hanging outside trousers which were tucked into brown hunting boots. Although there were cartridges for rifles in the loops on the jackets' chests, like the women, neither had any weapons in view.

However, while the girl found the massive woman and the men of some interest, they did not command much of her attention. Instead, she gave it to the black haired beauty; about whom she thought there was something familiar. As the Land-Rover carried her closer, she realized why this should be. Being a gymnast, athlete and swimmer of world class, although she had given up entering such events except at local level,[12] she recognized Katya Viskovsky as a leading Russian 'amateur' gymnast against whom she had won in her last international competition.

According to the reports Dawn had read in newspapers, the woman had retired after the defeat. For all that, if the play of muscles in her bare arms and visible beneath the

[12] The reason Dawn Drummond-Clayton retired from international athletics is given in the first paragraph of *APPENDIX FOUR*. J.T.E.

skin tight riding breeches was any indication, she still kept herself in excellent physical condition. Despite a pending marriage having been given as the reason for her retirement, she wore no rings of any kind to exhibit her marital status.

On climbing from the cab when Abu brought the vehicle to a halt in front of the four white people, the girl discovered that the recognition was mutual.

'Well, well!' the beautiful Russian said, with no suggestion of cordiality in her sultry voice, speaking English fluently. 'You are Dawn *Drummond*, aren't you?'

'Dawn Drummond-*Clayton*, Miss Viskovsky,' the girl amended, using the other's maiden name as she could not recollect having seen any mention of the husband's identity. 'I certainly didn't expect to see *you* here.'

'You have brought our lion, I see,' Katya stated, making no attempt to correct the way she had been addressed. 'What a magnificent specimen.'

'Isn't he,' Dawn agreed. 'But it's a great pity he has to be placed in a cage for the rest of his life.'

'It is,' Katya admitted, darting a glance filled with annoyance at the Africans who were gathering around the rear of the Land-Rover. 'But I assure you he will be given the finest of accommodation and good treatment.'

Wondering what was causing the woman's reaction, Dawn glanced over her shoulder. She was puzzled by the men's obvious excitement as they pointed at the lion and exchanged comments. While it was a fine specimen and of the type which was once classed as 'royal game', with the exception of the old man who had risen from the elephant's side and was approaching, their dress suggested they were moderately well-to-do town dwellers. Unless there was some advantage to be gained, many of their class took little interest in the wild life of the country.

Because there were men from both of Amabagasali's races present – as well as four Dawn identified as being respectively a Kikuyu, a Nandi and a Swahili from Kenya and a Tanzanian Wakeke – most of the remarks were in the *lingua franca* instead of their tribal languages. Hearing the words, '*simba nyeuse*', she realized they meant the lion and not the ruler of the country.[13] However, despite being familiar with the names Africans gave to various kinds of animals, she was unable to think of what a '*punda simba*' might be. The Swahili name for a zebra was, '*punda milia*', but she had never heard of a 'zebra lion'.

'May I introduce you to my associates?' Katya asked, diverting the girl's attention from the Africans and their remarks. 'They are Comrades Agasha Nefedovna, Philip Golitsyn and Boris Kravichenko.'

'Pleased to meet you,' Dawn said automatically, shaking hands with the younger man, Kravichenko, who alone offered to do so. Pulling free from his grasp when he attempted to maintain the contact, eyeing her as if trying to see beneath her clothing, she went on, 'Where are you going to cage the lion?'

'*Cage* it?' Katya repeated. 'But it is already in a cage.'

'Which belongs to the Department of Wild Life And Natural Resources,' Dawn pointed out. 'Besides, even if I was authorized to leave it, you'd need to put the lion in something larger unless you intend moving it straight away. The travelling cage is far too cramped for any extensive occupancy.'

'Very well,' Katya almost snorted. 'We will attend to it.'

'Do you want us to take the cage into the marquee?' Dawn inquired, sensing that her refusal to leave the cage was not received favourably by the former gymnast.

'Why should we?' Katya demanded, while the other women and the men, who clearly understood what was being said despite having made no attempt to join in the conversation or acknowledge the introduction, exchanged glances.

'I don't see any cages out here,' the girl explained. 'So I presume you're keeping your collection in the marquee. '

'Ah yes, of course,' Katya replied. There was a brief pause before she continued, 'But how remiss of me. You must both be very hungry. Why don't you tell your driver to go to the kitchen, while you join me for lunch in my tent. My associates will attend to transferring the lion to more suitable quarters.'

[13] '*Simba Nyeuse*': Swahili for 'Black Lion', literally, 'Lion Black'. J.T.E.

'Thank you for the invitation,' Dawn answered, but decided upon a way which would allow her to see inside the marquee. 'However, as I'm representing the Department of Wild Life and Natural Resources, I must assure myself that you have satisfactory accommodation available before turning the lion over to you.'

'You can take *my* word – !' Katya began.

'I don't doubt *that*,' Dawn interrupted and lowered her voice to a conspiratorial level. 'But you *know* what these Africans are like. The driver would be only too pleased to report me if I neglected my duty and there are those in the Department who are just waiting for a chance to have me dismissed so as to take my place. So you see my position.'

'I *do!*' Katya admitted, before she could stop herself, glancing at her associates. Coming from a country and society in which such behaviour was the rule rather than the exception, she was willing to accept the explanation. 'Very well. I'll take you inside.'

*　*　*　*　*

Walking into the marquee with the black haired beauty by her side and the other three Russians following on her heels, Dawn Drummond-Clayton found the resemblance to the 'big top' of a circus was not restricted to the external appearance. In the centre was the kind of enclosure made from steel bars employed in acts involving dangerous animals, but devoid of the hoops and stands upon which the creatures were made to perform tricks. For illumination, power being supplied via a generator truck which was one of the vehicles in the clearing, several lights such as those used by photographers in addition to the more usual type were suspended over the enclosure. Although there were signs on the grass indicating something had been moving around in the enclosure, it was empty at that moment and the barred chute through which ingress was possible disappeared behind the canvas wall across the centre of the marquee.

There was, however, no sign of any animals which had been collected. Nor anything in which captured creatures could be held prior to being taken to Russia.

'What is *that* for?' Dawn inquired, pointing to the enclosure.

'Comrade Nefedovna is probably our country's greatest lion tamer,' Katya Viskovsky replied. 'She has to test the temperament of those she will be taking back with her for use in her act.'

'I don't understand,' Dawn stated, having noticed that the massive woman's scowl deepened at the use of the word, 'probably' although she did not speak. 'I thought you were collecting for a zoo?'

'So we are,' Katya asserted, then gave a cluck of what might have been annoyance. 'Do you mean to say you didn't know we have been granted permission for her to capture lions for the State circus she is with?'

'I *didn't*,' Dawn stated, adopting the tone of a bureaucrat who had made a discovery regarding something of which she believed she should have been consulted. 'Do you have *many* of them to pick from?'

'Only one, until you came,' Katya claimed. 'It is in its cage behind the dividing wall, but I'm afraid you cannot see it.'

'Why not?' the girl demanded, still acting as she had seen pompous representatives of government departments behave when they believed their 'rights' were being challenged.

'Comrade Nefedovna *always* keeps a new lion to herself and allows nobody else near it,' the retired gymnast explained, but after a pause as if needing to think of a reason. 'She says this is the only way to build a rapport with it. She is doing so well that she will not permit myself, Comrade Kravichenko, or even Comrade Golitsyn, her assistant, to go near it.'

'That's all very well – !' Dawn commented, continuing her pose by displaying well simulated bristling self-important indignation.

'You can look, *if you insist*,' Katya authorized coldly. 'But we have been assured of complete co-operation by Com – *Mr* Utambi and if he should hear – !'

'Oh *very well*!' Dawn surrendered, knowing the man named was the Secretary of State For Overseas Relations. Having completed his education at the London School of

Economics, his sympathies were not in accord with the pro-West attitudes of Prince Simba Nyeuse and he advocated a policy of employing only Ambagasali nationals in positions of trust. He had, in fact, been one of the most vocal protestors when she and Bunduki were offered their respective positions. 'I *suppose* it's all right and I don't need to look.'

There was a more serious reason behind the girl's acceptance than a concern over possible repercussions instigated by Mr Utambi. Although she suspected something was wrong, her instincts warned she could be treading on dangerous ground should she try to find out what it might be. If she was to insist upon going to inspect the animal behind the dividing wall, she would be refused. Or, if she was permitted to do so and it was something which should be kept a secret, she had no doubt the Russians would take any measures necessary to ensure it remained that way. So she decided the best policy was to give the impression of being frightened of arousing the important official's ire. Then she could return and enlist the aid of Bunduki to solve and deal with the mystery.

'I didn't think you would,' Katya purred, exuding such smug condescension that Dawn was hard put to control her temper. 'Let's go and have lunch while my associates transfer the lion to more commodious accommodation.'

'Yes, *let's*,' the girl assented, contriving to restrain her annoyance. Then, instead of setting off immediately, she pointed to the powerful lamps erected around the enclosure. 'Are you making a film?'

'Why should we be?' Katya challenged, throwing a quick look at the other Russians as the lion tamer and her assistant let out sharp exclamations in their native tongue and Kravichenko gave a startled gasp.

'The lights are similar to those I've seen used when one is being made,' Dawn replied, noticing the women and the men had registered something closer to alarm than just surprise at her question.

'So they are,' Katya conceded, as if the point had only just occurred to her. 'But we are *not* making a film. Comrade Nefedovna used them to accustom the lion to working in such brilliance. Shall we go to lunch?'

'I am hungry,' Dawn answered, considering she would be ill-advised to take the matter further. 'So, unless you think your *assistants* need any help – '

'They *don't*!' Katya declared, scowling as she noticed that her associates were showing they did not care for the designation they had been given. 'Shall we go?'

Conscious of being watched by three pairs of coldly suspicious eyes, Dawn went from the marquee with the retired gymnast. Calling over the man she had recognized as a Kikuyu, Katya told him in English to take Abu to the mess hall for a meal and then led her to the largest of the tents. Facing the woodland, its front flaps were fastened open to show it was divided into a living section at the front and, hidden by a canvas wall, sleeping quarters behind it. From all appearances, it was equipped with the latest furnishings and devices intended to make life comfortable while on safari.

Escorting the girl inside and seating her on one of the folding chairs at the collapsible table, the woman asked if she had any preferences for lunch. Being told she had not, Katya nevertheless left with a comment about going to make sure the cook was preparing something suitable for a white person's palate.

Left to herself, Dawn's first inclination was to look around the tent in the hope of finding some clue about the Russians' activities. A moment's thought served to warn her such a course might be ill-advised. It was unlikely she would have been left alone and unobserved if anything informative was available. Or, in the unlikely event that it should be, there was almost certain to be some form of precaution against it being discovered by an authorized searcher. So, wanting to lull the quartet into a sense of false security by having them assume she harboured no suspicions, she remained seated and waited for Katya to return.

In spite of her misgivings, Dawn could not fault her hostess's hospitality. Like the majority of Communists with whom she had come into contact, Katya clearly had no qualms about living with the best possible standards. The food, served on china and a clean white tablecloth by a Gasali whose behaviour indicated he was long used to such

71

employment, was excellent and the wine accompanying it from a costly vintage. What was more, although refusing to discuss the reason for her Party's presence in Ambagasali, she proved to be a good conversationalist so long as the subject stayed on athletics in general and gymnastics in particular.

'What's *that*?' Dawn demanded, being interrupted by a savage roaring snarl which sounded from somewhere in the clearing, just as she was commenting upon the training she was giving to pupils at the University of Ambagasali.

'It seems your friend doesn't care for the idea of being moved to a larger cage,' Katya answered.

'So it seems,' Dawn admitted, but she was conscious of a partially developed thought even though its completion eluded her. 'What kind of methods does Comrade Nefedovna use for her training?'

'Probably less cruel than those used in the West,' Katya replied stiffly. 'And one can hardly expect a freshly caught lion to accept human beings close to it, much less moving it from one cage to another, without making some protest.'

'I suppose not,' the girl conceded, trying to decide what she found unsatisfying about the explanation.

'You were saying how good some of your pupils are,' the woman remarked. 'Do you have any who are up to *your* standard?'

'I've some who are very good,' Dawn answered and the conversation was resumed, continuing through the meal and until Kravichenko arrived to say the transfer of the lion was completed.

'Are you armed?' Katya inquired, and she and her guest walked to where the unloaded Land-Rover was parked.

'I've my bow and arrows with me, but that's all,' Dawn lied, having her knife and Smith & Wesson revolver locked in her overnight bag under the vehicle's front passenger seat. 'Why?'

'Aren't you worried about not carrying a revolver, or a rifle?' Katya asked. 'I mean while you are travelling through such desolate country.'

'I've never had the need for either,' Dawn replied. 'I only have the bow in case there is a chance of shooting something for the pot. Anyway, my game scout has a rifle.'

'Is he a good shot?' the woman wanted to know. 'From what I've heard, few Africans are.'

'I've seen better, I'll admit,' Dawn confessed. 'Anyway, here he comes. I'll not take up any more of your time, particularly as we've a long drive ahead of us.'

'Have a safe journey,' Katya said. 'Perhaps I'll find time to come and visit you before we leave the country.'

*   *   *   *   *

'You seem worried, Abu,' Dawn Drummond-Clayton stated, glancing at the Ambaga after he had driven the Land-Rover for something over a mile in silence.

'Those people back there are up to something,' the game scout replied. 'And it *isn't* just animal collecting.'

'Have you any idea what it *is*?' the girl asked.

'No,' Abu admitted. 'They wouldn't tell me anything in the mess hall. But some of them are members of the Ambagasali National Party.'

'Are they?' Dawn ejaculated, aware that the organization was in favour of breaking all connections with the West and were suspected of having connections with Communist-backed groups in other countries. However, before the conversation could be continued, she saw the old man who had been with the elephant at the clearing emerging from the undergrowth at the side of the road and waving to them. 'It looks as if he wants us to stop.'

'Shall I?'

'Of course.'

'*Jambo, memsaab,*' the old man said, as the vehicle came to a halt before him, applying the Swahili mode of address for a white woman which the younger people had let fall into disuse since their country was granted independence.

'*Jambo, m'zee,*' Dawn responded, employing a word which in such a context meant an older and respected person. She went on in Gasali, 'What can we do for you?'

'Can I ride with you?' the man inquired, showing no surprise at hearing his native tongue spoken so fluently.

73

'Of course,' Dawn assented, opening the door and moving across the seat. 'Come in.'

Studying the passenger as he climbed nimbly aboard, the girl liked what she saw. Crinkly white hair framed a wrinkled face with surprisingly bright eyes and a smile that displayed a well fitting set of false teeth. He had on an old British Army battledress blouse, shorts and a pair of sandals made from pieces of a tyre. Settling himself alongside her, he did not speak as the vehicle started moving. Instead, he started to hum.

'Fungua safari, fungua safari?' Dawn sang, recognizing the tune and having noticed the glances he directed at her. *'Amri kwa nani, amri kwa nani?'*

'Amri ya bwana captain,' the old man replied, in a cracked voice. *'Amri ya* K.R.'

'Who did you serve with?' Dawn asked, with a smile, at the conclusion of the old marching song, having deduced from the answer that the passenger had served in one of what used to be called the 'native' regiments of the British Army.[14]

'Sergeant Major Katabona, 12th K.A.R., *memsaab,'* the man announced proudly, using the traditional abbreviation for the King's African Rifles. 'Are you the daughter of *Bwana Mkubwa Sana?'*[15]

'I am of his house,' Dawn admitted. When no response was forthcoming, she commented, 'You have a fine elephant.'

'She's getting old, like me,' Katabona said, wistfully it seemed. 'These days, we're pleased to take any kind of work we're offered.'

'And what have you been offered?' the girl inquired, after another brief pause.

'Nothing,' the old man replied. 'I took *Kidogo* to the Russians hoping there would be something for us to do. They

[14] *Fungua safari;* Start the journey, *Amri kwa nani?*; By whose order? (literally, order by who?). *Amri ya* K. R.; by order of King's Regulations. J.T.E.

[15] *Bwana Mkubwa Sana:* 'Very Big Master' (literally, Master Big Very) one name by which the head of Dawn Drummond-Clayton's family was known throughout Africa. J.T.E.

said there wasn't, but I told them I'd wait in case something came up.'

'And did it?'

'Not yet.'

'Do you know what they're doing?'

'Collecting animals, they *say*,' Katabona sniffed. 'But the only ones I've seen are those town-living *shenzis*[16] and the four foreigners who came with the *mzungu*.[17] I've heard there's one of the four-legged kind in the marquee, but I've never seen it. They only let a few of the blacks go inside and I'm not one who can.'

'And you've no idea what it might be?' Dawn asked, forming the impression that the old man had no liking for the occupants of the camp and suspecting he was not only much shrewder than he pretended, but possessed considerable knowledge of animals.

'They *call* it a *"punda simba"*,' Katabona answered. 'But I've *never* heard of such a thing. One thing I do know, though. It doesn't sound like any lion I've ever heard, or zebra for that matter.'

'Or me,' Dawn admitted, then the memory which had eluded her in Katya Viskovsky's tent broke through. It was of a sound she had heard made by a predatory animal during a tour of wild life reserves in India and suggested why the name, 'zebra lion', had been granted. 'In fact, if it isn't a – !'

Before the girl could complete her explanation, the Land-Rover's engine began to splutter and lose power.

* * * * *

'Why's that happened?' Abu demanded, as the vehicle's motor stopped operating and it came to a halt.

'The tank's empty,' Dawn Drummond-Clayton stated, looking at the petrol gauge on the dashboard. 'But it shouldn't be.'

'I'll fill it from the jerry cans,' the trainee game scout

[16] '*Shenzi*' : Swahili for something cheap, shoddy, or an uncouth person. J.T.E.

[17] '*Mzungu*' : Swahili name for a white person, although it is only employed in a derogatory manner. J.T.E.

offered, although he too was surprised by the lack of fuel, opening his door and getting out.

'I'll lend you a hand,' the girl offered, feeling decidedly uneasy.

'I can manage,' Abu declared.

'It will save time if I come and help,' Dawn countered and looked at the old man. 'Can I go out, please?'

Although Katabona left the vehicle and moved clear of the passenger door, the girl did not follow him immediately. Instead, she removed the panel which concealed the compartment under the seat. Pulling out her overnight bag, she extracted the Smith & Wesson revolver. Tucking the weapon into the waistband of her slacks, but leaving its holster and her knife inside, she returned the bag and followed the old man.

Once again, however, Dawn did not carry out a stated intention straight away. Abu was already unclipping one of the jerry cans in which was carried a reserve of petrol for use in such emergencies. Neither going to join him, nor freeing another can, she looked back along the road. Because of its winding nature and the dense woodland on either side, she could only see about a hundred yards.

It was enough!

Even before the vehicle came into view and she identified it as the Ford Bronco she had seen at the clearing, the sound of its engine approaching had increased her ill-at-ease feeling. It was travelling slowly and, although she could only make out the faces of the pair on the front seat, there were four occupants. They were the two male Russians and, as the distance decreased, she decided the others were Africans. At that moment, however, she was less concerned with the composition of the party than over the fact that Kravichenko was driving and, at his side, Golitsyn was holding a rifle. Discovering the bearded man was armed did nothing to decrease her growing sense of foreboding.

Even as Dawn's suspicions with regards to the arrival of the Bronco were forming, something more struck her. She had been too engrossed elsewhere to realize it until that moment, but the old man was not to be seen. Which meant he must have gone directly into the undergrowth on leaving

76

the Land-Rover. His departure had passed unobserved because she was occupied with arming herself and her speculations about the possible reasons for the vehicle from the clearing putting in what might be considered a fortuitous appearance.

There was, however, little time for the girl to ponder over the reason for Katabona's absence. All she knew for sure was it added to her belief that no good would come from the arrival of the two Russians and their African passengers.

Watching the Bronco coming to a stop a few yards from the Land-Rover, Dawn was grateful for the realization that the contours of the road were such that she had been partially concealed from the Russians as they were approaching. While they could see the upper portion of her body, the revolver in her waistband was below their range of vision. Remembering Katya's questions about her carrying weapons, she felt sure the hiding place under the Land-Rover's seat had not been discovered. So, provided her answers had been accepted, the two men would not know she had such a potent firearm readily available. She also realized that she would be unable to alert Abu to the situation, although he clearly was not aware of it. Certainly, if his behaviour was any guide, he had no suspicions that their lives might be in jeopardy. He was merely pausing in his task and looking at the Bronco hopefully, anticipating an offer of assistance.

The passenger door of the Bronco opened and, followed by the Kikuyu and the Wakeke, Golitsyn hauled himself out. Although each of the Africans had a Tokarev Model TT30 automatic pistol in his waistband and was reaching for it, Dawn spared them no more than a glance. Nor did she devote any time to studying Kravichenko as he emerged from the other side of the vehicle. Her attention was upon the weapon in the bearded Russian's hands and she knew it made an already sufficiently perilous situation infinitely worse.

While the girl did not identify the 7.62mm Avtomat Kalashnikov with which Golitsyn was armed any more accurately than she had the firearms carried by the Africans – having only noticed them as being handguns of an unspeci-

77

fied type and a potential source of added danger – the long, curved magazine beneath the frame and its general shape warned her it was what, in military terms, was classified as an 'assault rifle' and, as such, was capable of automatic fire.[18]

Instead of advancing, the bearded Russian confirmed Dawn's fears almost as soon as he was out of the Bronco. Paying no attention to his African companions, he spread his heavy boots apart and, looking at Abu, began to raise the weapon.

'Surrender!' Dawn shouted in English, blessing her forethought in already having pulled the Smith & Wesson from her waistband.

Despite employing a word which she hoped would be understood and obeyed, the girl did not intend to wait and see if this happened. Even as she was speaking, crouching slightly so as to present as small a target as possible, she swung around the heavy revolver in both hands until her forearms rested on the bonnet of the Land-Rover. As she took aim along the barrel, her thumbs were drawing back the hammer.

Spitting forth an obscenity in his native tongue, Golitsyn began to turn the Avtomat in the direction of what he knew to be a target of greater priority than the young Ambaga. Seeing her command was being ignored and aware that he would not be deterred from shooting by considerations of her sex, Dawn had no qualms over her response. Squeezing the trigger, she caused the uppermost cartridge in the revolver's cylinder to be discharged.

Caught between the eyes by the .41 Magnum bullet, which passed through his head and onwards with hardly any loss of velocity, the bearded Russian was thrown backwards. His unexpected action caused even greater consternation to the two Africans. Already alarmed by the sight of his skull being burst open and the lead hissing between them, they still had sufficient presence of mind to spring aside in opposite directions. As the stricken Golitsyn went blundering by to crash

[18] Apart from their respective sizes, the chief difference between an 'assault rifle' and a submachine gun is that the former fires rifle and the latter handgun cartridges, so it has a superior range and striking power. J.T.E.

lifeless on the road, instead of attempting to retrieve the weapon discarded involuntarily when the bullet struck, each snatched at his automatic pistol. Taken equally unawares, Kravichenko nevertheless duplicated their actions by starting to draw the Tokarev he had put into his waistband before setting out from the clearing.

Remaining alert to everything that was happening by the Bronco, Dawn found herself on the horns of a dilemma. While she had removed the most serious threat posed by the quartet, the affair was still far from ended. The other three were armed and as unlikely as Golitsyn had been to accept a command to surrender. Between them, they would be more than she could handle unaided.

Before the girl could decide which assailant required her attentions most urgently, much of the need was removed. Drawing back the Smith & Wesson's hammer as an aid to rapid firing and a steadier aim, she saw a figure appear from among the bushes and behind the two Africans. Despite the speed at which he was moving, she realized it was Katabona even though uncertain of what the slender black thing in his right hand might be.

Even as the Kikuyu's pistol came out, the old man was behind him. The girl was unable to see what was taking place, but the way in which his back suddenly arched and his features were suffused by an expression of agony, she could guess. Dropping the weapon, he advanced a couple of staggering steps and, with his hands reaching behind him, collapsed on to his face.

Seeing the way in which the Kikuyu was behaving, the Wakeke started to turn with the intention of discovering the cause. Although he found out, he was not permitted to make use of the information. Still moving with the same surprising rapidity for one so advanced in years, Katabona lunged and swung his right arm in an upwards arc. The knife he held, its blade red with the blood from his first victim, laid open the Wakeke's throat almost to the neck bones. Giving an agonized gurgle that was intended as a cry, the man dropped his weapon and, clutching unavailingly at the mortal wound he had received, fell dying against the side of the Bronco. After delivering the second attack, the old man

79

exhibited a similar alacrity by darting behind the rear of the vehicle.

'Surrender!' Dawn repeated, aligning her Smith & Wesson at Kravichenko.

Darting a frightened glance about him, the surviving Russian assessed his situation and concluded it was desperate. Not only were all his companions rendered *hors de combat*, but the people they believed would be easy victims had proved anything except that. The girl had lied about the way she was armed and demonstrated considerable ability in using the heavy calibre revolver. Despite having displayed surprise, the Ambaga was sufficiently recovered from it to have dropped the jerry can and was pulling his British Army bolt action rifle from the Land-Rover. Furthermore, the two African's attacker might have disappeared from sight, but that did not mean he was no longer in the vicinity. In fact, he was almost certainly close by and ready to do whatever was necessary.

'Don't shoot!' Kravichenko yelled, throwing aside his Tokarev. 'I'm a Russian national and demand diplomatic immunity.'

'We *might* let you live long enough to ask for it,' Dawn replied, straightening up and glancing to where Katabona, still holding the blood-smeared all black Sykes-Fairbirn commando knife – which, she learned later, he carried in a sheath behind his back – advanced to retrieve the discarded automatic pistol. 'But only if you tell us what you intend to do with the *"punda simba"*.'

*　　*　　*　　*　　*

'How soon can we put them together?' Katya Viskovsky demanded, glancing from the black-maned lion – which was in an even smaller and more cramped cage than the one it had arrived in – to the tiger prowling around the enclosure.

'Soon,' Agasha Nefedovna replied, her voice implying resentment at what she considered to be an intrusion into her part of the affair.

'*How* soon?' Katya repeated and a person who knew Russians could have told from their different accents that she belonged to a higher class of their country's supposedly classless society than her bulky companion. 'When the "Drummond" girl doesn't return, others are sure to come in search of her.'

'Another day, at least!' Agasha stated. 'By then, my tiger will consider the enclosure belongs to him and will attack any other creature that enters. But, to keep *you* satisfied, although *I'd* rather have the lion full of food, but kept cramped and stiff for longer, I'll have everything ready tomorrow afternoon.'

The frown which came to the retired gymnast's beautiful face was more noticeable than a similar emotion on the other woman's sullen features. Experienced in her people's ways, she knew the other was paving the way to lay the blame upon her if anything went wrong. However, aware of just how much was at stake, she was too wise to antagonize her associate and was determined to keep the peace if that was the only way she could guarantee the success of the plan which she had hatched and had brought them, their equipment and the tiger to Ambagasali.

Although Katya had been attending her last gymnastic tournament prior to retiring, her defeat at Dawn Drummond-Clayton's hands resulted in the loss of the important and lucrative coaching job in Moscow she had hoped to receive. Instead, she had found herself directed to a far less exalted position at the university of a smaller city. Ambitious and an opportunist, she had sought for a way in which she might be able to regain favour.

The means had suggested itself one night after Katya had attended the university's cinema. Part of the programme had been a Hollywood action-escapism-adventure jungle movie, shown ostensibly to illustrate the exploitation of the African natives by the Capitalist Imperialists, but which she suspected the rest of the audience found as entertaining and enjoyable as she had after the usual round of 'message' ladened, propaganda-based films made in her homeland, or from British television, which were the usual fare. Part of the action had been a fight between a tiger and a black maned lion, ending in the latter's 'death'. A trio of Gasalis, receiving their education in Russia, were among the audience and she had been surprised by their reaction to the sequence. Instead of being amused by the sight of a tiger apparently roaming wild in Africa, they had behaved in such an amazed manner she had asked why. Learning of the connection between the black maned lion and Prince Simba Nyeuse, who her Government hoped to depose and replace by somebody more compatible, she had thought up a scheme she felt sure would produce her promotion.

Katya's idea was based upon an episode from a series of books she had enjoyed while in England,[19] although she was sure the hierarchy of her Government would not have approved of her reading them. On explaining, she had found the three Gasalis most appreciative and willing to supply their assistance. Fortunately, she had sufficient discreditable knowledge of a highly placed Party member's affairs to ensure his support. Calling upon him, she had obtained permission and the necessary funds for the scheme to be implemented.

On being returned to their homeland, the three Gasalis had set about spreading a story claimed to be an old legend that had been suppressed by the rulers of their nation. It told how a creature with the appearance of a lion, yet striped after the fashion of a zebra and known as a *'punda simba'* fought and killed one of the black maned 'royal' predators. Seeing this, the gods had decided that the royal family of Simba Nyeuse was no longer fit to rule and they were deposed to the benefit of the population.

Receiving reports that the improvised 'legend' was being accepted eagerly by the populace, although unaware that these were grossly exaggerated, Katya had been granted authority to carry on. Despite her flattering description to Dawn, Agasha Nefedovna was only a moderately competent lion tamer employed in a minor circus. However, she was the best who would accept the assignment and had agreed on being promised a successful outcome would be rewarded by promotion to a more prestigious appointment.

[19] The incident upon which Katya Viskovsky based her idea is recorded in: *Chapter VII, 'The Legender', LIEUTENANT BONES* (one of the *SANDERS OF THE RIVER* series of biographies by Edgar Wallace.) J.T.E.

Supplied with the largest and most aggressive tiger available and the means by which to transport it, Katya had travelled from her homeland accompanied by Agasha, Philip Golitsyn – the inevitable representative of the *M.V.D.*[20] who accompanied any party leaving the 'people's' paradise on Earth to ensure they all returned – and Boris Gravichenko, a not too important director-cum-cameraman, who was to film the spectacle. Landing in an African country with strong obligations to Russia, they had been joined by four men from Kenya and Tanzania, who were to assist them and supply any local knowledge they required.

Although the original intention was to find and catch a suitable lion, the news of the stock-raiders' capture had saved Katya's party from needing to do so. With the connivance of the Secretary of State for Overseas Relations, long an overt supporter of Russia, they had arranged for the black maned beast to be delivered. There had, however, been something more than a mere precaution behind her insistence that the people who brought it must be killed. Despite her claim that she believed they had seen and heard enough to become suspicious, her primary motive had stemmed from a desire for revenge upon the beautiful and capable English girl whose victory in the gymnastic competition she blamed for her fall from grace.

Over an hour had elapsed since the four men had set off in pursuit of the Land-Rover. They had not yet returned, but Katya saw no reason for concern. The vehicle's tank had been almost drained of petrol, but there was no way of estimating how much had been left to ensure it would start and leave the clearing. Nor had it been considered advisable that they should be killed there, with so many witnesses – not all guaranteed to remain loyal if it was considered an advantage to be otherwise – present. So the men were to follow until a depletion of the fuel brought the Land-Rover to a stop. Having disposed of the girl and her companion, Golitsyn was to make sure neither they nor their vehicle were found. Katya was convinced that nothing could go wrong. There had been a powerful hunting bow in the vehicle, but it

[20] '*M.V.D.*': *Ministerstvo Vnutrennikh Del* (Ministry of Internal Affairs) the secret police of Soviet Russia. J.T.E.

was disassembled into its component parts. Except for the game scout's rifle, no other weapons had been found. So it was agreed that the girl would be unarmed and, as it was to be unexpected, neither she nor the Ambaga would be able to oppose the attack when it was launched. ·

Always impatient, Katya had not been content to remain in her tent until the men returned. Hearing sounds which informed her Agasha was in the marquee, she had gone there. As she had expected, the woman was aggravating the tiger by prodding at it with a sharp stick through the bars of the enclosure. Despite knowing the other resented any interference, she could not resist the temptation to go over and request information about the possibility of commencing the filming.

'Very well,' Katya said, in tones redolent of an implied threat, as Agasha's estimation was delivered. 'Do as *you* wish!'

As the stocky woman was about to make an angry response, there came an interruption. From outside the marquee arose the squeal of an enraged elephant, the crackling of wood being broken and masculine bellows of alarm. However, there was something much closer to attract her attention. Nor was it overlooked by her companion.

Showing no sign of hearing the commotion behind her, the beautiful English girl was stepping through the gash she had slit with the knife she held down the side wall of the marquee.

*   *   *   *   *

'*You!*' Katya Viskovsky, too aghast to say or do anything more constructive, although she retained just sufficient presence of mind to speak English.

'*Me!*' Dawn Drummond-Clayton admitted, walking forward and returning to its sheath the Randall Model 1 'All Purpose Fighting' knife with which she had gained her entrance.

'What's happening out there?' Katya demanded, as the pandemonium continued, still unable to decide how to deal with the unexpected and unwanted visitor.

84

'Just *Kidogo* pushing down the mess hall,' Dawn explained, 'with your men in it.'

'*Kidogo?*' Katya repeated incredulously, knowing this was the name – meaning 'Tiny' – by which the aged owner spoke of his elephant. 'But that old fool told us it had been trained *never* to push against a human being's dwelling.'

'She forgot her training,' Dawn asserted calmly, reaching for the Smith & Wesson revolver in her waistband. 'And so would *you* if you were being bitten where she is by several *siafu*.'[21]

Frightened by threats from Katabona, Boris Kravichenko had told of the Russians' intentions. Knowing what the consequences of a successful outcome could mean, the girl and her companions had agreed something must be done. Merely contacting the authorities, they realized, would not be enough. The film might be completed before any official action could be taken and the conspirators gone into hiding. Then, after allowing the hunt time to die down, they would continue with the interrupted scheme.

Dawn's declaration that they must return to the clearing and try to liberate the black maned lion had met with the two men's approval. It had been Katabona's suggestion of how this might be achieved. Recollecting one important aspect of all domesticated elephants' training, on hearing how he planned to use *Kidogo* to create a diversion, she had pointed out how it could spoil the scheme. However, he had claimed he could overcome the animal's disinclination to damage property. While he had not gone into details, beyond saying he would require Abu's assistance, she had had sufficient confidence in him to accept the offer.

Placing Kravichenko, bound hand and foot and gagged, into the travelling cage, the trio had concealed the Land-Rover and bodies in the woodland by the roadside. Taking the Ford Bronco as their transportation, they had made the return journey without the precaution against being seen proving necessary. Leaving it out of sight of their destination, they had gone the rest of the way on foot. Guiding them through the forest, having armed himself with the Avtomat

[21] *Siafu*: Swahili name for the nomadic, voracious, carnivorous 'safari' ant. J.T.E.

assault rifle and two of the Tovarevs taken from the would-be killers, Katabona had insisted upon making a short detour to where a mass of safari ants were feeding upon the carcass of a bushbuck. Then he had shown why he had brought a small empty bottle from the Land-Rover with him, by scooping several of the voracious creatures into it and securing them with its stopper. Having done so, he led the way to the camp. As he had said might be the case, on hearing the snarls of the tiger being tormented, all the men were in the mess hall. This had become the policy while Agasha was working with the animal, designed to prevent any of the Africans from finding out what was happening in the marquee.

While the men had gone to collect *Kidogo*, the girl had made her way equally unchallenged to the side of the marquee. Waiting until they had brought the elephant to stand with its head almost touching the wall of the mess hall, she had began to cut a means of entering. As she commenced, she saw how *Kidogo* was to be persuaded to act in the required manner. Taking the stopper from the bottle, which he had been given, Abu placed its mouth carefully against the animal's sexual organ. Moving restlessly as they had since being confined, the little creatures soon began to emerge. The girl had not waited to watch the result when the ants started to bite with their huge pincer-like jaws, but *Kidogo*'s scream of mingled surprise and pain, followed by the other sounds, informed her that her assumption of what would happen had been correct.

Taking advantage of the girl's attention being on Katya, Agasha Nefedovna acted with considerable speed for her bulk. Although the pointed stick she sent spinning through the air missed its intended mark, her efforts were far from wasted. Striking the revolver just as it was drawn free, the missile knocked it from its owner's grasp. Nor did the lion tamer restrict herself to the throw, but lumbered rapidly forward.

Instead of trying to retrieve the Swith & Wesson immediately, Dawn faced the appoaching woman. Waiting until an instant before the outstretched hands were close enough to clutch her, she stepped sideways. The evasive action was only partially successful. While Agasha was unable to stop, she swung a blow as she went by. Caught between the shoulders with sufficient force to send her staggering towards the enclosure, the girl also lost her grip on the knife she had just completed drawing.

Bringing herself to a halt not many feet from where the tiger was prowling balefully beyond the bars, Dawn looked behind her. Already the stocky woman was advancing to the attack. Once again, the girl knew there would not be time for her to try to reclaim a weapon she had lost. So she sprang as if meaning to meet the other's charge. Showing just as good timing, she swerved at the last moment; but this time with greater success. Catching Agasha's right wrist in both hands, she put all her not inconsiderable strength into heaving at it.

Such was the force of the tug, aided by her own forward impetus, that the lion tamer was propelled helplessly by her intended victim. In spite of realizing in which direction she was hurtling, there was nothing she could do to prevent herself from going. A hoarse bellow of alarm broke from her as she crashed into the side of the enclosure. Seizing the opportunity with which it was presented, the tiger sprang towards its tormentor. Her bellow turned to a scream, which ended abruptly as one of the striped paws came between the bars to descend with sufficient power to crush the top of her skull and she crumpled like a punctured balloon.

For all the horror inspired by the sight, Dawn knew there was nothing she could do for the stricken woman. Nor would there have been time, even if she could have. Taking advantage of Agasha's intervention, Katya was running to where the Smith & Wesson had fallen. Having no doubt as to what use it would be put, the girl darted in the same direction. Throwing herself through the air for the last few feet in the fashion of a rugby player, she tackled the beautiful Russian around the waist with such vigour that they went reeling away from the weapon and, still in contact fell to the ground.

Rolling apart on landing, through no conscious effort on either's part, Dawn and Katya rose at almost the same instant. Oblivious of everything except one another, they took not the slightest notice of the sound of gunfire crackling

87

outside the marquee or the tiger as it continued to maul its victim through the bars. Hardly pausing once on their feet, they sprang together like two enraged wildcats and without offering to employ the unarmed combat techniques each had learned. Hands sank into hair, jerking and tugging, while feet flailed to land or miss as fortune dictated. Struggling in such a fashion, they swung around half a dozen times before losing their balance and once more going down together to roll across the grassy floor of the marquee. Nor did they adopt any more scientific methods during the close to three minutes they fought in that fashion before regaining their feet.

A punch thrown without conscious guidance by Dawn as they stood up landed on Katya's nose. Jolted backwards a couple of steps, realization of her position struck the Russian along with the pain she felt and blood which began to flow from her nostrils. She was fighting more than just the girl who had spoiled her hopes of attaining high office. If she should be beaten, the lion would either be killed or liberated by the victress. Then, even should her men succeed in rescuing her, the scheme to bring death to Simba Nyeuse – the last four words having been adopted as the conspirators' rallying cry – would receive a setback from which it was unlikely to recover. In which case, considering the expense incurred by setting it up, she was finished. Such a costly failure would never be forgiven by her Government.

With that sobering thought in mind, Katya forced herself to forgo a desire to spring recklessly into an attempt to repay the blow. Instead, as Dawn tried to deliver another, she countered it with a shoulder throw. Finding herself sent flying, the girl's superb reflexes and instincts fined by years of gymnastic practise just managed to assert themselves to save her from injury. As she broke the fall, which still hurt – if not as badly as might have been the case – she too became aware of how rashly she had been behaving. The appreciation came not a moment too soon. Running up, Katya launched a kick at her head. Although she had not previously been involved in a fight with another woman, the unarmed combat lessons she had received supplied the answer in time to save her from what would have been an incapacitating injury. Forming an X-block with her crossed arms, she halted and caught hold of the leg before the foot reached her and, with a twisting thrust, toppled her assailant over.

On rising as quickly as before, the combatants showed more skill in the way they continued the conflict. Instead of a wild, hair-pulling mêlée, each demonstrated how well she had absorbed her instruction in self-defence. Throws were attempted successfully or prevented, holds, grips and locks sought for and either obtained or countered, while punches and kicks flew, guided thoughtfully instead of sent indiscriminately.

For five minutes without a pause, except when one or the other was sent sufficiently far away to prevent an immediate resumption and even then there was no unnecessary delay in coming together, the embattled pair went at it. Nor did they pay the slightest attention to what was going on outside the marquee. Engrossed to the exclusion of all else in their fight, neither was aware that the men who had avoided injury when *Kidogo* smashed through the mess hall had armed themselves and were exchanging shots with Dawn's companions.

So well matched were they that, throughout the period, there was little to choose between Dawn and Katya. Each had lost her upper garments, but fought on naked to the waist. Perspiration soaked them, diluting the blood both were shedding from nostrils or grazes. Their exposed bosoms came in for punishment of the most gruelling kind, too, but neither showed any indication of giving in. Nor, although they had rolled over or otherwise passed the knife and revolver on several occasions, had either attempted to arm herself.

At last, however, Dawn's youth and somewhat better physical condition took its toll. Slowly she gained the ascendancy. This reached its climax when, caught in a full nelson, she broke free by forcing Katya's arms open with sheer strength. Reaching over her shoulders, she sank her hands into the Russian's matted, sweat-soddened hair which had long since been torn from its severe bun and reduced to an untidy tangle. Sinking on to her left knee and bending forward sharply while hauling on the hair, she catapulted Katya over her back.

89

Turning a half somersault, the Russian crashed supine without being able to apply the kind of break-fall which had reduced the impact of previous landings. Straddling her antagonist's head and kneeling so as to hold it down between her thighs, the girl began to deliver punches to the offered bosom and stomach. As the first blow arrived, Katya struggled weakly and tried to fend off those which followed. Failing to protect the vulnerable areas under attack and already on the verge of losing consciousness, her feeble efforts soon ended and her bruised, tormented body went limp.

Realizing that the woman beneath her was not longer resisting and with exhaustion threatening to make her collapse, Dawn became aware of the commotion outside the marquee. There was the sound of helicopters landing. Where the shooting had previously been confined to rifles and handguns, the harsh chatter of automatic weapons commenced. It was quickly followed by voices yelling in Ambaga, Gasali and, in one case, Swahili, that the speakers wished to surrender. Lastly, an instant before she slumped forward in a faint caused by extreme fatigue, she had a vague impression that somebody whose voice she recognized was calling her name.

It was not until some time later Dawn recovered sufficiently to learn what was happening.

Hearing hints of the plot to overthrow Prince Simba Nyeuse, the head of Ambagasali's Army Intelligence Service had instituted inquiries. Betrayed by an associate, the Minister of State for Overseas Relations had described the use to which the black maned lion would be put. Collecting Bunduki on the way, a force of troops in helicopters had been dispatched to deal with the conspirators. Although their arrival had been fortuitous in one respect they had found little remained to be done. Having taken cover behind the generator truck, Katabona and Abu had prevented any of their antagonists from reaching the marquee; but they were almost out of ammunition for their weapons when the rescue party appeared. Faced with such opposition, the survivors had surrendered with little further resistance. On investigating, Bunduki, the old man and the trainee game scout had found the organizer of the plot to bring death to Simba Nyeuse lying defeated beneath the girl who had once again proved capable of defeating her.

PART THREE

Woman Deputy Alice Fayde

In

A CONTRACT FOR ALICE FAYDE

A bullet flying by very close to her head, diverted Alice
Fayde's thoughts of how there were more onerous and less
worthwhile assignments than the one upon which she was
currently engaged in her capacity as a woman deputy of the
Rockabye County Sheriff's Office.

Three times in nine days, a killer had shot a woman to
death as she was walking in the residential Lasher Division –
as it was known to the local law enforcement officers – of the
county seat, Gusher City. As was the established procedure,
because their county-wide jurisdiction allowed greater scope
for the handling of such crimes, the Sheriff's Office had taken
charge of the investigation. Following the accepted mode of
operation,[1] the team who received the duty had been unable
to learn anything of use. Apart from living in the same
district, the victims had nothing in common. They were of
different ethnic groups, religious denominations and occu-
pations. So far as could be discovered, they had no connections whatsoever with one another.

When the usual routine had proved to be fruitless, Deputy
Sheriff Ian Grantley and his new partner, David Bulphin[2]

[1] Details of the procedure followed by the Rockabye County Sheriff's
Office during another series of apparently unconnected killings are given
in: *POINT OF CONTACT*. J.T.E.

[2] David Bulpin had transferred from being a sergeant in the Gusher
City Police Department's Detective Bureau to the Sheriff's Office. Why

wasted no time in asking for a special kind of assistance. While continuing the search for a point of contact which might offer a motive and lead to the killer, they arranged for female peace officers acting as decoys to walk the streets of the division. Which was how Alice, although belonging to the other Watch of the Sheriff's Office, had come to be involved.[3] What was more (and indicative of the esteem in which her abilities were held by Sheriff Jack Tragg and the two Watch Commanders) she was assigned to what they all knew would be the most potentially dangerous area to be covered by the operation.

Despite being aware that his female deputies and the selected members of the Gusher City Police Department's Bureau of Women Officers received thorough training in the use of firearms as well as unarmed combat,[4] the sheriff had no intention of allowing them to be placed into any greater jeopardy than was absolutely necessary. In addition to being armed as always with their handguns, each would carry a radio with which to keep in communication and wear a lightweight 'flak' jacket to offer protection against the .357 Magnum revolver with which the murders had been committed. Furthermore, there would be male officers following as closely as circumstances would allow without causing the killer to be frightened off by their presence. They would be ready to rush to the decoy's assistance at the first indication of the trap being sprung.

The distance at which the 'back up' team could follow depended upon the area through which the female officer would be walking. Acknowledged, even by the other decoys, as the most competent of them, Alice had been allocated to

Deputy Sheriff Ian Grantley required a new partner is told in: *BAD HOMBRE.* J.T.E.

[3] Details of the Rockabye County Sheriff's Office's two-watch rota system and other organization are given in *APPENDIX THREE.* J.T.E.

[4] Woman Deputy Alice Fayde had earned a grading of 'Expert' in the exacting qualification 'shoots' which every member of the Rockabye County Sheriff's Office and Gusher City Police Department had to attend once a month. It included handling various types of weapons under as near actual combat conditions as could be produced, in addition to conventional target practice. See *THE SIXTEEN DOLLAR SHOOTER* for further details. J.T.E.

the section of the Division where conditions precluded any close surveillance. She was patrolling the sidewalks of a wide, generally straight street that was adequately – or inadequately, from her point of view – illuminated by the lights from the apartment buildings which lined it. Each had a garden in front, either cultivated decoratively or with a small swimming pool and other furnishings. The buildings were separated from their neighbours by mostly unlit areaways.

The nature of the terrain and its state of visibility prevented Alice's partner, Deputy Sheriff Bradford 'Brad' Counter and the other member of her 'back up' team from staying closer than almost half a mile. However, this contingency had been taken into consideration when the plan of campaign was formulated. In spite of the precautions, she knew that should she be selected for an attack by the killer she would be dependent upon her own resources until the others officers could arrive. But she was confident that she could protect herself until help came should the need arise.

Because of the kind of duty she was engaged upon, Alice could not wear her official khaki uniform which – whether in the form of a skirt or slacks – was designed to be flattering to the wearer as well as functional. For all that, despite the need to have the fairly bulky 'flak' jacket concealed beneath a loose fitting and lightweight black coat, she still presented a far from unattractive picture as she walked silently, yet gracefully, in her low-heeled and rubber-soled black shoes.

Red hair, which had already grown long enough for Alice to have had it returned to the 'flip' style she preferred,[5] fringed a tanned face that – if not ravishingly beautiful – had charm and was very good looking. Beneath the outer garments, her five foot seven tall, well moulded, thirty-seven, twenty-five, thirty-five inch figure filled a dark blue blouse and denim skirt in a most shapely, yet not blatantly curvaceous manner. As a precaution against the killer 'making' her as a law enforcement officer, she was not carrying the bulky Pete Ludwig shoulder bag which was part of her ensemble when working in civilian clothing under less demanding circumstances. While the omission deprived her of

[5] The reason Alice Fayde had her hair cut is given in: *RUN FOR THE BORDER*. J.T.E.

94

the spare ammunition, a cased set of Stoeger-Zephyr 'Double-Lock' handcuffs and official notebook which reposed therein, she had her Colt Commander .45 automatic pistol – a present from her partner[6] – identification wallet, police whistle and the small two-way radio on her person. So she felt adequately equipped to deal with any eventuality.

Two hours of unceasing patrolling had passed uneventfully since the red-head commenced the duty. It was the first night of the assignment, but the killings had occurred at intervals of three days and this was the third evening since the last had taken place. So she had been constantly on the alert from the moment she entered the section to which she had been allocated. Despite that, such was the care taken by the assailant, she neither saw nor heard anything to alert her to the danger and she was completely unaware that there was a hostile presence in the vicinity until she received the unpleasant indication emanating from it.

Jolted from its state of partial reverie, Alice's brain instantly identified the eerie and unexpected 'splat!' just in front of her face as having been made by a bullet splitting the air as it flew onwards to sink into the trunk of a good sized cottonwood which grew in the garden of the apartment building she was passing. The departure of the lead was echoed by a sharp crack similar to the sound of a burlesque comic's slapstick[7] meeting the seat of a victim's trousers, but she knew nothing so innocuous as that had caused it.

The crack, Alice realized as she instinctively started to take evasive action, was produced by the detonation of the powerful powder charge contained in the cartridge of and giving a high velocity to the bullet from a revolver.

A .357 Magnum cartridge was one which possessed the requisite qualities!

According to the deductions of the ballistics expert at the Firearms Investigation Laboratory in the Department of

[6] When and why Deputy Sheriff Bradford 'Brad' Counter gave Alice Fayde the Colt Commander .45 automatic pistol is explained in: *THE ¼ SECOND DRAW*. J.T.E.

[7] 'Slapstick': a flat, thin, pliant double wooden paddle which produces a loud report when struck against a person or object, but does little damage. Its use by 'knockabout' comedians gave the name 'slapstick' to their form of entertainment. J.T.E

Public Safety Building – which also housed the Headquarters Division of the G.C.P.D. and the Sheriff's Office – the murderer used a Smith & Wesson Model 27 .357 Magnum revolver.

Even as the red-head's brain was registering the facts and coming to the conclusion that she had lured the killer into making an attempt on her life, there was the crack of a second shot, and another of the lethal missiles flew across the street. Yet, quickly as it had been dispatched in the wake of its predecessor, it too missed its intended mark. Alice was already diving over the low picket fence of the garden, silently blessing providence for there being a lawn instead of something harder upon which to land, and adequate shelter readily available. Although the margin was slight, the bullet passed through the space her head had occupied a moment earlier.

Putting to good use her training in unarmed combat and horseback riding, the red-head started rolling as soon as she landed on the grassy surface. Nor did she stop, as she knew she would still be visible between the rails of the fence until she had attained the protection offered by the trunk of the tree she had seen while making her hurried entrance to the garden. Swiftly as she was moving, a third bullet ploughed into the lawn not six inches to her rear before she reached her destination; proving that she was right in assuming that she was still within the would-be killer's range of vision.

Not until Alice had placed the cottonwood's comforting bulk between herself and the powerful revolver did she offer to rise and arm herself. Drawing the Colt from the holster designed to be carried *inside* and clipped to the nether garments – whether skirt, as now, or slacks[8] – on the left side with the butt forward to be accessible to either hand, she peered cautiously around the trunk. She was compelled to withdraw her head almost immediately and at greater speed. Although failing to penetrate all the way and emerge on her side, another bullet had come to gouge into the tree.

The latest attempt to kill her allowed the red-head to

[8] Further details respecting to the kind of holster used by Alice Fayde are given in: *'CAP' FOG, TEXAS RANGER, MEET MR J. G. REEDER.* J.T.E.

locate her assailant. Glowing briefly, the fiery muzzle flash came from the interior of the areaway between the two apartment buildings directly across the street. Although she knew that the sound of shooting would be bringing assistance, she felt the information should be put to use before the 'back up' team arrived. It was unlikely they would be able to reach the scene undetected and, on receiving a warning of their approach, the person who was firing at her was almost certain to take flight. If the escape bid was successful, as was at least a fifty-fifty chance under the circumstances, the miscreant would remain at liberty and either stop killing, or – far worse – transfer the activities to another location.

Much as Alice desired to prevent her attacker from escaping, she had no intention of shooting back. Good as she was, making a hit at that range – other than by pure chance – would require taking a more careful aim than was possible from behind the tree, even using the 'barricade stance' learned at the Police Academy.[9] To step into the open and employ one of the long range shooting stances she knew, or to try and close the gap by rushing forward, would be equally suicidal against such an obviously competent antagonist; who was in the darkness of the areaway while she would have to approach across a street not only illuminated by the buildings' lights, but with the glow of a threequarter moon.

Glancing around, as she listened for indications of the 'back up' team approaching, Alice decided she had one advantage. Because of being positioned back in the areaway, her assailant's field of fire was narrowly restricted. If she could move to a spot only a few yards on either side, she would be concealed from the revolver.

On the point of making a dart sideways, the red-head saw how such a course might be dangerous in the extreme. Her assailant had proved to be watching carefully and had probably anticipated her intended manoeuvre. Knowing she would be under fire the moment she left concealment, she realized a change of strategy was needed and saw a way in which one could be put into effect.

[9] A description of how a 'barricade stance' is performed is given in: THE PROFESSIONAL KILLERS. J.T.E.

The shadow of the tree extended at an angle towards the corner of the building and, sinking to her hands and knees, Alice began to creep along the blackness it created. She was aware that doing so put her directly in her assailant's line of fire, but was relying upon the combination of her dark clothing and the contrast of the shadow against the surrounding moonlight to camouflage her.

The hope materialized!

Despite another shot sounding, causing Alice to drop flat, the bullet joined its predecessors in the tree.

However, even as the red-head was on the point of resuming her advance along the shadow, she heard something which told her there was no need to continue with her plan although, for the time being, she would be ill-advised to emerge from the blackness.

* * * * *

Alerted by the shooting, Deputy Sheriff Bradford Counter swung astride the Honda Trail 90 motor cycle he had been pushing and, kicking its engine into life, set off at a rapid rate of acceleration to his partner's assistance.

Six foot three inches in height, with curly golden blond hair of moderate length and a tanned, exceptionally handsome face, Brad had the tremendously wide shouldered, slim waisted, physical development of a 'Mr Universe' type hero in an Italian-made action-escapism-adventure pseudo-epic movie. His looks were a hereditary feature of his family.[10]

As was the case with Alice Fayde, the blond giant was not wearing the uniform prescribed for members of the Rocka-bye County Sheriff's Office. However, in some respects, his attire seemed closer to that which might have been expected of a peace officer in Texas. His silver-grey Resistol Rancher 125 hat shaped with a Luskey roll crease, black leather vest to which was attached his badge of office, biege Klopman Ultressa shirt and faded blue Levi's pants might have been

---

[10] A similar physique was possessed by Bradford Counter's paterna great-grandfather, Mark, and his look-alike cousin, James Allenvale 'Bunduki' Gunn, q.v. Details of Mark Counter's career can be found in the author's *FLOATING OUTFIT* series. J.T.E.

worn by his great-grandfather, Mark, during the mid-1870s. Although he had on a gunbelt, it was not of the classic Old West *buscadero* pattern. It was a Bianchi Deluxe Sam Browne, without a shoulder strap,[11] to which was attached a pouch for spare ammunition, handcuff case and a key-ring. His Colt Government Model .45 automatic pistol – a heavier forerunner of Alice's Commander – action cocked and manual safety catch applied, was secured by an Elden Carl 'Fly Off' strap in a somewhat skimpy, forward raked Bianchi Cooper-Combat holster set high on his right hip. An Old West *pistolero* might have felt it could not be drawn quickly. Employing a technique perfected by master gun handlers of a more recent generation, he was able to do so and at speeds which would have been beyond the capability of even the legendary Rio Hondo gun wizard and his paternal great-grandfather's closest friend, Dusty Fog.[12] Furthermore, instead of the traditional high-heeled, sharp-toed footwear of the earlier age, he had on crepe-soled, calf-high brown hunting boots which permitted a far greater mobility. Lastly, he had a weapon in the boot of his vehicle that had been manufactured by the Winchester Repeating Arms Company. It was of a kind he considered more suitable for his purposes than a lever action rifle or carbine.

Because of the need to avoid arousing the killer's suspicions by being too close, Brad was some distance away from his partner. He had been walking fast, pushing the motor cycle, so as to turn a corner which was hiding her from sight when the shooting commenced. On turning the corner, he was at first unable to see anything of her. However, as he sped along the street in what he knew must be the right direction, the situation was rectified even though the second member of the 'back up' team had not yet put in an appearance from the other side.

[11] 'Sam Browne' belt: a military belt with one or two light shoulder straps running diagonally across the chest from right to left. It was designed by General Samuel J. Browne (1824—1901) of the British Army, allegedly as an aid to carrying a pistol or a sword after he had lost an arm in combat. J.T.E.

[12] Details of the career of Captain Dustine Edward Marsden 'Dusty' Fog, C.S.A., are given in the author's *CIVIL WAR* and *FLOATING OUTFIT* series. J.T.E.

Listening to the trail bike coming closer, Alice realised that her partner was unlikely to know where the killer was positioned. So she thrust herself erect and sprinted, still in the shadow thrown by the tree, until she reached the corner of the apartment building. Arriving unmolested, she knew that she had accomplished the easiest part of her task. Despite appreciating what could happen to her if the killer moved forward, or if she underestimated the width of the revolver's field of fire, she sucked in a breath and ran forward. As she left the sheltering darkness to cross the garden, she was alert for any hint that she had been in error. There was none and no shots came her way. So, hurdling the fence, she looked to where Brad was racing towards her.

'Down the areaway!' the red-head shouted, pointing in the appropriate direction.

Although unable to hear the words, Alice's gesture told the blond giant all he needed to know. Bringing the Honda to a stop in a sliding half circle that kept him clear of the entrance to the areaway, he was off it and slipping the weapon from its saddleboot before its motion had ceased. Transferring his left fist from the handlebars and allowing the trail bike to fall unheeded to the ground, he grasped the 'trombone action' cocking slide of the Winchester Model of 1897 twelve gauge riot gun he had extracted. A jerk of his wrist operated the mechanism and fed a shell loaded with nine .32 calibre buckshot balls into the chamber. With that precaution taken, he ran across the garden and flattened his back against the wall at the corner of the building at the right of the areaway. Once there, he waited for his partner to arrive and take up a similar position at the left. He was pleased to notice that neither of the fences on the garden at each side extended to the wall, but left a gap offering access to the areaway.

'Now!' Alice snapped, thumbing down the manual safety catch of her pistol – which she had carried cocked and safe – for the first time since drawing it. She gave the command by virtue of being the senior member of the team.

Showing perfect co-ordination that told of considerable practise, the red-head and the blond giant thrust themselves simultaneously from behind the buildings. They twisted around as they moved, halting with their weapons pointing ahead ready to be used. Each hoped the assailant would be caught unawares by their appearance, confused as to which of them posed the greater threat and, while vacillating in the choice, would allow them to escape injury by firing first.

The areaway was deserted!

'He's split!' Brad growled.

'Not out this end,' Alice replied, lowering her pistol from its double-handed hold. 'And there are no doors on either side, so he must have gone through.'

'How many did he get off at you?' the big blond inquired, as he and the girl began to run forward.

'Five!' Alice answered, having taken the precaution of counting.

'One left, unless he's reloaded,' Brad commented, being willing to accept the summation of the F.I.L.'s ballistic expert on the type of weapon used by the killer and knowing the cylinder capacity of a Smith & Wesson Model 27 revolver.

No more was said as the partners continued to advance. Instead, they strained their ears in the hope of detecting their quarry's footsteps and watched the exit from the areaway they were approaching. It gave access to a street similar to the one they had just left. Although the second member of the 'back up' team arrived at the other end, they paid no attention to him. Nor, when he had deduced what had happened and what their intentions were, did he attempt to call out and request information. Instead, carrying the telescope sighted sniper's rifle he had brought in case accurate long range shooting should be required, he followed them. On coming to the intersection, they paused to look out before exposing themselves on the sidewalk.

There was no sign of the killer.

However!

'Over there!' Alice hissed, pointing to where a hat lay on the opposite sidewalk in front of the areaway separating two apartment buildings.

Striding forward side by side, their footwear being such that it allowed them to step almost inaudibly without special care, the deputies reached the object which had attracted Alice's notice. It was a grubby white straw hat with a blue band decorated by white 'Ban The Bomb' symbols. However, neither gave it more than a brief glance in passing. There was something of far greater importance and urgency to demand their attention as they were given their first view into the areaway. It was somewhat better illuminated than the one they had passed through to reach the street, a situation for which they were grateful as it enabled them to see clearly what was happening.

The areaway had occupants, one of whom was behaving in a far from innocent fashion. Tall, lean, long haired and bearded, a young man clad in a loose fitting short kaftan, ragged blue jeans and sandals was standing looking down at a woman lying by his feet. He was holding two revolvers, the one in his left hand – a long barrelled Smith & Wesson Model 27 – was grasped around its cylinder; but the other, a shorter yet no less lethal at short range Colt Cobra was held ready for use.

'Peace officers here!' Brad shouted. 'Fr – !'

'Pig bastards!' the young man screeched, before the command could be completed, twisting around and bringing up the Colt to fire twice.

Neither bullet scored a hit, but the blond giant knew there was only one course open to him. The young man had already tried four times to kill Alice and seemed determined to continue shooting. Or he might turn the revolver on the woman at his feet and use her as a hostage with which to bargain for an uninterrupted escape. Either way, he had to be stopped and quickly.

Undeterred by a third bullet which almost touched his cheek in passing, Brad brought up and fired the riot gun in one continuously flowing rapid motion. The result showed the wisdom of having carried along such an effective weapon. Caught by some of the nine buckshot balls, the long haired young man was flung backwards with the revolvers flying from his hands.

Working the Winchester's pump action with a flick of his left hand, to eject the empty case and replenish the chamber, the big blond resumed his advance accompanied by his partner. While she went to examine the woman, trampling on a black cloak that lay near by, he walked to where the man sprawled supine and in the abandoned fashion of a

102

corpse. Brad had kept the riot gun ready for use, but saw it would not be needed. One of the .32 calibre balls had hit the man between the eyes and any of the other three to find their marks would have been equally, if not as quickly, lethal.

'Is she hurt?' the blond giant inquired, looking to where his partner was kneeling besides the woman.

'Just fainted, I think,' Alice replied, turning her gaze from the plain and angular blonde, who was already stirring. 'How about him?'

'He's dead!' Brad answered, knowing this to be the case without the need to make a closer examination. 'I reckon we've closed Ian and Dave's case for them.'

* * * * *

'Yes, sir, good buddies, England's a great lil country and I wouldn't want to come right out and say the television networks over there are just a mite biased politically. All I know is, one day while I was waiting in line for a cab at my hotel, I heard the fellow ahead of me say, "Hey, driver, take me to Communist Party headquarters." And the cabbie said, "Yes, sir. Which network, British Broadcasting or Independent?" '

Chuckling over the first comment to greet her as she switched on the television in her apartment to watch *The Virgil Grayne Show*, Alice glanced to the front door as its bell rang. She had met the comedian, who had recently returned from a successful tour of the British Isles, during a multiple murder case she and Brad Counter had handled. They had found him far more friendly and co-operative than a more 'liberal' entertainer who was also involved.[13] Remembering comments passed by two policemen from England who had paid a visit to Gusher City and having seen examples of that country's television programmes, she could see the point of the probably apocryphal anecdote.[14]

While the third member of the decoy team was using his two-way radio to report the incident, the red-head had

[13] Told in: *POINT OF CONTACT*. J.T.E.
[14] Although the English police officers do not take any active part in the proceedings, some details of their visit to Gusher City are given in: *THE DEPUTIES*. J.T.E.

ascertained nothing more serious than a faint was afflicting the woman. On recovering, the blonde had explained that her condition was caused by the sight of the armed man, with a cloak draped over his shoulders, rushing towards her as she was taking a short cut through the areaway. She had introduced herself as Eileen Beresford, a fashion designer based at Houston spending a working vacation in Gusher City. She gave the name of a nearby hotel as her temporary place of residence. Admitting that she had been perturbed by the sound of the shooting, she had asserted that she had neither seen nor heard anything of the young man until he appeared before her. Although she had declined the offer of having Alice or one of the male officers escort her, she had been allowed to return to the hotel. She had been informed before setting off that she would be required to visit the Sheriff's Office the following morning to make out and sign a formal statement regarding her participation.

Once Deputy Sheriffs Ian Grantley and David Bulpin, the team in command of the investigation, arrived in answer to the radio message, the initial routine aspects of the incident were speeded up so far as Alice and Brad were concerned. There were further details which had to be carried out immediately on the spot of the attack. Material evidence such as the bullets fired at them also had to be gathered and any witnesses to what had happened had to be located. Both pieces of information had to be presented at the mandatory inquiry into the fatal shooting of the young man. The search for and collection of such evidence would be performed by specialists from the Department of Public Safety's Scientific Investigation Bureau. Being aware that the red-head and her partner had already been on duty from eight o'clock that morning until four in the afternoon, dealing with their current case, and would be logging on for the Day Watch at the same time the following morning, Grantley had said they could leave the latter to those officers who had arrived and were working the Night Watch.

Although Alice and Brad, when reporting to commence the decoy duty, had driven to the Department of Public Safety Building in her Ford Mustang they had seen no point in both of them going to retrieve it from the municipal employees' parking lot. As the big blond had to return the Honda and riot gun, he had volunteered to collect the vehicle while she went directly to her apartment and cooked supper for them. Being given a ride in a black and white G.C.P.D. radio patrol car, she had arrived in time to catch the comedian's monologue at the commencement of the show.

Chuckling appreciatively at a joke of the kind various press releases had claimed was responsible for an appearance on British television being cancelled, in spite of the acclaim the entertainer had been receiving elsewhere in the country, Alice reached the door. Wondering why Brad had not used his key to enter, as she was not expecting to receive any other visitors at such an hour of the night, she unlocked and opened it.

Immediately, the red-head discovered she was in error over her assumption regarding the identity of the caller!

Nor was the disclosure of an enjoyable nature!

Still clad in the green cat suit she had been wearing in the areaway and which did nothing to flatter her gaunt and boney figure, but now carrying a shoulder bag, Eileen Beresford stood in the passage. Without waiting to be invited, she walked forward clearly with the intention of entering the apartment.

Taken completely unawares, the red-head stepped backwards without challenging the blonde's right to enter or to question her intentions. The short-barrelled Smith & Wesson Model 27 .357 Magnum revolver she held was providing all the authority and explanation required to ensure compliance, particularly as it had a bulbous silencer attached to its muzzle. Keeping the weapon lined at the pit of Alice's stomach, where a wound would cause terrible suffering before death came to end it, the uninvited visitor pushed the door closed with her left hand so deftly she did not offer any opportunity for measures to be taken against her intrusion.

'I might have known a "something" pig would be watching that "mother-something" neo-fascist son of a bitch,' Eileen stated, glancing to the television and back without allowing the revolver to waver from its steady alignment.

'And I don't imagine even a strung-out soft-shell would be so damned bigoted she'd feel the need to bring a piece to

105

stop somebody watching an entertainer she thought politically unsuitable,' Alice countered, deducing from the foul language and appellation applied by such people to anybody who did not conform rigidly to their ideals that her visitor was of liberal intellectual pretensions. 'So, as I don't imagine that's what brought you here, what do you want?'

'I'm here on business, pig, *business*,' Eileen explained. 'But I must admit it's a pleasure to be paid for washing one of you scum.'

'Don't tell me you're trying to be a hit-woman?' Alice scoffed, continuing to employ an air of disdain she hoped would provoke a response that offered a chance of taking some form of defensive action.

'A hit-*person*!' the blonde corrected, but the note of asperity was not accompanied by any relaxation of vigilance. 'And, after six successful hits since I started, I'm not just *trying* as you'll find out after we've taken a little ride.'

* * * * *

'Thank gawd I've caught you, guv! Is Miss Fayde with you?'

Answering the call on the telephone at his team's desk in the Deputies Squadroom of the Sheriff's Office, Bradford Counter identified the hoarse Cockney voice as the best of the small coterie of informers he had inherited from his previous partner and Alice's uncle, Deputy Sheriff Thomas Cord.[15] He could not recollect ever having heard the little Englishman sound so perturbed.

'No, "Mr Brit",' the big blond replied, using the sobriquet English Herb employed for security reasons when calling him at the Squadroom. 'What's up?'

'There's a contract been put out on her!' the caller replied.

'Who by?' Brad demanded, feeling as if he was being touched by an ice cold hand.

[15] Bradford Counter's association with Deputy Sheriff Thomas Cord and 'English Herb' is described in: *THE SIXTEEN DOLLAR SHOOTER, THE SHERIFF OF ROCKABYE COUNTY*, and *THE PROFESSIONAL KILLERS*. The latter also tells of the killing of Benjamin Blumfeld's wife by Alice Fayde. J.T.E.

'Word on the street has it that it's that feller whose wife she shot.'

'Ben Blumfeld?'

'That's him!'

'I heard he was out of the rackets,' Brad objected.

'It's around he's trying to move back in,' English Herb asserted. 'Only he's not got a hit-man.'

'But you said – !' the blond giant growled.

'He's brought in a bleeding hit-*woman*, Mr Counter!' the informer interrupted. 'And, from all accounts, she's bloody good. So good *I* can't get a lead on her, but you can count on it she's around.'

'Thanks, Herb!' Brad ejaculated, so perturbed that for the first time in their acquaintance he broke the other's anonymity over the telephone.

'Think nothing of it, guv!' the Englishman replied, ignoring the use of his name. 'Just make sure you look after her.'

'What's wrong, Brad?' the Night Watch Commander inquired, as the big blond lowered the telephone.

'There's a contract out for Alice!' the big blond answered, starting to dial his partner's home number. After the telephone at the other end had rung several times without its summons meeting any response, he hung up and went on, 'There's no reply. I'm going over to find out why!'

* * * * *

'You've been an expensive hit, pig,' Eileen Beresford commented in conversational tones, as Alice Fayde drove her car as instructed along the secondary road leading across the hilly range country in the direction of the town of Euclid. 'I won't get back either of my pieces. The Cobra I don't mind, but I paid a good price for the Smith & Wesson.'

'Did you use it on the three women you burned to get me out on the streets as a decoy?' the red-head challenged, making a shrewd guess as to how her capture had been manipulated.

'No way!' the blonde scoffed, delighted to show her captive was in error and making a slight gesture with the weapon she had handled so competently that there had been no opportunity to disarm her. 'I took them out with *this* and only used the other because I didn't think I'd be able to get as close as I had to them.'

'I think it was the man who did all the shooting,' Alice lied, still trying to provoke her captress into making a mistake.

'*Him?*' Eileen snorted. 'All that acid-head was good for was making sure I didn't get grabbed by those "mother-something" bastards I knew would be following you.'

Given that much information, Alice was able to envisage the whole of the diabolical scheme. It also gave her an insight into the completely ruthless nature of the woman who was using the name, 'Eileen Beresford'.

By deliberately murdering three innocent women, the blonde had caused the decoys to be put into operation. Deducing that the red-head – whose record she had learned – would be assigned to the duty, she had either guessed or found out in some other way where to seek her quarry. Leaving her male associate on the second street, she had laid the ambush clad in the straw hat and cloak as a means of concealing her identity. Making use of him had been another example of her ruthless nature. Realizing that she would be pursued very soon after the shooting, she had left the hat to guide the peace officers in the required direction. Discarding the cloak and giving the man the pistol she had used, she had pretended to faint when sure the pursuit was near at hand. As a result, her companion was killed and she had been permitted to leave the scene with less questioning than would otherwise have been the case. She had, however, been aware of the need for haste in completing her assignment. Even if no suspicions were aroused that night, or nothing occurred to make the peace officers realize she had lied, a ballistic test on the Smith & Wesson would be carried out the following morning and reveal it was not the weapon used in the three killings.

Everything Alice had seen since their face to face meeting at the apartment warned her that Eileen was a competent adversary against whom it would be fatal to take reckless chances. At no time, even while leaving the building and boarding the car, had there been the slightest opportunity of escape presented. Nor had the red-head been able to do anything to alleviate her perilous condition as she was driving through the city. The blonde had shown an awareness of every ploy she was envisaging and had kept the revolver pointing in such a manner that to try and speed up the car, then stop it abruptly, would have produced nothing other than a painful death.

'Who put out the contract?' Alice inquired, noticing the way her captress was studying their surroundings with quick glances as they were talking and deciding this was to select the place in which she was to be killed.

'Nobody you know,' the blonde replied in a taunting manner.

'Come on now!' Alice protested, glancing into the rear-view mirror and noticing the flash of another vehicle's head-lights showing briefly before a curve in the winding, wood-lined road hid them from view. Hoping her abductress had been less watchful, she continued. 'Don't try to shit a shitter. Nobody puts out bread to hire even a hit-*woman* without cause. Unless *you* work real cheap because you've picked up a social disease and can't turn tricks as a hooker, that is.'

'You won't needle me into losing my cool and pulling a boo-boo, *pig*!' Eileen warned, but her tone was brittle.

'Don't tell me you're annoyed by being called a hooker,' the red-head challenged, as she guided the car over a bridge across a small river. 'I thought, according to *Klute*, it was an honourable and praiseworthy occupation.'

'I've never before met a pig who could th – !' the blonde began, then she stiffened and, darting a look through the window, went on hurriedly, 'Stop here. But do it slow and easy or, *when* they find your body, they'll be digging lead out of your gut.'

'What was it Humphrey Bogart said in *The Maltese Falcon* about the cheaper the punk, the cheaper the patter?' Alice mocked, carrying out the instruction even more slowly than was necessary. She felt sure that, possibly because it had been selected during a reconnaisance since her captress's arrival in Rockabye County, they had arrived at their destination. 'Or should I say, the cheaper the *woman*?'

'I'm just going to love wasting *you!*' Eileen declared

savagely incensed by the references to an actor for whom she had a great admiration and the repeated derogatory mentions of her sex. However, for all her tendency to over-react as became a virulent exponent of 'Women's Lib', she contrived to retain control over her temper and did not allow the revolver to leave its alignment. She had chosen the area as the site for a second contract she had undertaken in Gusher City and she was too aware of her captive's well deserved reputation to want to take chances which might prevent her from carrying it out. Fumbling behind with her left hand as the car stopped, she found the handle and opened the door. Backing out with the same care she had employed when entering, she hissed, 'Dim the lights, leave the keys in the ignition and haul your arse this way.'

Watching the blonde retreating a few steps, without the Smith & Wesson being diverted from its target, Alice obeyed the orders she had been given. She accepted there was no hope of duplicating a ploy her partner had pulled against a cattle rustler in this instance.[16] Feeling perspiration running down her ribs as she emerged and stood alongside the car, she glanced in both directions. Other than the bridge some thirty yards away, there was no sign of civilization. Nor could she see the lights of the vehicle which had been following them.

Taking a flashlight from her shoulder bag, Eileen instructed the red-head to walk ahead of her in the direction they had come. While doing so, Alice studied her surroundings in the hope of locating some means of escape. Nothing sprang immediately to her attention.

Ordering her captive to keep going, the blonde quickly directed the beam of the flashlight over the bridge's two foot high concrete guard railing. Taking advantage of the illumination, Alice was even more convinced she had reached the site selected for her execution. Flowing through a gorge perhaps fifteen feet high and about twenty wide, the stream looked sufficiently deep and fast flowing for her body to be carried a considerable distance. Far enough, perhaps, to ensure it would not be found for days, or weeks, if ever. However, she also believed her attempts to provoke Eileen had

[16] Told in: THE DEPUTIES. J.T.E.

110

resulted in them travelling farther than had been intended; which could account for her insistence upon their returning to the other side of the gorge.

Being far from enamoured by the prospect awaiting her after crossing, Alice slowed her pace as she approached the bridge. She was aware that she would soon reach the crisis time where something must be attempted whether the occasion was propitious or not. Just as she was at the half-way point, the lights she had noticed earlier showed at the bend farther along the road.

'Get the lead out!' the blonde shouted, having no desire to be illuminated by the approaching vehicle. 'Run!'

Drawing a very rapid conclusion, Alice set off as if in obedience to the order. As soon as she heard the change in Eileen's gait, she swerved and plunged head-first over the low concrete railing. Being uncertain of how deep the stream was at that point, she launched herself in a shallow dive. Going down in what appeared to be slow motion, she prayed she would not alight in shallow water running over jagged rocks. She also braced herself for the shock of her arrival, the slashing of any rocks present into her body, or the impact of a bullet in her back.

Neither of the last two occurred!

Hearing a strident feminine profanity as she was entering the river in a flat glide, the red-head guessed her action had caught the blonde unawares. She went about four foot below the surface before her hands and bosom encountered gravel. Then, straightening out, she thrust herself downstream underwater.

The water was very cold, but a few seconds elapsed before Alice could feel its impact through her clothing. Staying beneath the surface as long as she could hold her breath, the drag of her saturated garments was counter-acted by the press of the current. When a lack of air forced her to come up, she found herself some thirty yards from the bridge. Floundering erect in waist-deep water, she peered back in the direction from which she had come. Apparently the vehicle had passed while she was submerged, for there were no longer oncoming headlights. Scanning the outline of the bridge's concrete railing against the night sky beyond it, she could not see the blonde.

In spite of discovering Eileen was no longer on what would have made an ideal point of vantage, one to which she could have already returned if she had retired just to avoid being seen by the occupants of the truck, Alice did not believe she had left the vicinity.

Wading towards the side of the river upon which the car was parked, the red-head found its bank was more sloping than at the point at which she entered. While it was still fairly steep, her hands encountered sufficient irregularities for her to believe she could make an ascent. However, before commencing, she paused to try and detect any sign that the blonde had already started looking for her. For several seconds there was only the gentle murmur of the current and distant calls of a night bird. So she started to climb. As she was approaching the top, however, other and more disturbing sounds reached her ears. First came the thunk of the car's trunk being closed. There followed a clicking noise which she recognized. The last time she had heard something similar was when Brad was operating the action of his riot gun to recharge its chamber after shooting the young man.

Appreciating the gravity of the latest development, Alice concentrated on completing the climb. Just as she was peering over the top, her left hand encountered a boulder about the size and shape of a baseball. Liberating it, she took it with her as she cautiously rose and started to make for the shelter of the nearest bushes. Employing the skill she had gained on numerous deer and turkey hunts in which she had participated firstly with her father and Uncle Tom Cord, and then after their respective deaths with Brad, she made her way towards the road in almost complete silence.

Alice was not kept for long in suspense before she discovered where Eileen was located. Seeing the beam of the flashlight being directed into the gorge from the bridge supplied the necessary clue. After scanning the sides as far as the light would carry, the blonde turned and walked into the woods. Her purpose was soon obvious to the red-head. Having failed in her search from the bridge, she was continuing it by moving along the edge of the gorge.

Even discounting the presence of the pump shotgun, another and equally serious problem confronted Alice as she searched for a place from which to tackle the hit-woman. Although confident she possessed the ability to approach undetected, at no point was there any concealment closer than twenty or so feet from the edge of the gorge. To cross that much open ground when up against a person who was skilled in the use of weapons and was armed with one capable of spreading a lethal charge of shot would be suicidal unless complete surprise could be attained.

Halting in a crouch between two clumps of bushes, the redhead watched Eileen approaching. She was walking slowly, holding the flashlight and the foregrip of a pump action shotgun with her left hand, the right wrapped about the wrist of the butt so she could pull the trigger. The ease with which she was carrying them warned Alice that she possessed sufficient competence to make her a formidable prospect to tackle when armed with nothing more than a rock.

Another factor was increasing Alice's perturbation. Already chilled by the immersion in the river, her necessarily slow progress through the woodland had failed to warm her. Nor was being compelled to stand still, the wet clothes clinging to her, doing anything to improve matters. It was all she could do to prevent her teeth chattering and she was unable to stop herself shivering with enough violence to cause the foliage she was brushing against to rustle.

Slight though the disturbance had been, Eileen heard it. However, at first she merely glanced towards the bushes. Her original belief that the sound was made by some woodland creature was very soon dispelled. Seeing the vaguely human shape among the shadows, she began to turn and swing the shotgun around.

At the first suggestion that she had been detected, Alice hurled the boulder with all the strength she could muster. The instant it left her hand, she sprang forward. Descending upon a protruding root, her left foot slipped inwards from it. Pain knifed through her leg and she felt herself falling. Going down on the verge of fainting, she heard a thud and saw the blonde's head jerk under the impact of the missile.

Tilting upwards involuntarily as the flashlight flew from

8

Eileen's hand, the shotgun bellowed in response to her right forefinger tightening spasmodically on the trigger. Its recoil, combined to the force with which the boulder struck her, caused her to step backwards. Her foot descended on nothing more substantial than air and, already unconscious, she toppled into the gorge.

* * * * *

'They've found her body,' Bradford Counter reported, having taken the telephone call which had been relayed to the telephone on his and Alice Fayde's desk in the Deputies Squadroom. 'Buck says to tell you that there wasn't any way you could have saved her even if you'd gone straight in. She broke her neck as she hit the water and was swept about three miles downstream.'

'That's a relief,' the red-head replied, sitting with her bandaged ankle resting on another chair.

It was half past eleven on the morning after Alice's abduction.

On recovering from her faint, the red-head had crawled to the edge of the gorge. Although she had located the flashlight, it was broken and she had not been able to see anything in the river. So she had made her way to the car and managed to drive it to Euclid. Deputy Sheriff Buck Shields, of the town's Sheriff's Sub-Office, was awake – having been called by Brad as a matter of routine when her absence had been discovered – and had taken charge. Leaving her in his wife's care, he had gone to the river and instituted a search. It had not been fruitful that night, but was continued in daylight with the result he had just reported.

'Ben Blumfeld isn't at home,' Brad stated, on hanging up the receiver. 'He's been in Europe for the past three months.' The phone buzzed and, picking it up, he listened then said, 'It's for you.'

'Don't bother asking my name, or trying to have this call traced, Miss Fayde,' a polite voice with a New England accent requested. 'I'm speaking from Las Vegas. It has come to our attention that, fearing the unfounded rumours of a former member of the board of directors coming out of retirement to take over the position he hoped to attain, a junior executive decided to remove the threat. He hired a hit-person to kill you and arranged for word to get out it was done by – '

'Ben Blumfeld,' Alice suggested.

'I prefer not to name names,' the voice replied. 'We have heard that such an attempt was made last night, but without success. Orders have been given which will prevent a repetition and arrangements have been made to recompense the next of kin of the three ladies who were killed. We deeply regret that they should have died and you were endangered, but I can assure you that the executive responsible has been – shall we say dismissed – from our organization *permanently* and you need have no fear of a recurrence. There will be no other contract for you, Miss Fayde.'

PART FOUR

Betty Hardin

In

IT'S OUR TURN TO IMPROVISE, MISS BLAZE

'Menfolk do so have *all* the fun and excitement and you-all *know* they do, Cousin Betty, for shame,' Georgina Blaze insisted, continuing to expound a point of view which she had always advocated and which had been resurrected by a comment from the person to whom the words were addressed. Looking at the other member of the small hunting party, she challenged, 'Now isn't *that* just so, Tommy?'

The three riders were leisurely traversing the thinly wooded terrain forming the boundary between the great OD Connected and Double B ranches – which occupied the far from diminutive whole of Rio Hondo county – in the warmth of a warm early summer afternoon. In several respects, they would have struck a chance onlooker new to the area as being somewhat unusual. All wore masculine attire and were armed, but only one of them was of the male gender and even he was undeniably out of the ordinary for the United States of America – an incorrect term under the circumstances, as the struggle by certain of the States to be allowed to attain the constitutional right to secede from the Union was taking place elsewhere in the country – during the early 1860s.

While none of them could be considered tall, seated astride the low horned, double girthed Texas-style range saddle of a spirited little *bayos azafranados* gelding[1] at the right of the trio, Betty Hardin was the smallest. Not yet eighteen years of age, bare headed, with her shoulder long black hair gathered at the back of her head in what a later generation would refer to as a 'pony tail', she was petite and very beautiful. There was a suggestion of an inborn power to command and an intelligence beyond average about her attractively tanned face and she comported herself with the assured composure that might be expected of one who was undeniably descended from General Jackson Baines 'Ole Devil' Hardin, C.S.A. Yet, for all that she was said to be the granddaughter of a man with such prominence in the affairs of the Lone Star State,[2] there was nothing arrogant or snobbish about her. Rather her demeanour was of competent, yet – unless the need to change it for something more positive arose – unassertive self confidence.[3]

A tartan shirt and yellowish brown Nankeen trousers, which were tucked into the legs of brown Hessian boots,[4] could not entirely conceal that Betty had a curvaceous little body budding into womanhood, despite the fact that they

---

[1] *Bayos azafranados*: a saffron coloured horse, something between a dun and a sorrel. For the benefit of new readers; because of the Spanish connotations of the word, 'cinch', Texans generally employed the term, 'girth' – pronounced 'girt' – for the straps which help hold a saddle in position on a horse's back. J.T.E.

[2] As is pointed out on the 'Family Tree' which appears in *J.T.'s HUNDREDTH*, there is some speculation regarding the exact relationship between Betty and General Jackson Baines 'Ole Devil' Hardin, C.S.A. However, the various members of the Hardin, Fog and Blaze clan with whom we consulted cannot, or *will not*, clarify the situation. Details pertaining to the career of the General – whose sobriquet arose out of the manner in which he emphasized the Mephistophelian aspects of his features during his youth and because his contemporaries claimed he was 'a lil ole devil for a fight' – can be found in the *OLE DEVIL HARDIN*, *CIVIL WAR* and *FLOATING OUTFIT* series. His death is reported in: *DOC LEROY, M.D.* J.T.E.

[3] One occasion when Berry Hardin found need to assert herself described in: *Part Two*, '*The Quartet*', *THE HALF BREED*. J.T.E.

[4] For the benefit of new readers: 'Hessian' boots were originally designed as footwear for Hussars and other types of light cavalry. The legs extend to just below knee level, with a V-shaped notch at the front. J.T.E.

117

had been made for a somewhat larger male wearer. A magnificent 'Hawken' plains rifle, custom built for her by John P. Gemmer – who had been trained by the Hawken brothers and, on their retirement in 1862, continued to produce excellent examples of the type of weapon for which they were famous – rested across her knees. Its powder horn and a buckskin pouch containing several .45 calibre round lead balls with which to load it were suspended on the left side of her saddlehorn and, at the right, was strapped an open topped holster holding an ivory handled Colt Model of 1851 Navy revolver. Although few of her sex and even less belonging to her social class would have considered using anything other than a side-saddle, she sat astride her mount in masculine fashion with the relaxed grace of one who frequently rode in such a manner. Nor, being possessed of the much sought after quality called *brio escondido* – hidden vigour – for which duns were justly acclaimed, was the gelding an easy animal to handle. While *brio escondido* produced first rate stamina, speed, agility and general hardiness, it also created a lively spirit requiring – demanding even – a considerable skill in matters equestrian.

In the centre of the trio, displaying an almost equal facility in the unfeminine style of riding and handling a fine fourteen hand blue roan gelding, Georgina Blaze was slightly taller, buxom without being fat, blonde and with a pretty, expressive face that looked meant for laughter even while registering indignation over what she regarded as unkind discrimination against her sex. Being more subject to the dictates of conventional behaviour than her cousin, she had on a light blue blouse and a black, wide brimmed, low crowned hat suitable for a young lady. However, once beyond the range of maternal scrutiny, she had exchanged her skirts for a pair of men's trousers and replaced her high-buttoned shoes with Comanche moccasins. She was nursing a 'Kentucky'[5] style rifle which had had its barrel's length reduced to offer greater portability and ease of handling and she carried its ammunition supply in a similar fashion to Betty, as she did a .31 calibre Colt Model of 1849 'Pocket

[5] Some authorities claim the majority of 'Kentucky' rifles were, in fact, made in Lancaster County, Pennsylvania. J.T.E.

Pistol' – a revolver in spite of its name – with a five shot cylinder and six inch barrel.

Not quite five foot six inches in height, the male member of the trio was considerably older than the girls, but his actual age was hard to determine. His cheerful, almond eyed yellowish features were undoubtedly those of an Oriental; but his short-cropped, grey-tinged black hair lacked the long pigtail by which, tradition claimed, a member of the Chinese race was drawn to the Celestial Paradise on dying. His garments consisted of a loose fitting and wide sleeved black shirt hanging outside trousers of the same material and these were tucked into the black Hessian boots he wore instead of going bare foot, or in sandals, as was usually the case among his race. He had a dark blue silk sash about his waist. Over this was strapped a black leather belt from which two swords – the one on the right longer than its mate – with slightly curved blades and small, circular hilts strange to Occidental eyes, were suspended by slings in sheaths made of bamboo. He had no firearms visible upon his person, or the saddle of his large black gelding, which he rode with no less competence than his companions. However, he had a quiver of arrows slung across his back, their flights rising over his right shoulder and he carried a long bow very different from those usually seen in the Western Hemisphere, strung ready for use, in his left hand.

Known as a *daisho*, the swords – called respectively a *tachi*, the longer, and a *wakizashi* – and the archery equipment were, in fact, traditional weapons of a Japanese *samurai*. Before his departure from his homeland, Tommy Okasi had belonged to that elite and very efficient warrior class.[6] What was more, he had lost little of his skill in the martial arts with the passing of the years. He was still able to deal adequately with the situation should he be abused by larger, heavier and stronger men who drew an erroneous conclusion with regards to his nationality.[7]

Although Tommy had accompanied Ole Devil in his

---

[6] For the benefit of new readers: details of Tommy Okasi's background, special qualifications and weapons are given in: *Appendix Two, OLE DEVIL AT SAN JACINTO*. J.T.E.

[7] One occasion when Tommy Okasi found need to demonstrate his

capacity of valet when the General had joined the Confederate States' Army, a private matter of considerable importance had caused him to return to Polveroso City, seat of Rio Hondo County.[8] Finding himself at a loose end, as the matter was not developing as swiftly as he had anticipated, he had willingly accepted a suggestion that he accompanied the girls on their hunting expedition.

There was something of considerably greater importance than just a desire for sport motivating the girls and the little Oriental. The previous afternoon, an eccentric old man – who went by the name 'Prospector Tuck' and who was allowed to live undisturbed on the OD Connected's range – had arrived at the ranch house with his right arm wrapped in a crude bandage.

The story of how the injury had been caused had created considerable concern. Seeing that one of the small herd of goats he had kept to supply him with milk, meat and skins had been pulled down by a pair of coyotes, the old man had left his cabin with the intention of retrieving the carcass. Instead of running away, as would normally have been the case at the sight of a human being, the male coyote had rushed towards him. Surprised by such untypical behaviour, he had shot at it and it went down. Not until he had approached and was bending over to make sure it was dead had he noticed there was saliva smearing its jaws. Even as an awareness of what the sight implied struck him, the coyote had expended the last dregs of its life in delivering a bite to his arm. Hurrying back to his cabin, he had cauterized the wound by burning it with a piece of blazing wood from the fire upon which he had been cooking a meal.

While sympathizing with Prospector Tuck over what had happened and being aware of how serious the consequences

skill at unarmed combat is recorded in: *Part Four, Ole Devil Hardin series*, '*Mr Colt's Revolving Cylinder Pistol*', *J.T.'s* HUNDREDTH. J.T.E.

[8] According to Alvin Dustine 'Cap' Fog – some details of whose career are given in, *YOU'RE A TEXAS RANGER, ALVIN FOG* and '*CAP*' *FOG, TEXAS RANGER, MEET MR J. G. REEDER* – the business was the commencement of Tommy Okasi's negotiations with certain Japanese authorities which paved the way for him to reopen communications with his family and allowed him to be joined by a young cousin who, in due course, taught 'Cap' *ju jitsu* and *karate*. J.T.E.

of the bite might prove if the coyote was suffering from rabies, Betty had considered the other news he brought demanded instant action, Unlike its mate, the female coyote had fled when he appeared. However, he had claimed that it too had shown a similar 'foaming' at the mouth which suggested it also was suffering from the dreaded disease.

After the old man had been dispatched in a buggy to Polveroso City, in the hope that the local doctor could give him some kind of treatment, Betty had called a council of war. With the ranch short staffed, so many of the hands having followed their employer into the Army, she had stated her intention of attending to the matter personally by going to try and find and kill the second coyote. Aware of how capable she was in such matters, her Aunt Elizabeth Fog[9] – who was acting as her guardian in the absence of her grandfather – had given assent to the proposal with the proviso that the little Oriental accompanied her. Although the girl had not been averse to company and had agreed, Georgina's participation was made without any official sanction. She had looked so downcast over the prospect of missing involvement in such an important affair that Betty did not have the heart to refuse when she suggested that she became the third member of the party.

The hour of Tuck's arrival had been too late for the search to be commenced that day. So the trio had waited until morning before setting out. None of them, not even the usually optimistic Georgina, had believed the task would be a sinecure as they were deprived by the particular circumstances of what would otherwise have been an invaluable aid. Because of the possibility that they would be in contention with a creature suffering from one of the most deadly diseases known that was transmittable to human beings, they could not make use of the pack of well trained big hounds which was Betty's pride and joy.[10] Instead, they would be

[9] Mother of Captain Dustine Edward Marsden 'Dusty' Fog, C.S.A., some details of whose career are recorded in the *CIVIL WAR* and *FLOATING OUTFIT* series and grandmother of Alvine Dustine 'Cap' Fog, q.v. J.T.E.

[10] One example of when Betty Hardin was able to use the pack is given in: *THE RIO HONDO WAR.* J.T.E.

compelled to depend upon their own resources and abilities. As both of the girls had done a fair amount of hunting, they were not at an impossible disadvantage.

Being slightly over a mile from Tuck's property and knowing something of the strong territorial habits of the species *Canis Latrans*, although none of them would have employed the term or scientific name for the coyote, the trio were not expecting to come across their quarry for a short while. They were scanning their surroundings more in hope than expectancy as they rode along talking. A remark by Betty about how much better off they were at that moment than their cousins, Dusty Fog and Red Blaze, who had recently left to become officers in the regiment recruited, equipped and financed by the clan, had provoked Georgina's response and question.

'Ancient and wise Nipponese saying – !' Tommy commenced, employing a sing-song tone he invariably adopted when making such a pronouncement, as the girls' looks implied they expected an answer.

'Which he's just now made up!' Betty and Georgina chorused in unison.

'Woman's place is in home, or *geisha* teahouse spending all her time making man comfortable, well fed and happy,' the little Oriental continued, paying no observable attention to the kind of comment with which his friends – and the girls came into that category – invariably greeted his opening gambit. 'That way, she not have time, or need, for fun and excitement.'

'I wish I'd *never* asked!' Georgina declared, making a wry face.

'Doesn't *everybody* who asks him?' Betty replied, her voice an equally well-educated and attractive Texas drawl showing that there was no malice to the comment.

'Nipponese women – !' Tommy began, but was not allowed to finish.

'Surely must have a dull time, the way *you* tell it,' Betty asserted, then looked at the other girl. 'And, anyway, Cousin Georgie, although I'm sure Mrs Greenhow and Belle Boyd don't think what they're doing is *fun,* there are two ladies who are playing an important part in fighting the Yankees.'

'Why they just surely are,' Georgina agreed, as the smaller girl realized her statement had been an error of tactics, knowing the women in question to be prominent members of the Confederate States' Secret Service.[11] 'And when you and I go to visit with Uncle Devil next year, we may get to meet one or the other of them.'

'It's not likely,' Betty smiled.

'Well, *if* we do,' Georgina stated emphatically, despite having a feeling that her cousin – who she was willing to admit was far more knowledgeable than herself – would be correct. 'I just know we can show her we'll be as good spies as she is.'

For once Betty was in error. The meeting Georgina desired was to take place and have tragic consequences.[12] However, the discussion was not permitted to continue.

'Look!' Tommy said, quietly yet urgently, pointing to his right, then reaching for an arrow from his quiver.

*   *   *   *   *

As they looked in the direction indicated by the little Oriental, the girls had no difficulty in seeing what had provoked his suggestion and action.

And neither of them was slow in responding to what they saw.

A sandy-reddish creature with a shaggy coat, a sharp, dog-like face and pricked ears had emerged from among some bushes about fifty yards away. Coming to a halt, but showing no sign of being aware of their presence, it stared towards the woodland to the south and sniffed the breeze. Its size and build suggested to the trio that it was a female, the male coyote tending to grow about a fifth larger than the bitch. What was more important about this particular specimen, however, was that there was something whiter than the usual greying caused by age around its nose and mouth.

[11] For the benefit of new readers, information regarding Mrs Rose Greenhow and Belle 'the Rebel Spy' Boyd is given in *APPENDIX TWO*. J.T.E.
[12] The tragic results of the meeting between Mrs Rose Greenhow, Betty Hardin and Georgina Blaze are recorded in: *KILL DUSTY FOG!*

Taking the latter factor into consideration, Betty released the split-ended reins and gave a signal with her heels which brought the *bayos azafrandos* gelding to an almost immediate halt. While the motion was being brought to cessation, she thumbed back the hammer of the Hawken rifle and swung its butt towards her shoulder.

Moving with a corresponding alacrity, being less trustful of her mount's training as it was borrowed for the occasion from the OD Connected's *remuda*, Georgina did not attempt to duplicate her cousin's actions. While she too dropped the reins, knowing the blue roan was range-trained to stop and stand still when they were released to dangle from the bit, she did not remain in the saddle. Tossing her right leg forward and over the saddlehorn, exhibiting agility of a high order in spite of her buxom build, she jumped to the ground. On alighting, she cocked the action and began to raise her shortened Kentucky rifle to the firing position.

Extracting the arrow deftly, Tommy turned his bow into a position ready to receive it. Designed for use by a person of his comparatively small stature, the handle of the six foot long stave was situated two thirds of the way down instead of centrally as was the case with Occidental bows. Notching the arrow to the string as he brought his mount to a stop, he commenced his draw after the fashion of a *samurai* warrior.

Obedient as the *bayos azafranados* might be, it did not stand as steady as a statue. Just as its rider was squeezing the Hawken's trigger, it moved a little. Not much, but sufficient to ruin her aim. Flying beneath instead of into the coyote, the bullet flung a spray of dislodged dirt against its belly.

Having its attention held by scents and sounds carried to it from the woodland, the little predator was unaware of the trio's presence until receiving the warning shot. Letting out a yelp of alarm, it bounded into the air like the doll of a jack-in-a-box on the lid being raised. The involuntary action proved to be its undoing.

Aiming hurriedly in the hope of beating her companions to the shot, Georgina failed in one respect. Her Kentucky barked slightly after the Hawken's deeper detonation. Although its bullet would have passed over the intended target, the bitch's bound caused them to converge. Struck by

124

the lead while in mid-air, the coyote gave another yelp and was knocked to the ground in a leg kicking tangle. An instant later, having made an alteration to its alignment, the arrow released by Tommy flew across the intervening distance and pinned the predator to the turf beneath it.

'Hold hard, hot head!' Betty ordered, watching the coyote's body contorting as is snapped spasmodically at the arrow's shaft, noticing her cousin was lowering the Kentucky and stepping forward, 'Let us not forget what happened to Prospector Tuck when he went up to one he *thought* couldn't harm him.'

'She won't be able to harm anyone,' Georgina objected, but refrained from advancing.

'*Maybe* not,' Betty conceded. 'But, if she has got rabies, I'd rather wait until I'm *sure* she can't.'

'Ancient and wise Nipponese saying, which I've just made up,' Tommy remarked, being equally aware of the potential danger and the blonde's tendency for impatience. 'When there is nothing to do, do something useful.'

'*That's* a *wise* saying?' Betty challenged.

'What would you like us to do,' Georgina went on, 'make you a cup of tea?'

'Not possible, as we don't have any,' the little Oriental pointed out. 'Would suggest instead, you reload round-eyes devil's rifles.'

Exchanging glances of simulated derision at the advice, the girls nevertheless showed no hesitation in carrying it out. Joining her cousin on the ground, Betty lifted the powder horn from the saddle. Taking a bullet and a small brass box from the buckskin pouch, she set about the process of reloading. With the powder and ball rammed home, the latter wrapped in a small leather 'patch' from one portion of the subdivided box, she took a percussion cap from the other section and fitted it to the nipple which gave access for the flame it would produce on being struck by the hammer to reach the main charge in the chamber of the barrel. With the task completed and the ramrod returned to its groove beneath the rifle, she hung the powder flask over the saddlehorn once more.

'*Now* can we go take a look?' Georgina inquired, a few seconds later, having carried out a similar procedure except that – the Kentucky having the older flintlock type of mechanism – she had had to put a small amount of powder into the priming pan to ensure detonation of the firing charge.

'Go ahead, there'll be no living with you until you *have*,' Betty authorized with a smile, knowing her cousin's impatience stemmed from a desire to find out whether they were correct in their suppositions regarding the coyote. 'And, as you're in such a rush, we'll give you-all the privilege of carrying the body back to Polveroso for the doctor to look it over.'

'Why thank you 'most to death, cousin dear,' the blonde replied. 'How *can* you-all be so *good* to lil – ?'

The mock derisory words were brought to an end as it became apparent why the coyote's attention had been directed elsewhere until the arrival of Betty's bullet had given it warning of their presence.

Although none of the trio had seen or heard anything to suggest there were other human beings in the vicinity, the sound of movement and the faint creaking of leather instinctively alterted them. Only a glance was needed to inform each of them that the riders who were approaching through the woodland about seventy-five yards away were strangers. Even at that distance, recognizing one of the dozen Mexicans who – accompanied by four Indians whose tribal origins were clearly south of the Rio Grande – were obviously stalking them, the girls were supplied with a further indication that the newcomers were far from being merely harmless travellers coming to find out why the shots were fired.

Shortly before their cousins had left to join the Texas Light Cavalry, the four of them had been hunting when they came into contact with a party of Mexican *bandidos* carrying out a reconnaisance to discover whether Rio Hondo County would be a fruitful area for depredations. Such had been the effectiveness of the tactics suggested by Dusty Fog that only one of the band escaped from the attack they had made.[13] Fortunately, he had been the most easily identifiable out of a far from prepossessing bunch. He had, in fact, tried to capture Betty and had received a response which caused him to forget his intentions. For all that, neither she nor Georgina – who had shot a man attempting to take her prisoner – were likely to forget him.

Having questioned the prisoners who had been taken, Judge Mannen Blaze – acting as head of the clan in Ole Devil's absence – and the county sheriff had been of the opinion that, on receiving what would almost certainly be a distorted account of their reception from the survivor, plans for further forays into Rio Hondo County by the rest of the gang would be cancelled.

Now, seeing the men and considering how they were behaving, Betty and Georgina concluded their uncle and the local peace officer's summation was incorrect.

Finding that their presence had been detected, the *bandidos* discarded the slow and stealthy approach which they had hoped would bring them close enough to allow them to rush from such a short distance that their victims would have no chance of escaping. With one exception, a burly Mexican who began to raise the rifle he was carrying, they let out yells and urged their mounts forward at an increased speed.

Although Tommy did not have the girls' advantage of recognizing one of the *bandidos* to guide him, he was equally aware of their status. So he had reached for another arrow as soon as he had received his first glimpse of them. Showing the kind of skill he had displayed when dealing with the coyote, he nocked, drew and loosed it in a smoothly flowing, yet rapid, sequence of motions.

Swiftly as the little Oriental acted, the missile he discharged flew where it was intended to go. Passing just above the head of the horse carrying the man who was preparing to shoot, it travelled beneath his weapon and sank through his chest until its point emerged from his back. He gave a scream of agony and, with the rifle tilting to fire harmlessly into the air, toppled from his saddle. None of his companions as

[13] Told in: *Part Five, CIVIL WAR series, 'A Time For Improvisation, Mr Blaze', J.T.'s HUNDREDTH.* J.T.E.

much as glanced around to find out if he needed assistance, or gave the slightest indication of caring what his fate might be. Ignoring the shrieks of pain he continued to utter for a few seconds, which ended in a harsh rattle as death claimed him, they continued to urge their mounts onwards inspired by a mutual desire to be the first to reach their intended victims and, by doing so, have the pick of the spoils.

Appreciating that to do so would merely delay their escape without halting the rest of the gang, neither girl offered to use the weapon she had just reloaded. However, while the methods they employed differed slightly, each was sufficiently cool and capable to make ready for taking flight in a commendably rapid fashion.

Grabbing the *bayos azafranado* gelding's reins in her left hand, Betty caught hold of the saddlehorn with them in it. Then, retaining the Hawken in her right fist, she made a bounding swing to alight astride the animal's back. The combination of a yell and jab in the ribs with her heels set it into instant motion.

Lacking her small cousin's agility and dexterity, Georgina nevertheless proved just as calm in a time of crisis despite her frequently impetuous nature. Quickly sliding the Kentucky into the leather boot attached to the blue roan's saddle, she too collected the dangling reins and grabbed the horn, but was able to employ both hands. Which proved fortunate. Startled by Betty's yell and seeing the *bayos azafranados* start moving, her mount followed suit with a jerk that would have dislodged one hand. Even having two in place, she needed all her strength to hang on. Contriving to do so, she was able to duplicate the means by which her cousin had mounted.

Unlike the girls, Tommy had remained in the saddle. He was prepared to continue using the bow, or draw and attack with his *daisho* if necessary to protect them, but a glance to his rear informed neither course would be necessary. No coward, he was far from reckless and realized that to stand and fight against such odds would be suicidal. Not only for himself, either. Knowing Betty and Georgina, he did not doubt they would turn to his assistance if he adopted such a course. So, waiting until both were mounted and moving, he

128

sent his black gelding after them.

Yells of fury burst from the *bandidos* as they saw the speed with which their intended victims were taking flight before they had covered more than half of the distance separating them. Knowledgeable in such matters, every member of the gang could appreciate how this would make their task more difficult. While being reasonably good riders and well mounted, as was obligatory for survival in their ignoble profession, their horses had done considerable travelling. On the other hand, not only were the two girls and the primitively armed small foreigner equally competent, they had other advantages. Their horses were if anything of superior quality and they were personally lighter burdens to be carried by the much fresher animals.

Sitting astride horses capable of running as swiftly as the proverbial Neuces steer and possessing the stamina required to keep up the pace for a long distance, the girls and Tommy were confident that, unless something untoward occurred, they could outrun their pursuers. Nor, with about fifty yards already separating them and likely to increase (being aware of how difficult it was to aim accurately from the back of a fast running horse), did they consider there was any great danger to them should the *bandidos* try shooting to halt them. Only by sheer bad luck, from their point of view, would a bullet be likely to find its mark on one or another of them.

On the negative side, the trio appreciated how they were being driven away from the town or either of the ranch houses at which they would be able to find shelter and protection. Having confidence in their mounts, they felt this could be overcome by taking a circuitous route to one of the havens. Furthermore, they hoped that the length of the chase, which showed no sign of being brought to a successful conclusion, might persuade the *bandidos* to give up the attempt.

There was, although Betty and her companions were unaware of it, little chance of that hope being brought to fruition.

Despite a growing realization that they could be in for a protracted chase, the *bandidos* were not swayed from their

9

determination to continue. They were driven by a much stronger motive than the chance of obtaining the trio's property and were not dissuaded from the pursuit in spite of knowing that the usual pleasures would have to be at least delayed when the girls fell into their hands.

Although the prisoners had not disclosed the fact to Judge Blaze and the sheriff of Rio Hondo County, one of them had been a participant in the hiding of the loot taken earlier in the foray upon which the gang were engaged. As he alone of those who had been responsible had survived the defeat of the scouting party, allegedly at the hands of about twenty well armed *Tejanos*, his associates wanted to secure his release and had, in fact, sent two of their number to Polveroso City the previous night to secretly advise him this would be done.

Having guessed who Betty and Georgina were when the Yaqui Indian scouting ahead had returned to tell of seeing them, without mentioning all he knew, the man who had escaped suggested they should be taken as hostages and offered in exchange for the release of the prisoners. Being disinclined to try and attack a town which they imagined to have a larger active population than was actually the case, the others had been in agreement with his plan. Nor were they put off when their attempt to effect the capture in an easy fashion came to nothing, knowing what was at stake.

By the time the trio were entering the large wood-encircled clearing in which Prospector Tuck had his home, the distance between themselves and the pursuers had opened to a good hundred yards. This had been achieved in spite of the precautions taken by the girls against their being forced to halt and fight for some reason. Returning the Hawken temporarily to its saddleboot, Betty had hung the powder flask and bullet pouch over her left shoulder. Then, having transferred the Navy Colt from its holster to her waistband, she took possession of the rifle once more. Seeing what her cousin was doing, Georgina made a similar adjustment to her armament.

Erected as a refuge in the days when depredations by hostile Indians as well as *bandidos* was an ever present possibility and maintained in an excellent state of preservation, despite the need having decreased prior to the War Between The States, the sturdily built cabin was situated in a very good defensive position. Occupying the whole of a niche in the sheer wall which formed one edge of the clearing, there was a trapdoor in the roof and a ladder of sufficient length inside to offer a means of ascending the fifteen or so foot to the top, otherwise an approach could only be made from the front and across the open ground.

Despite being aware of the potential for defence offered by the cabin, the trio had no intention of staying to make a fight from it. Nor were they swayed from the decision by noticing that the old man had left the door open in his haste to help to deal with his wound. They believed their chances were better by continuing the flight, but the matter was to be taken out of their hands.

How and why the mishap occurred, Betty had no conception, but the normally sure-footed *bayos azafranados* gelding stumbled and started to collapse. Displaying the superb skill she had acquired, even when riding under such adverse conditions, she quit the saddle the moment she felt the horse was going down. Although she contrived to alight on her feet and keep running, it was at the expense of losing the Hawken. Finding it an encumbrance threatening to make her lose her balance, she tossed it aside and continued to sprint towards the cabin's open door.

Seeing what was happening to her cousin, Georgina immediately started reining the blue roan to a rump-scraping stop. Before its forward motion had ended, she was dismounted and running after the other girl as fast as her legs could carry her.

However, while equally aware of what had befallen Betty, the little Oriental did not follow the blonde's example. Instead, paying no attention to the delighted yells given by their pursuers, he continued to ride across the clearing at the same pace and disappeared among the trees as his companions were entering the building.

*   *   *   *   *

'Blast the luck!' Betty Hardin ejaculated, slamming the

131

cabin's door as her cousin entered and shooting across the stout wooden bar which served as a bolt. 'I could use that Hawken of mine!'

'It's still lying where you threw it, for shame,' Georgina Blaze pointed out, going to the left side window and, closing the thick wooden shutter, peering through the aperture cut as a loophole. 'Shall I go and fetch it?'

'If you'd any sense, you wouldn't be in here at all, hot head,' Betty stated, treating the other window in a similar fashion. Then she picked up the double-barrelled shotgun which was leaning against the window instead of drawing her Navy Colt. She felt sure its owner would keep it loaded for just such an emergency. Then she continued, 'Well of all the nerve! Only *two* of them are going after Tommy.'

'I hope they've made their wills,' the blonde commented, showing no animosity over the little Oriental's apparent desertion. Having drawn the same conclusion with regards to the bell-mouthed blunderbus hanging on hooks beneath her window and being satisfied that it would be ready to carry on the fight, she thrust the Kentucky's barrel out of the loophole. 'I'd say we'll have to do something about the rest of them, though.'

'Let's do it then!' Betty suggested, bringing up the shotgun and drawing its twin hammers.

Starting to turn their horses towards the cabin, the remaining *bandidos* saw the weapons emerging. Any hopes they had that the girls might be bluffing, or unable to handle the weapons, were shattered as flame erupted from the rifle's muzzle and the shotgun's left barrel. An Indian let out a yell of pain as the bullet from the Kentucky caught him in the shoulder. With his horse collapsing underneath him, one of the Mexicans was swept from the saddle by mates of the buckshot balls which had struck it down. Seeing the rifle rapidly replaced by an even more potentially dangerous blunderbus and suspecting the shotgun still had a second barrel loaded, the rest wheeled their mounts and rode out of range.

'*That's* stopped them!' Georgina enthused.

'Not for long, though,' Betty warned. 'Keep watch on them

132

while I see whether Prospector has any other guns we can use.'

Leaving the shotgun extended through the window ready to be used again without delay if the need arose, the smaller girl started to conduct the examination. A glance at the roof satisfied her that the trapdoor was bolted. Passing the table in the centre of the room, she noticed there were a number of rock chips and a sheet of metal made by cutting open and beating flat a kerosene can on it. She paid little attention to the piece of new chimney pipe lying alongside the stove. Instead, she searched the cupboards and sidepiece without finding any weapons.

'There's only this keg of powder,' Betty reported, at the conclusion of her efforts, carrying the item in question from where she had located it beneath the old man's bed. 'The trouble is, we've no more shot for either the gun or the blunderbuss, or bullets for our revolvers.'

'We could always roll it outside and shoot into it when they're close enough,' Georgina offered hopefully, knowing the find would be of little use due to the lack of ammunition to be propelled by it.

'Which would be fine if they were obliged enough to come up to it,' Betty replied, her gaze returning to the stove. 'What are they doing?'

'Standing and talking is all,' the blonde answered, then ducked instinctively as one of the *bandidos* jerked up his rifle to send a shot which struck the shutter near the loop-hole but did not penetrate. 'No sense in answering him, they're too far away. What's wrong?'

'I've an idea!' Betty stated, straightening up from the examination of the chimney pipe which had provoked her cousin's question. 'They're going to rush us sooner or later and, when that happens, we may get a couple but the rest will be on us before we can reload.'

'We'll have our Colts,' Georgina pointed out.

'They don't know that,' Betty countered. 'And, anyway, we're neither of us close to as good as Cousin Dusty or Cousin Red with them.'

'We *could* go out there and throw ourselves on their mercy,' Georgina said dryly, although confident her cousin had some-

133

thing more positive in mind. 'But I don't really think *that* would be too good an idea.'

'Neither do I,' Betty seconded, still studying the object at her feet and thinking of the other things she had seen during her search of the cabin. 'So, as Cousin Dusty might say, it's our turn to improvise, Miss Blaze.'

'I suppose you'll finally tell me what you mean,' Georgina declared, giving what might have been a sigh or resignation.

'I will, I will!' Betty promised, but with reservations. 'Just as soon as I decide what I mean myself.'

There were, the black haired little girl told herself as she picked up the piece of pipe, a considerable number of factors against the scheme she was envisaging working. However, as she could not foresee any other alternative, she was determined to put it into effect if she could possibly do so.

Carrying the pipe to the table, Betty set it down. Designed to form the bottom section of the chimney, it had a stout cap firmly welded to one end and there was a hole a couple of inches above the appendage to connect it to the back of the stove. Collecting a roll of baling wire and box of matches from the kitchen, she put them on the table. Listening to her cousin's commentary on the *bandidos'* activities, she wrapped the sheet of metal securely around the pipe so it covered the opening near the bottom. Having done so, aware of the pressures to which the device would be subjected when her idea was put to the test, she began to bind it into place as tightly as she could manage. Nor did she stop when confident it was as secure as she could make it, but wound the rest of the wire around the remainder of the pipe. Then, fetching a hammer and a metal spike from a tool box she had located, she inserted the tip of the spike between the wire over the now concealed hole. Delivering a blow with the hammer, she created a small aperture which gave access to the interior of the pipe.

'I wish I knew what you're doing!' Georgina remarked, glancing around.

'I wish I could be sure it will work,' Betty replied fervently. 'How about them?'

'They seem to be arguing about what to do,' the blonde decided, returning her gaze to the loophole. 'I'd say none of

134

them are willing to take the lead when they attack.'

'Let's hope they all stay the same way!' Betty breathed, taking her contraption and one of the chairs to a position facing the door.

Setting the chair on its side, the girl inserted the strengthened pipe between the legs so that its base was resting on the floor and the hole she had made in the metal sheet was uppermost. Ensuring the inclined tube was pointing at the door, she gathered and weighted its lower end beneath sacks of provisions. With that done, she collected and placed the powder keg alongside the contraption.

'My god!' Georgina gasped, having taken another glance around. 'You're making a *cannon*!'

'No!' Betty corrected grimly. 'I'm *trying* to.'

With that, the girl continued her task by fetching over the keg of gun powder. As she did so, she thanked providence for her insatiable curiosity and having had the opportunity to acquire at least sufficient knowledge to make what she was hoping to achieve feasible. While not a tomboy in the accepted sense, she had taken an interest in the lessons her two favourite male cousins had been receiving at Judge Blaze's small military academy. Among the other manuals they and she studied had been a couple devoted to artillery. Possessing an excellent memory, she could recollect enough about the procedure to know something of how the loading of a cannon was carried out.

Knowing and putting the knowledge into practice were, Betty realized, horses of a *very* different colour. Unless using ready-made cartridges, a gunner in the Army employed a ladle designed to take only enough powder to ensure the gun fired properly. She had neither aid available. Yet too little would mean the charge would barely leave the barrel.

Too much, on the other hand, would explode the pipe and might even blow up the cabin!

Scooping a handful of the potent black grains from the keg, Betty gingerly tipped them into the tube. Deciding they would be insufficient, she sent a second after them. A glance informed her that the hole she had made was now concealed by the powder. So, taking off her shirt, she tore it in half. Placing one portion into the muzzle of the improvised cannon, she rammed it on to the powder with the aid of a broom-handle. Obtaining projectiles for the device proved the simplest task, a double handful of the rock chips serving in the place of more formal shot. These too were rammed home and held in place by the rest of her shirt. With that completed, she poured more powder through the small hole until the space below was filled and a small mound remained on top.

'Do you think it will work?' Georgina asked, unable to prevent herself from taking quick glances while keeping the *bandidos* under observation.

'I'll tell you *after* I've tried,' Betty replied, pulling the ramrod from its place beneath the Kentucky rifle.

'If it *doesn't* I'd rather not know,' the blonde asserted, watching her cousin fastening a piece of cloth to the end of the ramrod. Then, hearing a shout, she returned her gaze to the loophole. 'Somebody's coming!'

'Let's hope Tommy found some help,' Betty answered.

'It isn't them, even if he did,' Georgina declared. 'Whoever it is is coming from the wrong direction. There are two of them, which makes two more against us.'

Joining her cousin, Betty studied the two men who came from the woodland. One was a Mexican and the other a Yaqui Indian. From the pace they approached and the heated manner in which each was speaking while pointing behind them, she concluded they were bringing important and possibly alarming news.

'Whatever they're saying's stirring the others up like bees with a bear clawing open the hive!' Georgina estimated, also watching the *bandidos'* reactions.

'And it's enough to make them ready to rush us!' Betty supplemented, returning to the improvised cannon. Applying the light from a match to the piece of rag at the end of the ramrod, she went on, 'Wait until they're close, then open the door!'

* * * * *

Listening to the sound of the pursuit drawing closer as he slowed down his black gelding, Tommy Okasi glanced over his shoulder. He saw everything was progressing as he required. Not only were he and the two men who had followed him out of sight of the clearing, but their behaviour met with his entire satisfaction. Each was a Yaqui Indian and had already discharged the trade musket with which he was armed without scoring a hit. Because of the terrain they were traversing and the way in which the little Oriental had led them on a swerving course through the trees, neither had had an opportunity to reload. Furthermore, their upbringing as warriors was leading them to compete for the honour of being the one to reach and strike him down. Already the smaller had gained a lead over his companion of close to twenty feet and was striving to keep in the favourable position.

Satisfied with his latest observation and having no desire to be driven too far from the clearing, Tommy bounded off his saddle. As he alighted, he tossed aside his bow. However, he made no attempt to pull out either the *tachi* or shorter *wakizashi*. Instead, he did no more than turn and face his pursuers, standing balanced lightly on his spread apart and slightly bent legs.

Urging his fast moving pony eagerly, the leading Yaqui could hardly believe his good fortune. He was so delighted at seeing his intended victim dismount and discard the bow on turning to face him that he gave no thought to why the basic precaution of drawing one of the 'long knives' was not being taken. Nor, at the pace he was approaching, did he have much time to ponder on the matter. Droping his empty rifle, he snatched the knife from its sheath on his belt and, letting out a whoop of triumph, he dived from his horse's back towards what he regarded as being an easy means of counting coup and acquiring loot.

Tommy was far from being as incautious as his behaviour suggested. Like every *samurai* warrior, he was accomplished at *lai jitsu*, the extremely rapid withdrawal of the *tachi*. Waiting until seeing how the attack was being launched and considering it ideal for his purpose, he stepped aside. As he did so, he swept the long blade of the sword from its sheath to send its point into the ribs of the descending brave, Jerking the weapon free as its victim plunged dying to the ground, he swung to face his second assailant.

Startled by the fate of his companion, the taller and slightly older Yaqui was less inclined to be reckless, but continued to press home the attack. However, conveying the impression that he was intending to ride the foreigner down, he swerved his well trained mount at the last moment. Throwing his empty rifle butt first at Tommy, he sprang after it. Deflecting the missile with his left arm while retiring a long step, the little Oriental swung the *tachi* in an almost horizontal arc. Made of specially forged steel, the razor sharp blade bit into the Indian's skull like a length of wire slicing through a piece of cheese. Continuing the retreat to avoid being struck by his victim's body, he extracted the weapon and looked around.

One glance assured Tommy he had nothing to fear from the other Indian. Having ensured that no more of the *bandidos* were in the vicinity, he wiped the blade of the *tachi* clean on his second victim's shirt and returned it to its sheath. Then, collecting his bow, he went to where his horse had been brought to a halt by its dangling reins. Mounting, he guided it around and rode in the general direction from which he had come.

Instead of returning and entering the·clearing, the little Oriental turned aside while still out of sight of its occupants. Being a competent warrior, he wanted to discover what he would be up against when he arrived. From his knowledge of the area, he could remember a point of vantage which would allow him to achieve his purpose and also offer an opportunity of intervening without his presence being suspected in advance.

Before leaving the open ground, hoping to draw away more of the *bandidos* than had proved the case, Tommy had looked back to ensure the girls reached the safety of the cabin. If they had not, he would have returned to their aid immediately and regardless of the odds. He had heard the Kentucky and the shotgun being fired and, remembering having seen one in the building during a previous visit, deduced Betty was using the latter weapon. Although he had been surprised by how little shooting there had subsequently been, he considered this good rather than bad tidings. The girls would never have allowed themselves to be taken, particularly from such a sturdy refuge, without having put up a fight.

Dismounting on arriving at the slope, as ascending it on the black was out of the question, the little Oriental climbed to the top and set off through the undergrowth on foot. Before he reached his destination, he discovered to his relief that his summations were correct. There was no sign of the girls and the *bandidos* were gathered in a group at a safe distance from the cabin, with the exception of one who lay dead by an equally lifeless horse.

Coming to a halt among the bushes above the niche in which the cabin was situated, Tommy watched the arrival of the two newcomers. Like the girls, he could tell that their coming was a source of considerable interest to the assembled *bandidos*. Despite being unable to hear what was being said, he also concluded from their actions that an attack was imminent.

On noticing the way in which the assault was to be carried out, Tommy decided how he would respond. Realizing the way he meant to intervene could put him in danger from the girls, he envisaged a method of notifying them of his presence and hoped they would draw the correct conclusions with regards to his intentions. Sliding three arrows from his quiver, he thrust their points into the ground at his feet. Then, removing the quiver as an unnecessary encumbrance, he leaned it against a bush. Removing a fourth arrow, he set it in position on the bow and prepared to put his scheme into practice.

* * * * *

'Heavens to Betsy, they're playing it tricky!' Georgina Blaze gasped, taking a look through the loophole before she set out to follow her cousin's instructions. 'They're not riding, but are walking here with the horses ahead of them.'

'Are they?' Betty Hardin ejaculated and darted to the other window carrying the ramrod with its burning attachment. Keeping it in her hand, she peered through the hole. As she did so, she saw one of the Mexicans suddenly reel and clutch at the shaft of arrow which had appeared to sprout from nowhere out of the centre of his chest. Taking up her position behind the shotgun and gripping it without relinquishing her other device, she snapped, 'Fire the blunderbus when I shoot and try to scatter the horses. Then get ready to open up for them.'

Noticing another Mexican being impaled by an arrow, Georgina was too engrossed in doing as she was told to draw any conclusions from the sight. However, having no wish to harm the animals, she sent the charge from the blunderbus into the ground ahead of them. Dropping the weapon and springing towards the door, she saw that her cousin had fired in a similar fashion. She had also seen something else, but was moving before the implications of it struck her.

The horses did not scatter!

Despite the blonde's consternation, which she did not permit to stop her continuing with the instructions, Betty's purpose was achieved.

Allowing the shotgun to fall, the smaller girl watched the result of her ploy starting to take effect before turning and darting to the improvised cannon.

Concluding that the weapons had been discharged and abandoned in panic, the *bandidos* pushed between the horses and dashed forward. Having been informed by the newcomers that a large and well armed posse from Polveroso City were coming, they were so eager to take the girls hostage that none of them noticed the two men who were killed by Tommy Okasi's arrows. Nor did they pay any greater attention when one of the Yaquis was struck down in the same fashion. There was something else attracting their interest.

The cabin's door had swung open!

Because the interior of the building was in deep shadow, the men were unable to see what was waiting for them. So, although puzzled by the sight, they not only continued to advance with no reduction of speed, but began to converge so as to make the most of the opportunity that the apparently pointless behaviour of the occupants was presenting.

Sparing a glance as she stood holding the ramrod over the small mound of powder on the touch-hole of the home-made cannon, Betty found as she had expected that Georgina had shown a sound grasp of the situation. Having drawn the bolt and thrown open the door, the blonde had moved away from it.

There was, however, no time for Betty to think of anything other than the *bandidos*. Already they were closing upon the entrance, pressing together in their eagerness to reach Georgina and herself. Waiting until they were almost at the door, she lowered the burning cloth on to the powder. Dropping the ramrod as the grains ignited, she sprang aside and snatched out her revolver. Even as it was coming clear, she heard a thud on the roof of the cabin and guessed what had caused it. Once more, she was granted no chance of considering the possibilities suggested by the sound.

Spluttering and emitting a cloud of acrid white smoke, the flame cause by the rag passed through the hole. The main charge was detonated with a roar. Pushed along the pipe by the volume of gas this created, the bits of stone belched from the muzzle and spread like the charge from a shotgun while flying towards the gang. Taken totally unprepared, those men who were not hit found their troubles were far from over.

'*Banzai!*'

Having discarded his bow after the fourth arrow missed, Tommy had left his place of concealment. Hoping the girls would draw the correct conclusion from seeing the men he had hit going down, he sprang from the top of the cliff on to the roof. Although he was as surprised as any of the attackers when the explosion sounded from beneath him, he did not let it deter him from continuing with his plan of campaign.

Giving the traditional *samurai* battle-cry, the little Oriental leapt from the cabin to alight among the already discomfited *bandidos*. Bringing out the *tachi* on alighting, he struck left and right in rapid succession to disembowel the Yaqui whose shoulder wound had been no more than a graze, then almost remove a Mexican's head by severing the neck. As the second victim was falling, the girls opened fire with their Colts through the loopholes. While neither made a hit, their contribution proved too much for the five survivors. Deserting their wounded companions, the quintet raced after the horses which had bolted in fright at the explosion. Each one contrived to catch himself a mount and set off for safety as quickly as he could persuade it to carry him.

Emerging from the smoke filled cabin, keeping their eyes averted from the carnage they had helped to wreak, Betty and Georgina joined Tommy in the fresh air. Their concern over hearing shouts and hooves died away as they saw who was coming through the woodland. All knew the danger was past and the girls wanted only to get away from the clearing where they had so ably made use of their turn to improvise a means of defence.

Author's note: *An examination of the dead coyotes, the male's body being found where it was shot, established that neither had rabies. The 'froth' on their mouths had come from eating the remains of a batch of sourdough discarded by Prospector Tuck. J.T.E.*

PART FIVE

Belle 'The Rebel Spy' Boyd

In

THE 'BUTCHER'S' FIERY END

'Darling, I've never been so *frightfully* disconcerted, or embarrassed in my life,' Amelia Penelope Diana Benkinsop asserted, continuing the story of certain events in which she had recently participated and knowing she was approaching the portion in which the person she was addressing would be most interested. 'There I was in all "me finery", happily chatting with *Dusty Fog* and convincing myself he believed I really *was* Lady Winifred Amelia Besgrove-Woodstole, when a rather tipsy rancher joined us and said enough to give me just the *tiniest* suspicion I wasn't being quite as successful as I imagined.'[1]

'Good heavens, Benkers, what a *facer*,' declared the genuine Lady Winifred Amelia Besgrove-Woodstole – although she was currently known by another, less aristocratic name – employing the sobriquet with which her travelling companion was addressed by close friends and showing neither surprise nor annoyance over the disclosure that the other had been using her identity. 'Although *I* could have told you it was unlikely you would be.'

The speakers were holding their conversation while seated on opposite sides of the table in a well furnished and comfortable private railroad car. Each was a magnificent example of feminine pulchritude (although neither openly flaunted it), and had demeanour indicative of birth and

[1] The events are recorded in: *BEGUINAGE IS DEAD!* J.T.E.

breeding. Expensively and tastefully attired as fashion dictated for travelling and exquisitely jewelled, although not ostentatiously so, nor too excess, they were both clearly accustomed to making a journey in such a luxurious form of transportation. However, while their accents and the honorific preceding the name of the one and under which the other had been masquerading – unsuccessfully according to her story – indicated they were well educated, upper class English 'gentlewomen', the train upon which they were riding was carrying them eastwards across Kansas.

Close to five foot eight inches in height and in her late twenties, the genuine Lady Winifred had such a commanding presence that she appeared taller and older. There was, however, nothing of the formidable and domineering female dragon about her. She had elegantly coiffured black hair, cut somewhat shorter than was dictated by current fashion, framing an exceptionally beautiful face which radiated charm, backed by personality and considerable strength of will. Despite her costly black two-piece travelling costume and well-filled frilly bosomed white silk blouse being almost severely masculine in style and line, she contrived – without making any conscious, or deliberate, effort to do so – to make them seem as sensual and revealing as the most daring ball gown. They set off her richly contoured body magnificently.

For all that, the second passenger was in no way at a disadvantage as far as physical attractions went.

Lacking perhaps an inch of her companion's height, Benkers was about the same age. She too possessed a regal beauty which was enhanced by an aura of patrician distinction without affectation. Although lacking the letters patent to place before her name as an indication of a noble birthright, she clearly shared a similar social upbringing and family background. She too had removed her hat on settling down in the car and her longer honey blonde hair was drawn up in a large bun, being held in place by a net at the back of the neck. Like her friend's, her brown two-piece travelling costume and unadorned light blue blouse were an excellent fit, neither concealing nor deliberately seeking to show off an equally curvaceous and well developed figure.

'Of course, I *had* noticed that Mark Counter, the Ysabel

144

Kid and Waco gave me a few funny looks when I was introduced to them,' Benkers went on. 'But I'd been telling myself, where the Kid and Waco were concerned at any rate, it was only because they weren't accustomed to being in the company of a lady.'

'Some of my girls might be willing to give you an argument over *that*,' Lady Winifred asserted with a smile, having made the acquaintance of all the men to whom her friend was referring and being intimately acquainted in the case of Captain Dustine Edward Marsden 'Dusty' Fog, C.S.A.[2] 'Although I must admit Lon and Waco would tend to shy away from the company of "ladies", in your context, unless there was no way they could avoid it.'

'Be that as it may, Freddie, I still feel it was *most* inconsiderate of you,' Benkers complained, employing the abbreviation usually applied to her long-standing friend's name. 'I travel all the way over here to the "Colonies",[3] posing as you – rather adequately, if I may be excused for saying so – because I'd been *assured* by the staff at your family's hunting lodge in Melton Mowbray that you were gadding around India, hunting tigers, or whatever one does there – and what do I find when I arrive?'

'I can hardly wait to be told,' the black haired beauty replied. She knew sufficient about her friend's far from conventional family background not to ask why it had been considered necessary to pose as her while making the visit to the United States. She was, however, confident that it would not have been detrimental to her in any way.

[2] Along with Captain Dustine Edward Marsden 'Dusty' Fog, C.S.A., and Mark Counter, q.v., Loncey Dalton Ysabel – known as 'Lon', or the Ysabel Kid – and Waco were members of the OD Connected ranch's floating outfit. Some details of their respective careers are given in the *CIVIL WAR, FLOATING OUTFIT* and, in the latter's case, *WACO* series. J.T.E.

[3] Like many English people of that period, Amelia Penelope Diana 'Benkers' Benkinsop was of the opinion, perhaps a touch tongue-in-cheek where she was concerned, that the world was divided into two parts, Great Britain – as it was *then* – and its Colonies. See the dedication in: *KILL DUSTY FOG!*, the comments of 'Brit', the Earl of Hawkesden, in, *RIO GUNS*, also those attributed to 'Miz Freddie' Fog, née Lady Winifred Amelia Besgrove-Woodstole, in, *YOU'RE A TEXAS RANGER, ALVIN FOG.* J.T.E.

'I find out, at a *most* inopportune moment I might add, that far from being in India, you are over *here*,' Benkers explained, in aggrieved tones, waving her left hand languidly towards the nearest window of the car. 'Not only running a *music hall* – or whatever the "Colonials" call it – but also the *mayor* of a charming and most prosperous town in Kansas.'

All of which was true!

In spite of her family's servants having received instructions to inform everybody who asked – even such a close friend as Benkers – that she was travelling in India, Lady Winifred was making her home in the United States. Not only had she helped found the 'railroad' town of Mulrooney, Kansas – which derived much of its income out of the herds of longhorn cattle driven from Texas to its shipping pens – but she owned and operated its best saloon, the Fair Lady. Furthermore, being known by the residents and visitors as 'Freddie Woods', she had been elected mayor and was responsible for the policies which had given the town a well deserved reputation for honesty and fair dealing among the people who found the need to visit and transact business there.[4]

' "Colonies, *Colonials!*" ' Freddie sniffed, eyeing the blonde with mock disdain. 'You're beginning to sound like Pat Reeder, my girl.'

'Good heavens, am I?' Benkers ejaculated, displaying either real or well simulated horror at the prospect. 'I really *must* watch out for *that*, it could ruin me socially. But you shouldn't blame Pat, Actually, I haven't seen the dear boy since the night we celebrated his promotion to captain.'

'You should have been in Mulrooney a couple of weeks ago,' Freddie remarked, but out of consideration for the type of military duties upon which their mutual friend was engaged[5] and about which she felt sure the blonde was probably

[4] Some details of Lady Winifred Amelia 'Freddie Woods' Besgrove-Woodstole's career in Mulrooney, Kansas, are recorded in: *THE MAKING OF A LAWMAN*; *THE TROUBLE BUSTERS*; *THE GENTLE GIANT*; *THE FORTUNE HUNTERS*; *WHITE STALLION, RED MARE* and *THE WHIP AND THE WAR LANCE*. Information regarding her life after marrying Captain Dustine Edward Marsden Fog, C.S.A., q.v.. is given in: *NO FINGER ON THE TRIGGER*. J.T.E.

[5] For further information regarding the man in question, Captain

even better informed, she had lowered her voice to a conspiratorial level. 'He was passing through and we had dinner
together.'

'Are you two talking about *me*, heh?' demanded a strident
and indignantly querulous feminine voice from near the
door at the forward end of the car.

*　*　*　*　*

Surprised by the interruption, Freddie Woods and Benkers
Benkinsop looked at the hitherto silent third occupant of the
compartment. Clad from head to toe in a cheap black ensemble of the kind referred to as 'widow's weeds', which gave
her an appearance of being dumpy in build and made estimating her height difficult, a veil attached to the hat securely
pinned on stringy white hair served to conceal the speaker's
features. The timbre of her harsh Southern accent and her
posture suggested she was advanced in years. Although she
had announced herself earlier as 'Mrs Henrietta Turnbull',
the gloves she wore hid any rings which would prove this to
be her correct marital status.

The woman was not a member of the friends' party and,
if it came to a point, had no right to be sharing their comfortable accommodation. The private car belonged to an
important official of the railroad company and had been put
at Freddie's disposal for the trip to Chicago she was taking
with Benkers. On their arrival, although the Negro porter
had insisted he had locked the doors after making the compartment ready for them, Mrs Turnbull had been sitting inside. She had steadfastly and indignantly refused to leave,
waving a large and almost shapeless black umbrella – which,
along with a bulky old carpetbag of equally decrepit aspect,
appeared to be her only possessions – to emphasize her intention of staying where she was.

Amused by the woman's determination not to be put upon,
Freddie had told the porter she could remain in the com-

Patrick Reeder, Rifle Brigade, seconded to British Military Intelligence,
see *Footnote 13*, *APPENDIX TWO*, also *THE REMITTANCE KID*
and *THE WHIP AND THE WAR LANCE*. J.T.E.

partment. It had soon become obvious that her insistence had not stemmed out of a desire for feminine society. She had declined an invitation to join the friends at the table and, rebuffing their attempts to make conversation, continued to sit defiantly nursing her umbrella on the seat next to the forward door. Respecting her privacy, they had left her to her own devices and had spent the half hour or so which had elapsed since leaving Mulrooney chatting about various events that had transpired since their last meeting in England. It was, in fact, the first time the subject of Benker's visit to the United States had come up and her friend was looking forward to learning the details, as well as telling what little she knew about the assignment upon which Captain Patrick Reeder – otherwise known as 'the Remittance Kid' – was currently engaged.

Before either Freddie or Benkers could refute the accusation, the forward door of the car was thrust open. Once again, if appearances were any guide, the compartment was being invaded by unauthorized passengers.

Three of the intruders – and there could be no more apt description of them – were tall, lanky young men wearing the attire of town dwellers in the middle income bracket. Long hair trailed from beneath their badly fitting billycock hats.[6] Their hollow-cheeked, sunken-eyed, sullen-mouthed faces were alike in being unshaven and so sallow it was plain they spent little time out of doors. Although moderately costly, their three-piece suits were crumpled and stained. Their white shirts showed signs of having been worn for considerably longer than one day. The two shortest did not wear collars and that of their companion, embellished by a badly knotted red tie, was equally grubby from use. They were all holding cheaply manufactured revolvers of the kind which would come to be known as 'Saturday night specials', but these could be as dangerous as the products of the major companies making firearms of better quality.

Bringing up the rear, closing and bolting the door behind her, was a young woman. Straggly, untidily combed brunette hair showed from a brimless and unadorned toque hat. Her plump face was as sallow as those of her companions, but

[6] 'Billycock' hat: also known as a 'derby', or a 'bowler'. J.T.E.

148

suggestive of Gallic rather than Anglo-Saxon origins and, bearing an expression of almost fanatical intensity, no more prepossessing. Of medium height, she was stocky and filled her grey two-piece tailored costume in a way that was flattering neither to her figure nor the garments. She was empty handed, but the plain black vanity bag suspended from her left wrist was hanging in a manner that suggested there was something heavy and bulky inside.

'Start screaming and you're dead!' warned the tallest of the three men, darting a surprised look at the black-clad woman sitting by the door, as they walked forward.

Taking her duties as mayor seriously, as well as being aware of the advisability of keeping a watch for potential trouble makers in her saloon, Freddie made sure she kept in touch with everything of importance that happened in Mulrooney. While she had never seen the female intruder before as far as she could remember, she was able to identify the men. In order of size, they were Alan Fisher, Jamie Morris and Davis Basnett, a trio of political agitators who had arrived a few days earlier, apparently with the intention of stirring up unrest among the railroad construction gangs and other workers in the area.

'I've not the slightest intention of screaming, my good man,' Benkers declared, directing a quick and regretful glance to where her hat and vanity bag lay on the seat under the left side window. Although she did not recognize any of the intruders, she formed an accurate estimation of the men's characters and guessed the woman came into a similar category. 'Have you, Freddie?'

'None whatsoever,' the black haired beauty replied, throwing an equally quick and frustrated glance to where her hat and bag lay on the opposite side of the compartment. Then she returned her gaze, which became filled with disdain, to the approaching men and went on, 'May I ask what you mean by bursting into a private car in such an ill-mannered fashion?'

'Listen to that, Gertrude!' Fisher jeered, looking over his shoulder, his accent Mid-West and suggestive of a good education. 'This capitalist's "something-sucking" whore – !'

'You keep your talk clean around womenfolk.' Mrs Turnbull ordered, rising with more alacrity than her quavering old voice suggested she could attain.

'Sit down and shut up, you old fool! Gertrude Fioret ordered, speaking English with a noticeable French accent.

'Don't you dare talk to me like that, you foreign hussy!' Mrs Turnbull yelped, taking a pace forward.

'I said sit – ' Gertrude began, grabbing the body of the umbrella which was being brandished in front of her face with her left hand and putting the right against the old woman's veiled face so as to fend off what appeared to be a contemplated attack.

* * * * *

The Frenchwoman's words came to an abrupt and startled end!

Having first pushed with and then withdrawn her head, Mrs Turnbull was also giving a twisting tug at the umbrella. Feeling the pressure against her right hand, Gertrude Fioret instinctively grabbed hold of and began to bunch up the veil. As she did so, the old woman jerked backwards causing Gertrude's fingers to tighten and she felt the veil coming away.

So was the hat – and the white 'hair' to which it was firmly pinned!

What the removal exposed was not the face of an *old* woman!

Instead, there came into view black hair cropped almost boyishly short and, set in an expression of grim determination, the beautiful features of a girl about the same age as Freddie and Benkers.

So amazed was Gertrude by the remarkable metamorphosis, she gave no thought to the fact that while she still grasped the body of the umbrella, its handle – which ended in a small steel ball – remained in 'Mrs Turnbull's' right hand.

The Frenchwoman was not granted an opportunity to ponder at length upon either phenomenon, or how to act for the best. Rising swiftly, 'Mrs Turnbull's' left arm delivered a backhand slap to the side of her face. It landed with sufficient power to send her spinning uncontrollably to collide with the wall of the car.

Nor did the 'old woman' restrict her attentions to Gertrude. Still displaying the rapidity which had replaced her earlier slow and doddering movements, she advanced farther into the car. So swiftly and unexpectedly was she acting that none of the men had yet begun to respond to the change her intervention was creating to their plans. Before any of them could move, her right foot went to the seat of Basnett's trousers and shoved sharply to propel him forward. Losing his hat and with the revolver flying from his grasp, he landed in a helpless sprawl face down across the table between the two Englishwomen. Nor did his discomfiture end there. A strong hand dug from either side of his head into his back hair, raising and slamming his features against the top of the table. On being released an instant after the far from gentle impact, he toppled backwards to alight upon the portion of his anatomy which had been subjected to the shove.

Letting out startled and profane exclamations, the other two men had begun to turn around without waiting to see what happened to their companion. Nor would they have been greatly concerned if they had seen his fate. They were more interested in discovering what – if any – threat was posed to themselves.

Of the two, Fisher came off worst. Even as he was trying to turn his weapon upon the transformed 'old' woman, he saw the handle of her umbrella being swung horizontally in his direction. For a moment only, he thought he was beyond its reach. The supposition proved to be invalid, but he was unable to do anything to avert his fate.

Sliding forward under the impetus created by its wielder's movements, the steel ball proved to be attached to a short rod of the same metal. This in turn was connected to the end of a powerful coil spring. Having been telescoped into the handle of the umbrella, both emerged to make a substantial increase to the distance at which a blow could be delivered. Driven with the added force supplied by the whip-like action of the spring, the ball caught Fisher at the side of the jaw. There was a crack as the bone snapped and he twirled, almost gracefully, losing his hold on the revolver as he pitched headlong across the car until halted by its wall.

Having completed the attack on the tallest of the men, the 'old' woman reversed the direction in which her most effective weapon had been travelling. Swiftly and efficiently as she did so, she failed to achieve the success attained against her two previous victims.

Unlike Fisher and Gertrude, Jamie Morris was not caught unawares. Forgetting the firearm he was holding, he concluded some form of evasive tactics were called for. Possessing a healthy sense of self-preservation and an appreciation of the danger he was in served to put an added zest to his normally languid motions. Filled with alarm over the danger he was facing, he was able to leap aside and avoid what would otherwise have been an incapacitating blow. However, his misfortunes were not over and he failed to escape unscathed.

After the man who had been propelled on to the table was disposed of, with Benkers' able assistance, Freddie was not content to leave the rest of their salvation to the surprisingly competent 'old' woman. Before leaving England, she had seen games of football played in the style originated at Rugby School. Ever unconventional, a factor which had caused her to have to leave her homeland and live under an assumed name in the United States,[7] she had learned and practised various of the game's moves, acquiring a skill which – seeing how Morris was behaving – she proceded to put to good use.

Sending her chair skidding away as she rose, Freddie left the table and dived towards the young man. Her lunging body crashed against him and, locking her arms around his legs, she brought off as fine a tackle as she had ever managed. Although some Rugbeian exponents of the game might have found minor faults with her technique, she felt no cause to complain over the results. Caught while he was still in the throes of his hasty withdrawal beyond the reach of the 'old' woman's weapon, Morris was swept from his feet. As he fell,

[7] On being asked by the author why his grandmother had been compelled to leave England, Alvin Dustine 'Cap' Fog. q.v., stated that – as was the case with Tommy Okasi – his family considered it inadvisable to make the information public. J.T.E.

his head struck the wall of the car and he lost all further interest in the proceeding for some time to come.

Although the cracked rib she had acquired shortly after her meeting with Dusty Fog was now healed, Benkers felt she would be ill-advised to duplicate the spectacular methods being employed by Freddie and she lacked the means to produce the effect that the 'old' woman had achieved. Nevertheless, her contribution to the affair was not to be discounted. She too had come to her feet and, seeing that Basnett had not been rendered *hors de combat*, made him the object of her attentions.

Ignoring the blood which was gushing from a nose made even less attractive by the impact against the top of the table, the young agitator was reaching towards the revolver he had dropped while falling. Stepping forward, the blonde stamped upon his outstretched hand and pinned it to the floor with her heel. Incensed by the pain-filled profanity which burst from him, she decided to show her disapproval in no uncertain way. Hitching up her skirt as high as was necessary and displaying shapely legs encased in black silk stockings, she pivoted and delivered a kick to his jaw which brought the tirade to an abrupt end. Receiving no provocation from him after he had slumped silent and unmoving to the floor, she tentatively removed her foot from his hand. From the absence of response, she concluded he would not be causing any further trouble in the immediate future.

Glancing around and showing no surprise at the competent way in which her travelling companions had behaved throughout such a desperate situation, 'Mrs Turnbull' swung her gaze to where the Frenchwoman had fallen to the floor. Spitting obscenities in her native tongue, Gertrude was sitting with her back to the wall and trying to open the vanity bag.

'I'm an expert at *savate, Mademoiselle* Fioret,' the 'old' woman announced, speaking French fluently – if with the accent of a New Orleans' Creole – in a far younger voice than she had previously employed. Stepping close enough to be able to put the threat into effect and drawing up the skirt to show lower limbs attired in skin tight black riding breeches and matching Hessian boots, she went on, 'If you don't throw that bag aside and shut up, I'll kick your teeth

153

down your throat and you'll have to mumble the answers to the questions I'm going to ask.'

'I'd listen if I was you,' Freddie advised, showing just as great a facility in the use of Gertrude's native tongue. 'Colonel Boyd could – and *would* – do it if need be.'

'C – *Colonel* Boyd?' the Frenchwoman gasped, staring at the beautiful and grimly determined face which might otherwise have appeared incongruous topping such archaic mourning attire. 'B – But you can't be the one they call the Rebel Spy?'

'All you have to do to find out is keep trying to take out whatever you have in that bag,' Freddie declared, as she and the blonde started to collect the three men's discarded revolvers. 'And you'll soon have the matter settled, although perhaps not to *your* delight and satisfaction.'

*   *   *   *   *

'Belle, I'd like you to meet Benkers, a dear friend of mine from England,' the mayor of Mulrooney, Kansas, introduced. 'Although, if we're going to be formal, I suppose I should say, Colonel Boyd,[8] allow me to present Miss Amelia Penelope Diana Benkinsop.'

Half an hour had elapsed and the three beautiful young women once more had the private car to themselves. However, the formerly uninvited passenger no longer conveyed the impression of being a person advanced in years and in deep mourning. Nor was she continuing to behave in the previously unsociable and uncommunicative fashion.

Accepting that 'Mrs Turnbull' really was the woman who had earned the sobriquet, The Rebel Spy, for her exploits on behalf of the Confederate States during the War of Secession, but who now served just as loyally and efficiently in the United States' Secret Service, Gertrude Fioret had tossed away her vanity bag with the revolver it held undrawn and surrendered. Nor were any of her male associates in a

---

[8] As was the case when she was serving the Confederate States, Belle 'the Rebel Spy' Boyd was granted the rank of colonel on her enrolment in the United States' Secret Service to give her the necessary authority when dealing with military personel. J.T.E.

condition to essay further hostilities, or resistance.

After the Frenchwoman had been questioned by Belle Boyd and – although too frightened by the proposed repercussions to lie – proving unable to supply the desired piece of information, Freddie Woods had summoned the porter and the train's conductor. She had explained that a hold up had been attempted, but was thwarted by the intervention of 'Mrs Turnbull', an operative of the Pinkerton National Detective Agency. Such was the fear inspired by the Rebel Spy's apparently ruthless nature and the willingness of the Englishwomen to support her in the threats she had uttered, that Gertrude had not refuted the story or disclosed Belle's true identity. Help had been procured from among the male passengers, along with the services of a doctor, to remove the prisoners to the caboose. They would be held there, under the watchful eye of the armed brake-man, until being turned over to the authorities on arrival in Kansas City. Being well known and respected by a number of influential people in that city, Freddie had declared she was confident she would be able to prevent any awkward questions being asked about Belle's participation and would be able to ensure their journey was not delayed.

With the compartment to themselves, the Rebel Spy had discarded the 'widows's weeds'. Underneath, she was wearing a man's dark blue, open necked shirt, black riding breeches and Hessian boots which did full justice to her slender – yet anything except flat chested and skinny – figure. She had, however, covered the masculine attire with a dove-grey two-piece travelling costume and green cravat which came, along with an equally realistic brunette wig, from the commodious old carpetbag. Having reassembled the umbrella and stripped off the outer covering to convert it into a more dainty looking parasol, she placed the black material and the rest of her previous disguise in the bag. At the completion of the task, she had joined the other two at the table and Freddie performed the introductions

'I'm pleased to make your acquaintance – at last – *Benkers*,' Belle declared.

'At last?' queried the honey blonde with a smile.

'We've something of a dossier on you,' the Rebel Spy explained. 'And I believe I had the pleasure of meeting one of your uncles not too long ago.'[9]

'One of my *uncles*?' Benkers repeated.

'A corpulent gentleman with the grandiloquent name of Octávious Xavier Gulliemot,' Belle informed.

'The Ox is only a honorary uncle,' Benkers corrected, employing the sobriquet by which the man in question was known to the police of four continents and showing no annoyance at the suggestion that she was related to a notorious international master criminal. 'He's quite nice when you get to know him.'

'I'll take your word for that,' Belle stated, but without any trace of animosity or disbelief. Then she slapped a slender and shapely thigh with her right hand and went on, 'You must be the "Lady Winifred Besgrove-Woodstole" who was with the European crown prince down in Texas.'

'I *was*,' Benkers admitted, smiling wryly. 'Not knowing that the genuine Lady Winifred had been so dashed inconsiderate as to be very good friends with certain people who it was imperative should accept my bogus identity. I say, though, may I state you're all I've heard. That disguise was perfect.'

'I'd no idea it was *you*,' Freddie supplemented. 'And it's not all that long since I had dinner with you and Pat Reeder.'

'Thank you,' the Rebel Spy said quietly, far from displeased at receiving such compliments from two women for whom she had considerable respect.

'But how did you come to be here so providentially?' Freddie asked. 'The last time I saw you, you were going up to Stokeley, Montana, with Calamity Jane and Pat to try to stop that *Metis* chap causing a rebellion in Canada.'

'We did it,' Belle answered, but did not go into details. 'I was passing through Mulrooney on my way to Chicago when I was told there might be an attempt to rob and kill you on the train. So I thought I'd better see what could be done to stop it.'

'Rob and *kill*?' Freddie queried, refraining from asking questions about the Rebel Spy's source of information. 'I

[9] The meeting is described in: *THE QUEST FOR BOWIE'S BLADE.* J.T.E.

know I talked a bunch of dandy dancers[10] out of going along with their, "Workers of the world unite" ideas, but that hardly seems cause enough for even their kind to deliberately set out to murder two women.'

'From what I was told, you weren't their primary target,' Belle explained. 'Although, apparently your disruptive efforts gave the prospect of killing you as well as "Lady Winifred" an added attraction.'

'You mean they were after *me*?' Benkers asked, showing puzzlement. 'Or, at least, who they thought me to be?'

'So I was informed,' Belle confirmed.

'But I've never seen any of them before today,' the honey blonde protested.

'Apparently you helped cause Mademoiselle Fioret's sister to be killed,' the Rebel Spy countered.

'But she *can't* be related to the *Comtesse de* Petain!' Benkers objected, referring to one of the conspirators who had sought to cause the assassination of the visiting Crown Prince and who Benkers had shot in self defence.

'No,' Belle agreed. 'But her sister was the *Comtesse's* maid. It appears she blames you as much as Dusty Fog for her sister being killed and, probably, considered your collection of jewellery made you a more profitable as well as safer subject for revenge.'

'But what did you think she might have to do with that "Butcher" chap you were asking about?' Freddie wanted to know, after having heard a brief resumé of the events to which her companions had been referring.[11]

'Not much, really,' Belle sighed. 'It was just a chance she had. He's an illicit salesman of arms, ammunition and explosives. In fact, he's the reason I'm going to Chicago. He operates from there and I'm hoping to find him.'

'To stop his activities?' Freddie said, the words being more of a statement than a question.

'To stop *him*!' Belle confirmed, her tones showing deadly earnest.

'How much do you know about him?' Benkers asked.

[10] 'Dandy dancer': a railroad section construction worker. J.T.E.

[11] The events are recorded in: *BEGUINAGE* and *BEGUINAGE IS DEAD!* J.T.E.

'Very little, I'll admit,' the Rebel Spy replied. 'I'm sure he lives in Chicago and, as he's called *"die Fliescher"*, he is probably German.

'Then how do you propose to find him?' the honey blonde inquired, being aware that *"die Fliescher"* meant, "the Butcher" in German.

'Ask around and hope I'll get on his trail,' Belle answered.

'Perhaps *I* can help,' Benkers offered, out of gratitude for having been saved from robbery and murder. 'At least, I'll try.'

'Thank you, Benkers!' Belle said sincerely, being aware of just how useful help from the beautiful Englishwoman might be.

According to the dossier at the headquarters of the United States' Secret Service, although this was her first visit to the New World, Amelia Penelope Diana 'Benkers' Benkinsop was just as prominent and successful in international criminal circles as Octavius Xavier 'the Ox' Gulliemot. Such a person would possess contacts with far greater and more diverse sources of information than were available to the Rebel Spy, or the United States' Secret Service.

*   *   *   *   *

'Howdy there!' Belle Boyd greeted the tall, buxom blonde. a Germanically good looking maid who answered the door in response to her pull on its bell. 'I've come to see *"die Fliescher"*.'

'Who?' the servant asked, the one word being sufficient to establish her ethnic origin.

'*Die Fliescher*, Dutchy,' the Rebel Spy repeated, with an accent far different from her usual cultured Southern drawl. 'Go tell him it's Calamity Jane and I've been driving for good ole Jebediah Lincoln.'

Only three days had elapsed since Belle's arrival in Chicago. Using sources the nature of which Belle had not questioned, Benkers had obtained the name and address of the man she was seeking. Although the information she required was delivered on the first evening, along with details of an unusual form of entertainment to which Ernst *'die Fliescher'* Kramer was partial, she had spent the intervening time making preparations for the visit to his home.

Once again, the Rebel Spy was demonstrating her ability at disguising herself and giving a convincing portrayal of the character she was pretending to be. She was helped in this instance by being well acquainted with the person she was impersonating. Furthermore, despite being more slender in build, she was confident that she could pass herself off as the Martha 'Calamity Jane' Canary whose exploits were frequently reported in the *Police Gazette* and similar magazines commanding a large sale throughout the East.

Belle had dyed her hair a fiery red and wore thin leather gloves to conceal that her hands were less work-roughened than might be expected from one employed as the driver of a six-horse freight wagon. She was sufficiently tanned to preclude the need for make-up to aid her pose of being a person who spent most of her life out of doors. A search of the city's shops had procured the requisite attire, although the low crowned, wide brimmed black hat she was jauntily wearing should have been a battered U.S. Cavalry kepi to obtain absolute authenticity. She had on a tight fitting, open-necked tartan shirt, a fringed buckskin jacket and matching trousers, with Indian moccasins for footwear. As the laws of Chicago prohibited carrying firearms in such a fashion, she had not donned a gunbelt and was unsuccessful in acquiring a bull whip such as Calamity Jane almost always wore attached to the waist belt. She did, however, have an ivory handled Dance Bros. copy of the Colt 1851 Navy revolver tucked into the left side of her trousers' waist band, its butt turned forward to be readily available to either hand.

In addition to supplying the information, Benkers had insisted upon helping Belle. Wearing masculine attire and made up to look like a moustached young man, she had driven the Rebel Spy in a fringe-top Surrey[12] to the high rent north-eastern district of the city and was waiting in it outside the grounds of Kramer's large mansion.

[12] 'Fringe-top Surrey': a light, four-wheel, four-seat passenger vehicle having a decorative hood and considered more stylish and elegant than a buggy. J.T.E.

'I don't understand!' the maid stated, starting to close the door.

'Who is it, Gretchen?' barked a harsh masculine voice in German.

Taking advantage of the maid looking around, Belle pushed by and gained access to the mansion. She found herself in a large entrance hall and was given her first glimpse of the man she had come to find.

Close to six foot in height, heavily built, although much of his bulk was fat, Kramer was in his late fifties. He had on stylish and expensive city clothes, but they neither flattered his appearance nor distracted from his all too obvious corpulence. Being cropped very close, his greying hair emphasized the bullet shape of his head. He had florid, porcine features and a well fed air which contributed to his sobriquet, 'the Butcher', although he also pretended his source of income was attributable to participation in that business.

'Howdy, "Mr Butcher",' Belle said, thrusting her hat into the hands of the clearly indignant maid. 'Good ole Jebediah Lincoln said I should drop by and visit a spell any time I was in the Windy City. So here I be to do it.'

'He *did*, did he?' Kramer barked, in guttural and Germanic-accented English, the man in question being his chief agent in the Montana region and, as such, knew his address. However, he was aware of something else and it lead him to continue in his native tongue, 'Shut the door, Gretchen.'

'*Ja wohl, Herr* Kramer!' the maid answered.

'Why sure,' Belle agreed. She spoke sufficient German to understand the order and she waited for it to be carried out. 'Only, seeing's how poor ole Jebediah gotten his-self sort of killed by those jaspers he left behind afore he went on his last trip, I reckon's how you'd maybe be pleased to see me.'

'*Ach*, so!' Kramer grunted, pronouncing the second word, '*zoe!*'. '*And* who are you?'

'Calamity Jane,' Belle lied.

'*Calamity Jane?*' Kramer repeated and nodded his head.

'What the – ?' Belle yelled, as two hands gripped and jerked the buckskin jacket over her shoulder to pin her arms.

'So you are the famous Calamity Jane, are you?' Kramer challenged, stepping forward to pluck the revolver from the

160

girl's waistband and withdrawing a hurried couple of paces as she tried to kick at him.

'You just bet your god-dammned life I am!' Belle continued to prevaricate heatedly. 'Now what the hell's the son-of-a-bitching idea?'

'I have heard you are a *very* tough young lady,' the Butcher replied, allowing the weapon to dangle uncocked at his side as he moved farther away. 'But, although I am *not* from Missouri, I always need to be shown – Gretchen!'

Hearing her name and knowing what was expected of her, the maid released her hold on the jacket in a shoving motion which propelled Belle into the centre of the hall. Having done so, she removed her white cap and tossed it on to the black hat she had dropped when carrying out her employer's unspoken instructions. Kicking off her shoes, she reached behind her back.

'God damn it!' Belle screeched at the fat man as, remembering the information she had received from Benkers, she wriggled from and discarded the jacket. 'What the hell's your son-of-a-bitching game?'

'Gretchen is tough also,' Kramer replied, running the tip of his tongue across his thick lips in a gesture suggestive of licentious anticipation. 'So we will see which of you is the tougher, *nein*?'

'*Gretchen?*' Belle spat out, looking over her shoulder at the maid. 'If you mean *her*, it'll be more son-of-a-bitching "stretchen" than Gretchen time I'm through with her.'

'That we will see!' the Butcher claimed and continued in German, 'Thrash her good, little one!'

Eyeing the slender girl with sadistically malicious pleasure, having understood the derogatory comment, the maid tugged at the waist band of her skirt. It opened and, accompanied by the frilly white apron which completed her uniform, the garment slid down to reveal a pair of brief white underpants from which suspender straps made scarlet stripes along the milky white of her bulky – if shapely – thighs until joining black silk stockings. Stepping clear of the skirt and apron, she clenched her fists after the fashion of a male pugilist and advanced.

'She's going to get hurt!' Belle warned over her shoulder,

keeping her gaze on the taller, heavier woman.

'That is what she will be paid for,' the Butcher replied.

Despite having heard of Kramer's penchant for watching women fighting,[13] the Rebel Spy had not anticipated that she would be compelled to participate in his erotic pleasures. Neither was she caught entirely unawares, due to Benkers' information, when he decided to force her to defend herself. What was more, some of her own clothes were designed to be discarded in a similarly rapid fashion. Yet, studying the maid's posture, she sensed she was up against a very competent opponent.

For her part, Gretchen felt no qualms whatsoever. Since coming into Kramer's employment, she had been required to tackle other women. Every one had been larger and heavier than the slender 'red-head' and she did not doubt that her knowledge of pugilism, backed by her far from inconsiderable strength, would offer her a similar advantage to those earlier occasions.

Coming into range of the apparently unprepared Belle, the maid swung a looping round-house left punch. Ducking at the last moment and allowing it to pass over her head, the Rebel Spy shot her clenched right fist on to the point at which the black blouse and white panties joined. It was a good blow and, despite the rubbery hardness of the muscles beneath the garments, elicited a sharp intake of breath from its recipient.

But nothing more!

Instead of being winded, or even compelled to step away, Gretchen delivered a back-hand swing with her right arm. Caught at the side of the face, Belle was knocked staggering for a few steps. While she managed to remain on her feet, she was given no chance to recover. Moving in swiftly, the maid grabbed a double handful of her short 'red' hair and used it to precipitate her across the room. Sent in a wild

[13] As is recorded in: *Chapter Nine*, '*This Is Purely A Social Visit*', '*CAP*' *FOG*, *TEXAS RANGER, MEET MR J. G. REEDER*, members of the Pinhole Club in Leicester Place, London, during the mid-1920's had a similar predilection for watching women fighting. So, more recently in Gusher City, Rockabye County, Texas, had Mr and Mrs Oscar Burgenhof, as is told in: *BAD HOMBRE*. J.T.E.

twirling reel, she could not prevent herself from colliding against the wall. Although much of her momentum had gone, she was still dumped in a sitting position with her back to it. Nor were her troubles over.

Walking forward, aware of the kind of things her employer enjoyed watching at such times, Gretchen bent and thrust both hands into the open neck of Belle's shirt, causing its buttons to burst from their fastenings and the material to rip to the waist. Sliding beneath the bodice, the fingers and thumbs dug into the mounds of the two firm breasts. Crushing and grinding at them, as if kneading dough for bread, she lifted her victim erect. While doing so and ramming the slender girl backwards against the wall, she could not resist looking at Kramer for evidence of his approbation.

The inattention proved to be an error of judgement!

Tormented from the punishment being inflicted upon her bosom, Belle did not allow it to render her incapable of resistance. The moment Gretchen looked away, she thrust up her right knee. Passing between the spread apart legs, it rammed into a portion of the feminine anatomy very susceptible to such an attack. Although it was not delivered at full strength, because of the pain the Rebel Spy was suffering, she was brought immediate relief.

Letting out a strangled squawk, Gretchen staggered towards the centre of the hall. On emerging from the bodice, her hands went to clutch at the stricken area. For all that, when Belle approached to continue the attack, she threw a punch. Although missing its intended mark and only catching the shoulder, it halted the slender girl. An instant later, however, a set of hard knuckles dug into her left breast. As the thin black blouse was all that covered her bosom, there was nothing to protect it and she let out a little yelp of protest. A punch to the face, which started her nose bleeding, one just as hard to the other breast and a third to the jaw, delivered in rapid succession, drove her into an involuntary retreat of which she felt sure her employer would not approve. So, shaking her head, she lunged forward. Failing to achieve her desire by pinning her opponent's arms down, she encircled the slim waist with her own and began to squeeze.

163

Croaking in agony, Belle found herself being compressed against the maid's hard body and lifted from her feet. As she was borne backwards across the hall, she knew she must free herself quickly. With that in mind, she clenched her hands and dug the knuckles of each forefinger into the mastoid region behind Gretchen's ears. Such was the agony this inflicted, the woman could not stand it. Giving a screeched out obscenity in German, she opened her arms and used her bosom to thrust the Rebel Spy away.

Alighting on her feet and in control of her movements, despite her ribs feeling as if she had just emerged from the coils of a boa constrictor, Belle sprang aside to avoid the maid's rush. Making a fast pivot as the blonde blundered by, the girl performed a bounding *savate* kick which drove both moccasin-covered feet into her shoulders. Hurtled forward, she crashed face and bosom foremost into the wall and bounced, dazed and helpless from it. Catching her right wrist in both hands, Belle swung her around and propelled her to land and roll until supine a short distance from her employer. Darting over, the girl sank until crouching astride her stomach. Taking her hair and raising her head, the girl banged it hard on the floor.

Delivering a second bang with the head and feeling the big woman's already feeble struggles end, the Rebel Spy looked up. Kramer was standing a few feet away. Perspiration soaked his face as he stared with rapt attention. His left hand was thrust into the pocket of his trousers and he had allowed the Dance Bros. revolver to dangle unheeded at his side.

Thrusting herself from the recumbent body of the maid, Belle butted the Butcher in the stomach with her lowered head. As she did so, hearing him belch out his breath in a croaking profanity, she caught hold of the weapon with her left hand. Plucking it from his grasp as he stumbled backwards and fell on to his rump, gasping to replenish his depleted lungs, she transferred it so the butt was in her right fist.

'All right, you son-of-a-bitch!' The Rebel Spy hissed, cocking the weapon and lining it at the startled face of the fat man, her tone closer to normal than that of Calamity Jane.

'You've had your god-damned pleasure. Now listen to *mine!*'

*　　*　　*　　*　　*

Kicking open the door of the only room in the derelict building from which there was a light showing, Ernest Kramer entered with a short-barrelled Colt Storekeeper Model Peacemaker revolver in his right hand. Following on his heels, armed in the same way, were two tall, husky-looking, blond haired and Germanic young men. One of them had brought him to the building in an almost deserted portion of the slum area on the fringes of the Streeterville district and, despite his misgivings, he found his journey had not been a wild-goose chase.

'So!' the Butcher barked, pointing the revolver towards where Belle Boyd and Amelia Benkinsop were seated on the two chairs at the rickety table which comprised the remainder of the room's far from luxurious appointments. In fact, apart from a fair-sized leather trunk beneath the table, they were its sole furniture. '*That* is the way you are!'

There was a reason, if not justification for the cryptic utterance.

Apart from having changed her torn shirt for one which was undamaged, the Rebel Spy was dressed as she had been during the visit to Kramer's mansion. While Benkers had removed the false moustache she had worn and the hat with which she concealed her golden blonde tresses, she still had on the rest of the masculine attire.

'I like *fellers's* well,' Belle replied, in her 'Calamity Jane' voice, showing no more concern than her companion at the three armed men's eruption into their presence. 'We wondered how long it'd take you to get here, didn't we, Benkers?'

'Yes,' confirmed the blonde, keeping her reply to a minimum to lessen the chance of her English accent being noticed.

Having kept the Butcher covered with her revolver, effectively preventing his two men from intervening when they had appeared in the entrance hall from the rear of the mansion, the Rebel Spy had explained the supposed reason for her visit. She had been gambling upon his not knowing the full facts, even if he had heard of Jebediah Lincoln's death at the hands of three former employees, regarding the agent's last and abortive assignment.

The gamble had paid off.

While Kramer had heard of Lincoln's demise, he did not question the version of the events prior to it which Belle had given. The arms which should have been delivered to equip the proposed *Metis* and Indian uprising in Canada had been returned to his depot in Stokeley. However, the precautions which were always practised to prevent treachery on the part of the purchasers – removing a small and vital piece of each weapon's mechanism and hiding them – had been carried out by Lincoln on the night before the rendezvous was to have been reached. Circumstances had prevented him from recovering them, but Belle had claimed they were in her possession. Her story of having followed Lincoln when he buried the parts, then returned to collect them after he had deserted her, went unchallenged. She had prevented it from being questioned by offering to sell them, along with some incriminating documents obtained from Lincoln, to their rightful owner. Then, telling the Butcher she would inform him later when, where and how much money he was to bring in exchange for the property, she had made the men lie on the floor face down and took her departure without impediment.

As the girls had anticipated, on rejoining Benkers and driving away from the mansion, they had soon been followed by one of Kramer's young men. Showing no indication of knowing he was behind them, they had driven across town and returned the Surrey to the livery barn in the Streeterville district from which it had been hired. Still allowing him to keep them under observation, they had walked to the small and derelict house in a street of equally dilapidated and practically deserted properties in a slum area which was being cleared to make way for more habitable dwellings. He had kept watch on the house until nightfall, then left – as they had assumed correctly – to bring his employer to call upon them.

'You knew we would come?' Kramer barked, realizing what was implied to the response his comment had elicited.

'Why sure,' Belle declared, making no attempt to touch the Dance Bros. revolver which lay on the table between her and Benkers. 'I don't know how that big feller stacks when it comes to dogging city folk, but he wouldn't last five minutes up again' a ten-year-old button raised west of the Big Muddy. We let him trail us here, figuring he'd fetch you.'

'Why?' the Butcher asked, frowning.

'To show you I wasn't bluffing about what I'd got,' the Rebel Spy explained, moving the trunk forward with her foot. 'It's all in here.'

'Everything?' Kramer inquired.

'Could be everything,' Belle said, in a cagey fashion. 'Or, then again, I might not've left anything in it.'

'Open the trunk, Fritz!' Kramer snapped, speaking German.

'Happen you're telling him what I reckon,' Belle remarked, as the man who had followed them stepped forward. 'It's locked.'

'You have the key?' the Butcher wanted to know, reverting to English.

'Right here in my pocket,' Belle agreed.

'Give it!' Fritz commanded, making a threatening gesture with his Colt and holding forward his left hand. 'Carefully!'

'Whatever you say,' the Rebel Spy assented, reaching into her jacket's right side pocket and extracting a sturdy brass key with her thumb and forefinger. 'Just so long's your boss don't mind you seeing what's inside.'

'What do you mean?' Kramer demanded, as Fritz glanced at him.

'Could be there're things in the trunk you'd's soon nobody else saw,' Belle replied.

'I trust my men!' the Butcher asserted.

'You know 'em better'n me,' Belle countered, having detected a slight note of uncertainty in Kramer's voice and making a motion as if eager to allow the trunk to be opened by the younger man.

'No!' the Butcher barked, again in his native tongue. 'Give me the key, then take them both outside and wait for me.'

167

'*Ja wohl!*' Fritz assented, taking the key from Belle. Having handed it to his employer, he picked up her revolver and said in English, 'Go outside, both of you.'

'Hold on just a god-damned minute!' the Rebel Spy protested. 'Are you going to buy back that stuff?'

'Buy back what is mine?' Kramer snorted. 'I am *taking* it back!'

'By grab!' Belle hissed in what appeared to be fury. 'If that's the game, you just open that trunk and you're going to wish you hadn't.'

'I will take my chances on that!' the Butcher declared. 'Take them outside.'

'What do we do with them, *Herr* Kramer?' the second young man asked.

'Keep them quiet until I come,' the Butcher replied. 'Then we take them with us and see if Miss Calamity Jane can defeat Gretchen, a second time, or some other of the girls.'

Waiting until his men had escorted the girls from the house, Kramer went to the trunk. Bending down and thinking he had never seen such a large, sturdy lock on any other piece of luggage, he inserted and turned the key.

*   *   *   *   *

The sudden crack of an explosion, followed by a 'whoosing' roar and rapidly growing glow of flames came as the two young Germans were hustling Belle Boyd and Amelia Benkinsop towards the fringe-top Surrey in which they had travelled from Ernst Kramer's mansion. The sound was followed by a brief, but horrifying masculine scream of mortal agony.

'Now!' the Rebel Spy hissed, as the Germans let out startled exclamations in their own language. She turned to snatch the Dance Bros. revolver from Fritz's unresisting grasp and, swinging the base of its butt against the side of his jaw, tumbled him unconscious to the ground.

Showing commendable presence of mind, considering she was taken just as completely unawares as their escort, Benkers reacted almost as quickly as her companion. Jerking her arm free from the second German's grasp, she spun and kneed him in the groin with sufficient force to drop him in a moaning, writhing heap at her feet.

'Come on!' Belle ordered, glancing at the glare which told the fire inside the room was spreading at a great rate. Accompanied by the Englishwoman, she ran to the Surrey. Jerking free the weighted hitching rope, she climbed aboard and, as soon as Benkers joined her, set the already restless horse into motion. 'Let's get away from here.'

'What was in the trunk?' the honey blonde inquired, after the vehicle had covered about a hundred yards from the now freely blazing house.

'A powder charge to set off a bottle of Berney's "Liquid Fire",[14] which had pieces of phosphorus in it to ensure it burned once air got at it,' the Rebel Spy replied. 'The lid of the trunk opened from what appeared to be the back. Its lock was a fake, fitted with percussion caps which were detonated and set off the powder charge when the key was turned. The Yankees nearly killed me with something similar during the War,[15] so I took a chance we still had some around and, sure enough, one was sent along when I telegraphed for it.'

'Did your people know what you wanted it for?' Benkers inquired.

'My superior knew who I was after,' Belle answered. 'And it was he who authorized the issue. I don't regret what I've done in the slightest, Benkers. The Butcher has made a fortune peddling death for years.'

'I know,' Amelia Benkinsop said quietly. 'He certainly deserved his fiery end.'

[14] A composition of benzole, crude petroleum, coal tar, turpentine, residium and coal oil used in the 'Shell, Liquid Fire' projectile patented by Alfred Berney of Jersey City, New Jersey, on November the 11th, 1862 (Patent No. 36,834). J.T.E.
[15] Told in: THE REBEL SPY. J.T.E.

PART SIX

Martha 'Calamity Jane' Canary

In

MRS WILD BILL

'Hey, fellers, will you just look who's coming along here so high-faluting and head-in-the-air proud?' requested a mocking voice with a well educated New England accent. 'It's Mrs Wild Bill Hickok in person!'

The comment was uttered by one of six young men who were grouped in an almost proprietary fashion outside Battling Binnie's Ring Saloon in Cheyenne. Although none showed any sign of caring, they were forming an obstruction to those people who were taking the air, either for business or pleasure, on that late July afternoon in 1876.

Fairly tall, slim, his good looks marred by an arrogant expression, reddy-brown Dundreary side-whiskers and a thin moustache which emphasized rather than improved a loose-lipped mouth suggestive of a dissipated nature, the speaker was in his early twenties and obviously in superior financial straits to his companions. He wore a well cut, short, double-breasted black reefer jacket, all three buttons being left unfastened, a white silk shirt with an attached collar and embellished by a wide-knotted dark green tie, yellowish-brown Nankeen trousers and Hersome gaiter boots, the ensemble being completed by a brown billycock hat seated on the back of his head of longish hair. However, a black Western style gunbelt slanted downwards around his waist. In its holster, the tip of which was fastened to his right thigh, was an ivory-handled Colt Civilian Model Peacemaker.[1]

To eyes which could read the signs, the young man's five companions were typical of the kind of loafers to be found in any fair-sized town west of the Mississippi River. Of varying heights and builds, they were all about the same age as the speaker. Although their attire might have implied they were cowhands to less initiated eyes, none had had more than as brief an association as possible with the frequently gruelling work entailed by participation in the cattle business. One thing they all had in common, regardless of differences in their appearances, was that each wore a gunbelt with a holstered revolver.

Under different circumstances, the beautiful features of the woman at whom the sneering words were directed would have been merry and pleasant, but they took on a frown of annoyance when she heard what was said. Perhaps five foot six in height and in her mid-thirties, she had a buxom, yet firm-fleshed figure with attractive contours and she walked gracefully, in a manner that suggested she possessed excellent physical health. A wide-brimmed white bonnet, to which was attached a cape-like *bavolet* offering shade for the neck, showed little of her brunette hair and framed her face. She had on a dark blue day-dress. The *basquin* bodice, buttoned to the waist, had its V-neckline and turned-down collar edged by a narrow lace frill. Its bell-shaped sleeves showed the sleeves of a white chemisette which were puffed and fastened at the wrists. Enhanced by multiple flouncing, the skirt was full to the ground and, except for brief glimpses of the toes, concealed her black high-buttoned shoes. Tight-fitting, short day gloves covered her hands, the left holding a reticule which matched her dress.

'One thing's *very* obvious,' Agnes Hickok said scathingly, coming to a halt as the young men showed no sign of moving. 'You all *know* my husband *isn't* in town.'

'It wouldn't make no never mind to *us* good old boys if he was!' declared David Ennals, the tallest of the Westerners.

[1] For the benefit of new readers: information regarding the different varieties of the Colt Model P revolver, introduced in 1873 and commonly known as the 'Peacemaker' can be found in various volumes of the *FLOATING OUTFIT* and *WACO* series. J.T.E.

'He don't spook us none, does he, Albie?'

'He didn't while he was here,' Albert Booth stated, negligently brushing at the lapel of his reefer jacket and ignoring the fact that he and his companions had steered well clear of James Butler 'Wild Bill' Hickok since the day the famous gun-fighter had taken residence in Cheyenne. 'And, from what I saw of him, "Tired Old Bill" would have been a better name.'

'You-all want for me to swat a couple of 'em, seeing's you's a lady and can't, Miz Agnes?' inquired the large black woman who had been walking and talking with Mrs Hickok until the interruption. She sounded hopeful. She had a spotted bandana knotted around her head and the arms which emerged from the rolled-up sleeves of her gingham dress were well muscled. There was an angry expression on her broad, normally jovial face as she went on, ' 'Cause that's all they's worth, the shiftless good-for-nothings.'

'Watch your mouth, you uppity nigger!' ordered Royston Hattersley, his accent that of one who had been raised in Kansas. 'We don't take that kind of lip from your kind.'

'I'm whiter'n *you*, seeing's I wash more regular,' commented a feminine voice from the opposite side of the quintet to the two women. 'And I don't reckon any one of you're worth somebody pissing in your face was your mouth on fire.'

Incensed by the disrespectful statement from a member of the 'weaker' sex, the five young men turned to find out who was addressing them in such a fashion. They had no trouble in identifying the speaker. Even if the people closest to her had not started to back away hurriedly, she would have stood out in that – or any other – crowd.

A battered and faded blue U.S. Cavalry kepi tilted jauntily on a mop of shortish, curly red hair. It topped a freckled, tanned, pretty face with sparkling – or, at that moment, disdainfully flashing – blue eyes, a slightly snub nose and a full-lipped mouth which was set in unsmiling lines despite the grin quirks at the corners. Like her headdress, all her attire was masculine; but what it clothed definitely belonged to a person of feminine gender. A fringed buckskin shirt clung like a second skin, the swell of an imposing bosom forced the open neck apart to a level that let it be seen she did not consider undergarments a necessity, and the sleeves were turned up to above the elbows of a pair of strong arms. Trimming down without needing artificial aids, her waist widened to curvaceous buttocks and sturdy, shapely legs emphasized rather than concealed by buckskin trousers which – like the shirt – gave the impression of having been bought a size too small and further shrunk in washing. Her raiment was completed by a pair of Pawnee moccasins and a brown gunbelt slanting down from her left hip to where an ivory-handled Colt 1851 Navy revolver rode butt forward in a low cavalry-twist holster held by a pigging thong to her right thigh. On the left side of her waist belt, its handle tucked through a broad leather hoop, hung a coiled and long-lashed bull whip which looked far more functional than decorative.

'What the hell is it?' asked Mike Leigh; a thickset and ugly young man whose voice implied an upbringing in Nebraska.

'I'll damned sure find out!' promised gangling Chris Hitchens, being nearest to the contemptuously voiced speaker and, followed by Leigh, he started to slouch forward in a manner redolent of menace.

Although the young man attained his intention, it was not in the way he envisaged or desired!

Bringing up her left arm, the girl deflected the blow Hitchens threw at her. Then, exhibiting an equal dexterity and the precision of a male pugilist, she whipped over her clenched right fist to connect with the side of his jaw. It was propelled with sufficient power to send him in a sprawling rush, compelling Leigh to jump aside hurriedly, until he collapsed on the sidewalk at his other companions' feet.

Despite having avoided being struck by Hitchens, Leigh failed to achieve any more satisfactory a result from his point of view. He threw himself forward with outstretched hands, but they closed on nothing more substantial than the space occupied until a moment before by his intended victim. Having stepped clear without allowing him to grab her, she turned to deliver a kick to the seat of his pants as he blundered by. Sent staggering onwards, he contrived to prevent himself from falling by catching hold of and clinging to the saloon's hitching rail.

'Get her!' Booth yelled, conscious of how much the liberties he and his companions were allowed to take around the town depended, in part at least, upon their reputation for being tough.

Being equally cognizant of the point, Hattersley was already rushing forward. Like his predecessors, however, he found the girl was exceptionally well able to protect herself against such reckless tactics. She came to meet him, in an act he had not contemplated, catching his left wrist in both hands to tug at it so hard he momentarily thought the limb would be wrenched from its socket. The apprehension was only briefly retained, then he had other problems to displace it.

Swivelling around, without relinquishing her grasp, the redhead caused Hattersley to make a hurried and involuntary turn in a half circle. On being released unexpectedly, he went in an arm-flailing and uncontrollable rush in the direction from which he had come. Showing the kind of loyalty he was aware he could expect, the remaining three of his companions sprang aside and allowed him to reel onwards unchecked. He found his progress halted by another means, but it was not the one he would have selected. Caught by the right shoulder with a massive black hand, he received a shake of such violence that it rattled his teeth together. Then he was flung, apparently effortlessly, towards the knot of people who were watching. Although he crashed into the wall of the saloon with some force, he had sufficient control over his faculties to splutter a furious obscenity and grab at the revolver in his holster. Seeing that Mrs Hickok's maid had not turned to keep him under observation, he was confident he could avenge the treatment he had received from her and the redhead.

Having disposed of her third attacker with the same efficiency that had saved her from the other two, the girl clearly did not assume there would be no more attempts forthcoming. Using her turning momentum after releasing Hattersley's arm, she darted across the sidewalk. Slapping her left hand on to the hitching rail, she vaulted over it and, on alighting, backed into the centre of the street. It was obvious, however, that she did not contemplate the flight which might have struck some people as being an advisable precaution. Instead,

174

she turned to face the sidewalk and, with arms akimbo, stood on spread apart feet in a posture of challenge.

'Come on, damn it!' Booth ordered Ennals and Ben Murray, the heavy-set and unprepossessing sixth member of his party, taking the lead by jumping to the street through the opening left between the two sections of the saloon's hitching rails which gave access to the front entrance.

* * * * *

Snarling in fury, Mike Leigh began to thrust himself away from the portion of the hitching rail against which he had stumbled. His intention of rejoining and accompanying his three companions in tackling the girl came to nothing. Taking his first step, he felt something hook around his rear ankle and tug it upwards. Thrown off balance, he went sprawling to the sidewalk.

'Land-sakes a-mercy!' gasped the author of the young man's misfortune, in an almost plaintive feminine Southron drawl indicative of a good upbringing. 'Did *I* do *that*, for *shame*?'

While asking the rhetorical question, the speaker deftly liberated the crook of the parasol with which she had tripped Leigh. Equalling the red head in height and a few years older, she presented a less attractive sight. In fact, she had a mousy demeanour which matched her tone. Stringy brunette hair, taken into an unflattering bun and upon which an unadorned dark blue 'jockey' hat sat with almost military squareness, did nothing to improve pallid features which a pair of horn-rimmed spectacles and a somewhat large nose already placed at a disadvantage. Any improvements her figure might have offered were effectively concealed by a shapeless dark blue two-piece travelling custume. A plain black reticule that was bulky rather than dainty dangled from her left hand, which was gloved and so her marital status was hidden.

Rolling over, spitting out more obscenities, Leigh began to rise. His intentions of prior to the fall were forgotten or, at least, shelved until after he had done something to repay the indignity he had just suffered.

175

At the other side of the gap in the hitching rails, Royston Hattersley was also being thwarted in his desire to take revenge. Even as his fingers were closing on the butt of the revolver, he felt his wrist caught in a grasp as powerful as the one inflicted by the big black woman upon his shoulder and a solemn sounding voice with the accent of a Texan came to his ears.

'Like the Good Book says, brother; dispute not in violence, else violence is plumb likely to come right back and copper your bet!'

Possessing little more knowledge of the Bible except that it existed, Hattersley did not know whether the quotation was to be found in its pages. Nor was he particularly interested at that moment. Instead, he swung his furious gaze around and prepared to take punitive action against the man who had uttered it. What he saw lead him to assume, despite the strength with which his arm was being held, he would have little difficulty in doing so.

Of medium height and in his early thirties, the deliverer of the quotation had a heavily moustached, ruggedly good looking face that seemed as solemn as his voice had suggested. Apart from the black Texas-style J.B. Stetson hat tilted back to show rusty red hair and a pair of black, sharp toed, high heeled cowhand boots, his attire – a black three-piece suit, white shirt with an attached collar and sober dark blue necktie – was such as a member of one of the stricter minor religious sects frequently wore. However, if he was ordained in such a sect, he clearly believed in the church militant. At his right side, riding slightly higher than was usual on a two and a half inches wide and stiff belt, was a Rogers & Spencer Army Model revolver with bell shaped black walnut grips in an open fronted, spring retention holster of unconventional design.

Filled with anger at being accosted in such a manner, Hattersley's only thoughts regarding the Rogers & Spencer was that the way in which it was carried appeared poorly positioned for rapid withdrawal. Nor did he let the possibility that he might be in contention with a member of the cloth influence his actions. Snatching free his wrist, he swung around and lashed a punch with the solemn face as its target.

Watching Booth leading the trio from the sidewalk, the red-head proved she was far from as imprudent as her behaviour implied. Going across, her right hand closed on and drew free the handle of the bull whip. Swinging her arm around, she caused the long lash to uncoil and, reversing the limb's direction, sent it outwards as neatly as a master fly fisherman casting a double tapered line to a waiting trout.

Except that the effect was less pacific!

Guided by either luck or considerable skill, the whip's lash wrapped around Booth's ankles while he was in mid-leap and snapped them together. What little equilibrium he had left as he alighted was ruined by the girl jerking sharply on the handle and causing him to topple backwards. Proving that skill rather than chance had produced the effect, she freed and brought back the lash ready for further use as he lost his balance.

In one respect, Booth might have counted himself fortunate as he tumbled into the hands of his companions. Catching him by the arms, they saved him from what might have been a dangerous fall. Having done so, they hoisted him erect and pushed him towards their intended victim. Then, spreading out to offer divergent targets intended to confuse the girl, they followed him.

Halfway to his feet, Leigh became aware that two menacing figures were moving past the be-spectacled woman. Although they wore the attire of working cowhands, they had moccasins on their feet. Each was tall, lean, yet powerful looking, with black hair and a deeply tanned aquiline face indicative of a proportion of Indian blood. They were each armed with a revolver in a fast draw holster and a sheathed knife of impressive size.

Catching the young man by his arms, the pair hoisted him erect with no more observable difficulty than if he had been a new born baby. Before he could decide upon what action he might take, they flung him in a whirling rush along the sidewalk. By doing so, they added to the further misfortunes about to befall Chris Hitchens as he was getting up from where the red-head's blow had knocked him.

Showing an aptitude equal to that exhibited by the buckskin clad girl earlier, the solemn-featured man blocked his assailant's attempt to strike him and retaliated just as effectively. Rising with considerable power, a set of hard knuckles took Hattersley under the jaw. Knocked backwards, he passed without drawing any conclusions from Agnes Hickok's actions, between her and her maid. The manner in which he had been struck sent him in an uncontrollable spin, offering the advantage of allowing him to see where he was going. In spite of the information this supplied, he found he could do nothing to avert what he knew was forthcoming.

Converging rapidly upon Hitchens, with Leigh approaching if anything more precipitously from the other side, Hattersley tried in vain to escape the inevitable. They came together with considerable force and a precision which might have been created by weeks of rehearsal. Letting out mutually profane and alarmed howls, they collided and went down in a heap of tangled, flailing limbs. Grinning broadly, the maid strode forward and flopped her far from light weight down to sit on top of the pile they had made.

Advancing across the street in a rough arrowhead formation, the remnants of the hard-cases were putting the red-head on the horns of a dilemma. For all her confidence in being able to handle the whip skilfully, she realized its limitations as a means of defence under the present circumstances. No matter at which of the trio she struck, the other two would be able to close to a proximity at which the lash would be useless. The matter was taken out of her hands, however, as was the need to select the next man to receive her attentions.

Showing a justifiable reluctance to receive a blow from the whip, Ennals sought to prevent it by reaching for his holstered revolver. It was an act, if he had given the matter any thought, calculated to bring about what he was trying to avoid. In addition to drawing the red head's attention to him, it settled his hope that the way she had toppled Booth was a fluke. Sending the lash snaking forward, she proved that the rapidity she was employing in no way detracted from her aim. Hard, yet supple, plaited leather encircled his wrist with a numbing constriction and caused him to miss the weapon's butt.

The sharp crack of a light calibre revolver mingled with the yelp of pain that was forced from Ennals, both being echoed by a startled yell as Murray felt the bullet tear off his hat. An instant later, although Booth had somehow contrived to retain his billycock so far, another shot sounded and it was sent spinning from his head. Each of them swung around to glare in the direction from which the bullets had come. What they saw prevented either from attempting to complete the draw he had commenced.

Standing at the edge of the sidewalk, Agnes Hickok was demonstrating that Wild Bill was not the only member of their family to possess ability in the use of firearms. Retaining the double handed hold she had adopted on taking it from her reticule, she had already cocked the hammer of the profusely engraved Colt Model of 1862 Police Pistol and was turning its four and a half inch barrel so it menaced Booth and Murray equally. What was more, as the weapon was a revolver despite its official name, each was aware there were almost certainly more bullets in the cylinder and concluded these could be dispatched with no less accuracy if necessary.

'I think that's just about enough from you!' Agnes stated calmly.

'All right!' put in a female voice with an English accent, its tone filled with indignation and suggesting the speaker was used to being obeyed. 'What the hell's going on?'

*   *   *   *   *

Unless illiterate, there was no excuse for a stranger to fail to identify the woman who was stalking from Battling Binnie's Ring Saloon as the person who had supplied part of its name. Nor, if it came to a point, was it hard to discern why the name was given to the establishment even without needing to enter. Flanked by posters advising the citizens of Cheyenne to vote for Hubert Kretzmer for mayor, she was depicted on life-size placards – clad in a sleeveless bodice, black tights and calf length heel-less boots, in the stance of a masculine pugilist and wearing boxing gloves – at each side of the building's main entrance.

179

Seen in the flesh, Battling Binnie Gates was even more impressive than her portraits. Slightly over five foot six in height, her hair hung to just below shoulder level in what a later generation would call a 'flip' style and was remarkably blonde for her something over forty years of age. There was no visible evidence about her features, as to how she had acquired her sobriquet, nor any suggestion of exactly how old she might be. She was good looking, even though her features suggested an arrogant and self-willed nature. She had prominent lips that might a few years earlier have been indicative of sultry promise. Clad in a scarlet dress that was revealing to the point of being indecorous, she had a very full figure. However, the extreme décolleté left no doubt that there was nothing except flesh and bone beneath the upper portion of the garment and a bulkily shapely leg showed tantalizingly through the waist length slit in the skirt, encased in a black silk stocking and ending in a high heeled silver coloured slipper.

Two men were following Binnie and each, in his own way, was almost as well known as she was to those spectators who were residents of Cheyenne.

At the left, the candidate for mayor of the town was not an inspiring physical specimen. While it was unlikely anybody would guess he was fifty-five, few people would have thought he was much less. Of moderate height and build, clad in expensive town dweller's clothes to which he did no justice, he had a balding grey head and a thin, pallid, sanctimonious face which suggested a mid-European origin and was not enhanced by a thin moustache. Darting glances about him as he emerged from the saloon, it was obvious he disapproved of everything he was seeing.

The second man was close to four inches taller than Kretzmer and about twenty years younger, and unless his attire lied, he was a successful professional gambler. Certainly he was as elegant as his companion was dowdy. Carrying an ebony coloured walking stick in his right hand – which, like its mate, was embellished by diamond rings as large as those sparkling on the woman's fingers and wrists – although nobody had ever seen him place its ferrule on the ground, he sported a pearl handled and nickel plated Colt Storekeeper

Model Peacemaker in a cross draw holster on the left side of his well polished black waist belt. He was, as the majority of the onlookers knew, Warren Gates and, in addition to being Binnie's husband, he was acknowledged as a coming man in the affairs of the town. There were also those who, with varying depths of profanity depending upon how much they had suffered at his far from scrupulous or gentle hands, would have attested to his completely ruthless nature.

'Well?' Binnie demanded, bringing her gaze to rest upon the wife of Wild Bill Hickok. 'What's it all about?'

'Your *brother* and his *friends* have been up to their usual tricks, *Mrs* Gates,' Agnes replied, her tone indicating that the dislike implied by the blonde's demeanour was mutual. She did not take the Colt from its alignment or look around sufficiently long to allow the men at whom it was pointed to take advantage of the lapse in vigilance. 'Only this time they've bitten off more than they can chew.'

'Their *usual* tricks?' Binnie challenged, continuing to show an animosity that was apparent to everybody in the vicinity.

'Blocking the sidewalk and generally making nuisances of themselves,' Agnes elaborated, provoking a rumble of concurrence from the assembled spectators. Her voice hardened as she went on, 'And if your *brother* tries to pull the gun he's fingering, I'll put a bullet in his knee which will stop him ever being able to duplicate *your* – ability – in the boxing ring.'

'Stop *scratching* yourself, Albie, or Mrs Hickok might jump to the wrong conclusion and start shooting for no reason like her husband's been known to,' Binnie ordered, her cheeks having reddened. There was only one thing annoyed her more than having what had clearly been a doubt cast upon her ability as a boxer. That was for somebody she knew to be aware of the true situation suggest a direct blood-link between herself and her half-brother. She knew Agnes had learned he was her father's son by a second marriage and they had only met for the first time since her arrival in the United States from England. As the young man obeyed, although more in response to the threat he felt sure would be carried out than from a desire to please her, she swung her gaze to where the big black woman was still seated

181

upon the weakly struggling and gasping trio. 'Hey you. Get up!'

'Don't recollect's how you pays me my wages,' the maid answered calmly. 'Which means I don't take no orders from you-all. What does *you* want me to do, Miz Agnes?'

'Get up, please, Mattie,' the brunette answered, lowering the revolver although she kept it in her hands.

'Whatever *you* says,' the maid assented, rising and ignoring the hate-filled glare being directed at her by the buxom blonde. 'They wasn't so all-fired comfortable to sit on, anyways.'

'My wife asked what was going on!' Warren Gates put in, his accent telling he had been born in the East Side of New York, as he stepped to Binnie's side. 'So it's time she was given an answer.'

'Well now,' a laconic and drawling voice remarked, before any reply was forthcoming. 'With all due respect to Miz Gates, I'd say it was up to *me* to do such questioning. Just put up your gun, Miz Agnes and you, Calam-gal, come on over here so's I can get to doing it.'

Even before Binnie and her husband looked at the two men who were approaching, they knew who had spoken. It was not the big, jovial looking, heavily built and well dressed Harlon Drysdale, currently mayor of Cheyenne, but the other who had made the comment.

Ambling in the manner of one long used to sitting on a horse, Marshal Grover Rymer was tall, lean and leathery looking. His hair might be grey, but he had the keen-eyed expression of a man much younger than his fifty-odd years. Clad in clean, if not new, range clothes, he had his badge of office to the left breast of his calfskin vest and the Colt Civilian Model Peacemaker holstered at his right thigh had its walnut grips worn by considerable use.

If any of the people who were gathered in front of the saloon had had eyes for other than the group who were the centre of attraction, they might have noticed that – although he had been in conversation with the mayor and marshal as they walked along prior to his intervention – the solemn man did not accompany them as they went forward.

'There's *some* might think,' Gates stated loudly, as if

182

addressing a political rally. 'That, with a peace officer on hand, it shouldn't have been allowed to start in the first place.

'Well now,' Rymer answered, directing a contemptuous glance to where the three young men on the sidewalk were untangling themselves slowly and painfully. 'Happen I'd've been a mite closer, I might've been able to stop it. Only, seeing's I'm not so spry's I used to be – like *some* 've been spreading the word around town – damned if it wasn't all over bar the shouting afore I could get here. But, like you-all 'n' Miz Gates, I'd admire to know what happened.'

'I suppose you're set on proving Albie and his mates started it,' Binnie accused, her attitude showing as much animosity towards the marshal and mayor as it had for Agnes.

'I'm set on finding out who did,' Rymer corrected, as he and his companion came to a halt and looked at the buckskin clad girl. 'How about it, Calam?'

'Well now, I wouldn't go so far's say it was *them*,' the red-head replied, indicating her would-be assailants with a sweeping gesture from her whip filled right hand. Having released the lash from Ennals' wrist, which subsequently proved to be broken, she was coiling it as – ensuring she did not come between Agnes and the three men on the street – she walked forward. 'But, what *they* was doing, they sure's hell's for sinners looked to be asking for somebody to, which I obliged.' Her gaze flickered to the mayor and she continued, 'Howdy, Mr Drysdale, I was looking for you to let you know I've brought in that load of supplies you ordered.'

'*Supplies!*' Binnie scoffed, studying the girl's attire, which was just as revealing as her own. 'That's a *new* name for it. Who do you think you are, Calamity Jane?'

'No,' the red-head answered, stepping on to the sidewalk and returning the handle of the whip to the belt loop. 'I don't *think*, I *know* I'm Calamity Jane.'

'You are, are you?' Binnie barked, allowing a note of disbelief into her tone although something told her she had heard the truth. 'And is bringing in the Mayor's supplies *all* he's had you come for?'

'What else have you in mind?' Calamity demanded, her gaze flickering from the blonde to the placards and back.

'I wondered, you being so tough from all accounts,' Binnie answered, speaking in a carrying voice. 'If he might have brought you in to take up my challenge.'

'I most certainly did – !' Drysdale began, but was not permitted to finish his denial.

'I've allus been one for taking up a challenge,' Calamity put in. 'So what'd it be?'

'To get in the ring with me,' Binnie answered. 'And see how long you can last before I flatten you, or have you crying for me to quit.'

'Well now,' Calamity replied, the light of battle glowing in her eyes. 'I reckon's how I might just give it a whirl. So, any time you're wanting, let's me and you get in that ring of your'n and see who gets flattened, or starts crying to quit!'

*　*　*　*　*

'Blast you, Calam!' the solemn-faced man growled, sounding and looking like a particularly strict bishop confronted by a consistent sinner. 'If *anybody* can stir things up faster and wilder than *you*, I hope I never get to meet them.'

'Don't you go mean-mouthing me, Solly Coles!' Miss Martha 'Calamity Jane' Canary protested, the introductions which had been performed a few minutes earlier having shown it was all right for her to use the speaker's real, if abbreviated, name. There was a suggestion of genuine liking for him beneath the note of asperity in her voice as she continued, 'What the he – What *should* I have done when that half-dressed, big-ti – lard-gutted, white-haired tail-peddler called me down, back off like she scared the shi – like she scared me?'

The changes in the red-head's spirited response, mild as they were compared with some of the expletives to which she could put tongue when an occasion demanded, were made out of deference for where and in whose company the conversation was taking place.

Two hours had elapsed since the fracas outside Battling Bonnie's Ring Saloon. What amounted to a council of war was being held in the private living accommodation of the small hotel which had been purchased as a home and business by Mr & Mrs James Butler 'Wild Bill' Hickok. In addition to the speakers, Agnes, Mayor Drysdale, Marshal Rymer and half a dozen of Cheyenne's most prominent citizens were present. The latter group were among the mayor's stoutest supporters in his campaign to stay in office. That factor and recent developments had led them to seek him out with the disturbing news which had provoked the exchange between the girl and United States Marshal Solomon Wisdom 'Solly' Cole, although as yet his official status was known only to her, Agnes, Drysdale and the local peace officer.[2]

Being aware of how delicate the situation was with the municipal elections so close, and mindful of rumours which had been circulated since the campaign commenced regarding the possibility of his showing hostility to those who opposed his and Drysdale's return to office, Rymer had shown masterly tact in the way he handled the aftermath of the fracas. While satisfied Calamity was justified – if impulsive and ill-advised – with her intervention, he had craftily left the onus of responsibility for whatever action he had to take upon Binnie and Warren Gates. Or rather on the six young men known to be their adherents, which amounted to the same thing. When asked whether they wished to have the girl and the others who had been involved arrested for assaulting them, Albert Booth had clearly been on the point of answering in the affirmative. He was prevented from doing so by a furious glare from his half-sister and a prohibitive head shake by her equally reluctant husband, who knew his bullying and vindictive nature just as well as she did. Both appreciated, although he did not, how the response would be received by the onlookers if he insisted upon the charges being enforced.

On receiving Booth's negative reply, albeit given reluc-

[2] A United States Marshal received his appointment via the Federal Government, sometimes at the instigation of the President, which gave him jurisdiction throughout the country. Elected locally, a town marshal acted as chief of police and had jurisdictional authority only in the municipality which was employing him. Law enforcement elsewhere in the county wherein the town was situated was the responsibility of the county sheriff, whose jurisdiction was restricted to its boundaries. J.T.E.

tantly, the marshal had requested the onlookers to disperse. Before this could be done, Binnie had prevented an immediate departure by returning to the subject of the challenge she had made and had had accepted by Calamity. Repeating the suggestion that Drysdale had brought the girl to Cheyenne for just such a purpose, she had asked if he would be willing to help put up a 'purse' to reimburse the winner. Her husband had offered to donate one thousand dollars and, being aware of how adversely public sentiment could be affected by a refusal, the mayor was compelled to donate a similar amount. Asked if he also wished to make a side bet on the outcome, his hesitancy produced an offer of five to one odds from Binnie. Goaded by his awareness of the audience's reaction and being by nature a gambler, he had agreed. However, his intention of restricting the wager to a moderate sum came to nothing. Mocking comments about his lack of faith in his contender had led him to match the two thousand five hundred dollars proposed by Gates.

The matter had not ended with the completion of the arrangements and dispersal of the crowd. Nor was it likely to have done. Such an unusual sporting contest would have been of tremendous interest under any conditions. That its principals were from opposing sides in the forthcoming and hotly contended municipal elections gave the affair an added zest. In a remarkably short time, there was hardly a person in Cheyenne who had not been informed that Calamity Jane and Battling Binnie Gates were to 'have it out' with each other in the boxing ring, three minute rounds to a finish instead of to a set number, that evening at nine o'clock.

It transpired that more than just the news had been passed around.

Visiting each of Drysdale's main supporters individually, Gates had induced six of them to respectively wager considerable sums of money on the girl at the same odds offered by his wife. Nor had the gambling on the event been restricted to them. Apart from the multitude of transactions being carried out all over the town and which were not connected to the actual participants, Gates had men going around taking bets from anybody who wished to accept the odds. Having been approached, without his official status being exposed, Cole had mentioned the matter to Rymer. Both were experienced peace officers and, sensing something suspicious might be afoot, they had visited the business-men known to support Drysdale. Collecting the mayor and those of his adherents who were involved, on learning the extent of the wagering, they had come to the Hickok Hotel where Calamity had taken a room. On being informed of the reason for the visit, its proprietor had offered the privacy of her living quarters in which to discuss the matter.

'I don't see *you* backing off, anyway, Calam,' Agnes stated. 'Not if all Jim has told me about you is true.'

'No more she would,' Cole declared in a sombre voice. 'I mind one time she let a gal who she'd caught after trying to rob a stage she was on get the jump on her just so she could find out who was toughest.'

'She'd whomped me on my head first time we met!' the red-head pointed out in exculpation, but made no attempt to refute the accusation.[3] 'Anyways, don't tell me you be-grudge a hard working gal a mite of fun, now do you?'

'*Fun!*' yelped one of the businessmen, who had wagered considerably more than was wise upon Calamity being victorious. 'Is that all you regard *this* as, *fun?*'

'Easy, Barney!' Drysdale injected soothingly. 'We've all heard tell how Calam can hold up her end in a fight should she need.'

'Well, yes,' Barney Josephson admitted, considering and deciding it might be inadvisable to mention there was one occasion when the red-head had suffered a defeat in a fight with another woman.[4] 'But she's not a trained boxer like Binnie Gates.'

'I one time took on and whupped a gal's was reckoned to be woman fist fighting "champeen" of the whole damned world,' Calamity pointed out, having considerable pride in her prowess in such matters.

'But was that in a ring and under rules, Calam?' Agnes inquired, feeling sure such an event would have been

[3] Told in: *CALAMITY SPELLS TROUBLE*. However, at the time of writing, we had not learned of United States Marshal Solomon Wisdom 'Solly' Cole's full name. J.T.E.

[4] Told in: *Part One, 'Better Than Calamity', THE WILDCATS.* J.T.E.

accorded considerable mention in the newspapers or magazines which devoted space to highly spiced accounts of the girl's activities and unable to recollect ever having seen reference to it.

'Well, no,' Calamity confessed, grinning a little at the memory. 'It was tooth 'n' claw again' her and a gal who set us to fighting, but I had a cute lil schoolma'am backing my play.'[5]

'Boxing in a ring's different – I should imagine,' Agnes warned, although the second portion of a statement which began in a fashion suggesting knowledge, or experience in such matters, appeared to have been inserted as an afterthought. 'I know the exhibitions Mrs Gates has given while she's been here have always been against girls who work for her, but from what I've s – heard, she's a competent enough performer.'

'Likely,' Calamity admitted amiably, having taken a great liking to the woman who was married to an old and valued friend and whose expert handling of a revolver had saved her from a precarious situation. 'But I'm a heap younger, I'll bet fitter and, by cracky, I reckon's I can take *anything* she can hand out 'n' give back a whole heap more.'

'But she's a trained boxer!' Josephson reiterated.

'Do you reckon you'll have any trouble with those big gloves you'll be using, Calam?' Drysdale inquired, remembering the equipment he had seen employed in the exhibition bouts put on by Binnie since her arrival in Cheyenne.

'Not so long's they don't stop me hitting her just's hard's I can,' the red-head declared confidently.

'It's not as if the bout is over a set number of rounds and with points being awarded to get a winner if there isn't a decision,' Agnes went on, showing what might have been considered a surprising knowledge of how boxing matches were generally conducted. 'And, with Wally Siddons as referee, it will be fair enough.'

'There's nothing more certain than *that*!' Drysdale asserted, knowing the man in question was not only a noted referee who was frequently called upon to officiate at major male boxing bouts throughout Wyoming and the surrounding

[5] Told in: *TROUBLE TRAIL*. J.T.E.

States, but was also one of his supporters in the election. 'And, like Calam said, she's younger and fitter than Binnie Gates. So all she has to do is keep going until Binnie's all tuckered out and she'll win.'

Listening to the mutter of concurrence, in which Josephson gave only slightly grudging support, Solly Cole was worried. Not so much over Calamity's welfare, as he shared the mayor's confidence in her ability to succeed under those conditions, but because he realized that more than a considerable sum of money was hanging on the outcome. If she was defeated, it would almost certainly cause Drysdale to lose the election and see Rymer, a competent and scrupulously honest lawman, removed from office. What was more, from all he had heard of them and deduced outside the saloon, he could not imagine Binnie and Warren Gates offering odds of five to one, or taking the large sums which had been wagered, unless they believed she was certain of victory.

* * * * *

'We've got her, Warrie,' Albert Booth announced triumphantly, as he entered the owners' private office at the rear of Battling Binnie's Ring Saloon shortly after half past six in the evening. Then, because it went against the grain for him to give praise to anybody, his tone lost some of its enthusiasm as he elaborated, 'She went to the livery barn to 'tend to her horses just as you said she would.'

'I told you she would, Mr Gates!' Hubert Kretzmer put in, reluctant to allow the saloonkeeper to be credited with his deductions. 'Did you have any trouble?'

'Naw!' Booth scoffed, eyeing the politician with thinly disguised disdain. 'Chris and Mike jumped her while she was fetching hay for the horses.'

'Did she *see* either of them?' Kretzmer demanded.

'No.' Booth replied. 'Chris gave her a bang on the head from behind and before she got her wits about her again, they'd put her in a couple of sacks, with a gag over her mouth and trussed up like a turkey ready for the oven at Thanksgiving.'[6]

[6] 'Thanksgiving', also known as 'Thanksgiving Day': usually the last

189

'Where is she now?' Warren Gates inquired, having an even lower opinion than Kretzmer of the intelligence of Booth and his cronies.

'In the buggy out back,' the young man answered, with the air of one expecting approbation for work well done.

None was forthcoming!

'Then tell the stupid bastards to get her the hell away from here!' Gates bellowed, springing to his feet while his wife and Kretzmer exhibited just as much alarm. 'I said for them to take her to that cabin along Crow Creek when they got her.'

'S – Sure, Warrie!' Booth gulped, being too aware of the saloonkeeper's far from amiable disposition when crossed or roused to raise any arguments.

'You remembered to bring away that buckskin saddle-horse of hers and any of her gear that was with the wagon, didn't you?' Kretzmer asked, as the young man began to turn.

'Yes we did,' Booth confirmed, showing more indignation than would have been the case if the question had come from his half-sister or her husband. 'She hadn't took her war bag to the Hickoks' so we brought it along like *Warrie* told us.'

'Good!' Gates grunted, having hoped to receive the latter piece of information and slightly mollified by the way in which the latter part of it had been given. 'Tell them to get her to the cabin and stay with her.'

'Sure, Warrie,' Booth assented.

'And tell those mates of yours to forget any ideas they've got about paying her back for what she did to them outside,' Binnie Gates put in, her tones coldly menacing. 'Or having what they might think is fun with her. I want her in good shape when she comes back. Tell them you'll be bringing a couple of the girls to look after her later tonight and to make bloody sure she doesn't see any of them, or hear any names that would help her say who's involved.'

'I'll see to it,' Booth promised with a touch of asperity, disliking the repetition of orders he had already been given.

Thursday in November, set apart in the United States of America as an annual festival of thanksgiving to God for the year's blessings and upon which turkey is a traditional item of food. J.T.E.

'But, after the election tomorrow, it'll not matter any too much whether she can, or can't.'

'The hell it won't!' Gates contradicted savagely and Kretzmer nodded vehement agreement. 'You do as you're told and leave the thinking to those with brains for it.'

'God damn it, Warrie,' Binnie complained, after her half-brother had fled from the room even more precipitately than he had entered. 'I still don't see why you can't just let me have her in the ring tonight and hammer seven shades of shit out of her.'

'*I've* told you *why*!' Kretzmer put in, before the blonde's husband could speak. His voice had a grating whine which did little to enamour him to prospective voters, or to promote a friendly atmosphere even with the people upon whom he was depending to acquire the requisite support to win the election as mayor on the following day. 'After the way your brother and those other fools behaved outside, just doing that might not be enough.'

'We'll win all the bets,' Binnie pointed out, finding the would-be civic official's condescending attitude as irritating as it always was in her dealings with him.

'*We'll* win them anyway,' Kretzmer countered, wanting to establish that he expected a share of the money and having the kind of mentality which detested any argument or disputing of his wishes by people he considered to be underlings hired to do his bidding. 'The bets will be forfeit by default when she doesn't show up, but that won't be the end of it. Even the people who haven't bets down, are going to blame Drysdale for their disappointment when Canary doesn't come and fight.'

'She'll come straight back here when she gets loose,' Gates continued. 'So you'll be able to get her into the ring then and, that way, we'll get two dips into the cracker barrel instead of one.'

'The second time'll get even more attention and a bigger crowd,' Binnie mused, half to herself. 'Because everybody will know it's going to be a real, out and out grudge fight to a finish.'

*   *   *   *   *

'She's nowhere to be found!' U.S. Marshal Solly Cole announced, coming into the living quarters at the Hickoks' hotel. 'Her gear and the buckskin aren't at the livery barn and nobody there's seen hide nor hair of her!' She hasn't even finished feeding her team.

'Then something's happened to her!' Agnes Hickok stated and her maid nodded vigorous concurrence, the possibility of Calamity Jane having been afraid to go through with the boxing bout and fleeing from the town never occurring to either of them. 'And, in that case, Binnie Gates and her husband know what it is.'

'You-all won't get any argument from *me* on *that*,' Cole declared, having just as much faith in the red-head's courage and integrity, so he too did not believe she would let down her supporters by running away. 'The trouble is, what they did and how to prove it.'

'There's some's'd say *that* should be asked,' Matilda Boomer said, with the air of one stating the obvious.

'"Grove" Rymer dropped by the Ring, as if he was just looking in while making his rounds,' Cole answered. 'Gates told him without being asked, that he'd sent Booth's five *amigos* out of town so they wouldn't try to get evens with Calam. "Grove" didn't push it, nor let on we know she's gone missing.'

'Did Gates say where they'd gone?' Agnes wanted to know.

'Out to Velma Tickman's chicken ranch,' the marshal replied. 'Wherever that might be.'

'It's about five miles west of town,' Agnes informed them, showing neither embarrassment nor disapproval as she gave the location of a well known local brothel. 'But I know Velma and she wouldn't stand for anything like that. Having Calam taken and held there, I mean.'

'Which's what "Grove" told me,' Cole admitted.

'Do you think they're holding her at the saloon?' the brunette asked pensively.

'I wouldn't reckon so,' Cole replied. 'They'd not be willing to take such a chance in case we insisted on searching it.'

'Maybe you and me ought to go down there and make sure, Massa Cole,' Matilda suggested, her long association with Agnes having allowed her to be present during the conversation. 'I reckon 'tween us we could do it, one way or another.'

'Not quickly enough,' the brunette pointed out, glancing at the clock on the mantelpiece. 'It's half after eight already. Darn it, Solly, I wish I'd called you sooner.'

'You didn't miss her until half after seven,' the marshal consoled. 'And it took Mattie a while to find me. No, it's my fault. I should've watched her instead of Wally Siddons.'

'You thought you were taking the right precaution in doing so,' Agnes stated.

While that was true enough, Cole found little comfort in the thought.

The marshal had suspected the Gateses might be unwilling to rely solely upon Binnie's ability with so much at stake. However, he had been completely wrong in his assumption over how the precautionary measures would be taken. That Calamity might be prevented from competing had occurred to him, but he had discounted the idea. There was so much interest in the contest that its postponement would create resentment and hostility which might not be restricted to the girl and her supporters.

On the other hand, Cole had considered the saloonkeeper and his wife might regard Wallace Siddons as better suited to their purpose despite – or perhaps because of – their insistence on having him act as referee. If he could be compelled by some means to conduct the affair with less than his usual scrupulous fairness, their ends could be achieved in a way which would prevent suspicion falling upon them.

Having drawn the conclusion, Cole had acted upon it in the only way possible. As Rymer was unable to supply assistance, needing every deputy to help control the town which was in a restless and excited mood as a result of the impending contest, he had been compelled reluctantly to keep only one of the possibilities under observation.

Events had proved the wrong person was selected!

'I still reckon me 'n' you should go down there, Massa Cole,' Matilda insisted, folding a large black fist and shaking it in a gesture of grim determination. 'We – !'

'Even if there was time, the end result might make things worse instead of better,' Agnes warned. 'The Gateses and

Kretzmer would claim you're trying to shield Calamity, who's turned yellow and is either hiding, or has run away.'

'Don't say we's just going to sit on our butts 'n' let 'em get away with it?' the maid almost yelped, but was prevented from continuing by a knock on the door.

'I've got the hosses, Cole,' Marshal Grover Rymer announced, on being admitted by the indignant black woman.

'*Bueno,*' the solemn-faced man replied, then gave his hostess and her maid an apologetic smile. 'We figured that Gates would try to head us in the wrong direction from where they've got Calam hid out. So, remembering there's an empty cabin down along Crow Creek a ways and having noticed Mrs Gate's buckboard's not where it's usually kept, we reckoned's how we'd drift along there to see what's doing.'

'Do you think she's still alive?' Agnes asked.

'Yes,' Cole replied. 'With the friends she's got, they wouldn't want her turning up dead.' His voice hardened and, at that moment, nobody would have taken him for a member of the cloth even one who practised the church militant, as he continued, 'But, by God, if I'm wrong, Gates and Kretzmer won't live to see the election tomorrow.'

'There goes a man I'd hate to have riled at me,' Matilda declared, after the two peace officers had taken their departure. 'But, much's I hates them Gateses and Kretzmer, I surely hope he find that Calam girl alive. 'Cause, happen he don't, he's going to have to share 'em with *me.*'

'They can't get to the cabin and back in time, though,' the brunette pointed out and stood up. 'So something will have to be done until they arrive. Go and get out my gear, Mattie.'

'You means your – ?' the maid began.

'That's just what I mean!' Agnes confirmed and her face was set in determined lines.

*　*　*　*　*

'Where the hell's that son-of-a-bitch Chris got to?' Mike Leigh grumbled, so filled with impatience and a sense of grievance he forgot the instructions received with regards to avoiding the use of names. 'If he's stopped to watch the fight Bonnie's going to put on so's the fellers won't be too riled with her for that whore not showing, I'll fix his wagon good.'

'He's had plenty of time to get here,' Royston Hattersley mumbled, his speech somewhat impaired by a badly swollen jaw, studying the watch he had taken out and which had survived without damage his misfortunes earlier in the day. 'It's coming up to a quarter for nine.'

There was cause for the comments. Ignoring the orders given by Warren Gates once he and his companions had delivered Calamity Jane to the cabin about five miles south of Cheyenne along Crow Creek, Chris Hitchens had set out for the town. While they had brought their bedrolls and sufficient other supplies to let them spend the night at the cabin without too much discomfort, liquor had not been included. So he had said he would fetch some, obtaining it at another saloon. A similar idea had occurred to the others, but he had taken his departure before any of them could try to assert a better right to do so.

'We 'n's could be having fun if he is,' Len Murray complained. Looking across the room to the cause of their present discontent, he went on, 'Which we can *still* have some with *her*, only not the same kind.'

'You know Warren said we was to keep our hands offen her,' David Ennals reminded, rubbing his injured wrist, which throbbed painfully despite being in splints and bandaged.

'He's not here!' Murray countered, glancing at the other two and trying to estimate whether he could count upon their support. 'And what can he do when he finds out it's already been done?'

'You want to find out, go ahead!' Ennals replied. 'But, knowing what he's like when he's "riz" – and who he's got behind him – I'm not figuring to.'

'I'll tell you something else,' Leigh supplemented. 'Happen you go again' him, stay far clear of Cheyenne.'

'There's other god-damned towns!' Murray pointed out sullenly, possessing a nature which rejected advice no matter how sound it might be. 'And I'm fed so my guts're

195

full with taking rawhiding from him'n' *her*. So I don't con-clude's how missing meeting 'em again'll make me sleep any the worst once I've had my pleasure.'

Listening to the conversation without being able to see the men who were making it, as she sat on the floor where she had been dumped unceremoniously on arrival, Calamity awaited the answer to the comment in a state of trepidation. She was still swathed in the sacks which had been draped around her from each end after she had been stunned at the livery barn and the gag was still in position. Nor, after a few tentative tugs had disclosed she could not free herself from the bonds encircling her coverings, had she wasted time in struggling futilely. They were less tightly fastened than they could be and she had not wished to have the situ-ation rectified to her further disadvantage. Accepting that escape would be unlikely to succeed while they were watch-ing her, she had remained passive and was awaiting a suit-able opportunity to take action. Forcing herself to remain motionless, she was nevertheless prepared to defend herself in any way possible should the speaker – who, like his com-panions, she had identified by the names each had inadvert-ently used – obtain support for his proposal, or start to put it into effect alone should they turn him down.

Before either situation could eventuate, something hap-pened to take the men's attention from the subject they were discussing. The creaking of the front door's hinges drew their eyes in that direction. What they saw in the light of the two lamps they had brought and which were sus-pended from hooks in the ceiling diverted their thoughts away from the captive red-head.

A very shapely and obviously female leg clad in a black stocking, which added to its attraction, was ex-tended through the partially open entrance to the building. Although the rest of the body to which it belonged remained tatalisingly out of sight, a feminine voice with a seductively Southern drawl said, 'Howdy, you-all in there. Miz Binnie's sent Millie-Sue and lil ole me out with some goodies for you. Who-all's going to help us tote them in? First one here gets to see how smooth these stockings of mine are afore you start.'

196

There was no hesitation, or debate, over the response to this proposal.

Even Murray, who had been experiencing serious misgivings in view of his companions' reaction to the suggestion that they rape the red-head, joined the unanimous rush to make the most of the invitation.

The leg was withdrawn as, with Murray slightly in the lead, the four eager young men were approaching their goal. Even as he was reaching to open the door, there was a thud such as would have been made by somebody kicking the planks. Which, as the way it flew open proved, had happened. A howl of agony burst from Murray as it struck his outstretched hand, breaking two of his fingers. While he staggered backwards, his companions changed their advances into even more hurried retreats and began to grab for their revolvers.

Neither of the leading pair of figures to spring across the threshold was the cause of the mass rush to the door. They were, in fact, the pair of Indian-featured men in cow-hand's attire who had hurled Leigh along the sidewalk outside Battling Binnie's Ring Saloon to collide with Hitchens and Hattersley. Furthermore, as each had a Winchester Model of 1873 carbine in his hands, they seemed even more menacing upon this occasion.

Following closely upon the newcomers' heels, carrying what appeared to be a light calibre Colt revolver in her right hand,[7] was the young woman they had saved from Leigh's wrath; although he might have been excused if he had not recognized her. Gone were the spectacles and primly-proper garments, the latter being replaced by attire which was far more creditable to her. While her hair was the same, her beautiful features had lost the obviously false nose which reduced their charm and were set in an expression implying grim and deadly earnest intentions. The man's dark blue shirt and Levi's pants she had on, one leg still being rolled up from allowing the limb to be exposed as bait – she had

[7] The weapon was a Manhattan Navy Percussion revolver, a close imitation of the Colt Model of 1851 Navy, except that its cylinder took only five instead of six bullets and there was a spring plate between the percussion caps and the hammer. J.T.E.

removed and was carrying its Indian moccasin in her left hand – proved she had contours just as full and curvaceous as those of Calamity.

Swinging the butt of his carbine around vigorously, the taller of the masculine intruders drove its butt against the side of Leigh's jaw and, to the accompaniment of a crack of breaking bone, sent him spinning across the cabin to crash unconscious on the floor. Having retreated farther, Hattersley was out of the second man's range where such an attack was concerned. This did not save him. As his revolver was coming from its holster, the Winchester which could not have reached him for a blow barked and sent a bullet into his head. Encumbered by the broken wrist, although he had commenced his draw instinctively, Ennals snatched his hand away from its weapon and howled for the pair not to shoot him. Frightened to such an extent that he forgot the pain from his injured fingers, Murray joined in with a yell that he too surrendered.

Leaving her companions to cover the cowed and terrified pair, the beautiful young woman hurried across the cabin. Tucking the revolver into her waistband and donning the moccasin, she knelt alongside and began to unfasten the ropes around the prisoner's coverings. Despite the assurance she had been given when obtaining the information which allowed the rescue to be effected, she showed relief as the removal of the upper sack revealed Calamity gagged, blinking in the light of the lanterns, but otherwise clearly unharmed.

'This's *twice* in one day *I've* had to pull *your* hot chestnuts out of the fire, Martha Jane Canary,' the female rescuer announced, in what might have been chiding tones, removing the gag. 'Why, land-sakes a-mercy, girl, it's becoming a *habit*.'

'B – B – Belle – Starr!' the red-head gasped, once her mouth was liberated, staring as if hardly able to believe the evidence of her eyes. The other girl had withdrawn into the crowd, accompanied by the two men, avoiding being brought into the discussion which followed the affray and had therefore gone unnoticed by the red-head. 'By cracky, Belle-gal, I don't know when I was more pleased to see you.'

'I should think so too, for shame,' the rescuer replied, making no attempt to deny she was the notorious lady outlaw, Belle Starr, as this was indeed the case. Continuing the work of liberation, she went on, 'I'm sorry we couldn't get here sooner, Calam, but that ham-headed yack we caught sneaking out of town fainted when Blue-Duck and Sammy started to ask him where they'd got you and it took longer than I expected to find out.'

'I don't know's I blame him for that,' the red-head declared, throwing a grateful glance at the two men and knowing they possessed the effectiveness of their Indian forbears when it came to eliciting information from reluctant donors. 'Only I wish you could've got here a mite sooner. I surely hate to keep a lady waiting, even when she's no son-of-a-bitching lady. Anyway, they do say anything worth doing's worth waiting for and I'm figuring it's going to be worth doing what I'm going to do to *her*.'

Unlike U.S. Marshal Solly Cole, Calamity was unaware of the possible repercussions which her failure to appear on time was threatening to bring about at that moment.

*　*　*　*　*

'Where's your girl, *Mayor* Drysdale?' Binnie Gates called, having signalled for and brought silence to the packed-to-capacity bar-room. She leaned over the top rope of the boxing ring which was erected in its centre. 'Don't tell me she's ate crow and run away?'

As always was the case when participating in a boxing bout, the blonde had entered the ring with her hair taken into a bun at the back of her head and with her face as heavily made up as if attending to more conventional business in the saloon. Her bulky figure was encased rather than clad in a very tight fitting sleeveless white satin bodice, which was all too clearly her torso's sole covering, and she wore black tights and flat soled, calf high ring boots. Her whole demeanour was redolent of triumph and satisfaction as she asked the question to which she already was aware of the answer.

Before the clearly perturbed civic official could reply, an excited rumble of comment arose and the crowd between the saloon's main entrance and the ring began to part so two new arrivals could pass through. One was the big black maid, Matilda Boomer, carrying a towel, bucket and a square wooden box. It was, however, the other who had produced the eagerness to allow them to go by. While this one also gave the impression of being feminine, the hood of a long black cloak entirely concealed her features and gave little indication via her build as to her identity, other than glimpses of footwear beneath its floor-trailing hem, similar to that worn by Binnie. Studying her, as she and the maid climbed the three wooden steps and ducked beneath the ropes to enter the ring, Binnie was as puzzled as the spectators. However, even if she had known it could not be Calamity Jane, she could have deduced the person who clearly intended to replace the red-head was slightly shorter and bulkier. Nearer to her own size, in fact.

Neither the blonde nor the almost entirely masculine crowd filling the room were kept long in doubt over the second newcomer's identity.

'As you *may* know, *Mrs* Gates,' Agnes Hickok announced, with just as carrying tones which reached everybody else present in the silence which followed her tossing back the hood and starting to open the cloak, disclosing that her brunette hair was also secured in a bun. 'Calamity Jane is – indisposed – So, rather than allow everybody here to be disappointed – ' She turned her gaze to the tall, well built, middle-aged man clad in a black turtleneck sweater, slacks and ring boots starting to come forward from the third corner and went on, 'With Mr Siddons' permission, I am offering myself as a substitute.'

'Under the same rules and conditions?' Binnie asked eagerly, when the excited chatter aroused by the proposal died away and before the referee could speak.

'Exactly the same,' Agnes confirmed. 'May I substitute, Mr Siddons?'

'Well – !' the referee began, not sure what to make of the unexpected development, although he was aware of

Calamity's disappearance. 'I – I – What would Wild Bill say?'

'That I'm acting to his complete satisfaction,' the brunette stated. 'And I'll absolve you of all responsibility for anything that may happen to me.'

'All right!' Siddons assented, albeit reluctantly, but taking a warning from the crowd's shouted demands for the offer to be accepted. He was aware of the issues involved outside the actual bout and believed Agnes was bravely, if perhaps foolhardly, trying to rectify the situation by ensuring the spectators were given some consolation for the red-head's absence. Silently promising himself he would end it the moment she showed signs of being in danger of injury, regardless of public opinion, he went on, 'You can substitute for Calamity Jane.'

A hiss of satisfaction broke from Binnie, being drowned by the tumultuous applause greeting the referee's decision. From the day of her arrival in Cheyenne when what was intended as a grand opening of the Battling Binnie's Ring Saloon, had failed and lost customers due to a function planned much earlier by Agnes, she had developed a growing antipathy where the brunette – who she knew had been some kind of performer in a circus prior to marrying Wild Bill Hickok – was concerned. The dislike had become mutual when each had found herself on the opposing sides in the competition to attain office as the city's mayor. However, never in her wildest dreams had she hoped to be given such an opportunity to work off her animosity.

Watching the brunette remove the cloak revealing that she was dressed in an almost identical fashion to herself, even to the extent of wearing nothing beneath the bodice, the blonde gave thought as to how she might be able to extract the fullest vengeance. She drew similar conclusions to those of Siddons, including on how *he* would behave once the battering she wanted to inflict was commenced. So she was determined to subject her hated rival to the utmost humiliation and, if the means she employed caused a withdrawal from the bout, it would serve her husband and Hubert Kretzmer's purpose as effectively as if the substitution had not been proposed.

'All right, *Hickok*!' Binnie shouted, drawing off the bodice and tossing it to one of the saloongirls who were to act as her seconds. Standing with arms akimbo, feet apart and thrusting forward the naked mounds of a bosom that was firm in spite of its size, she continued, 'Let's have it out *this* way and show the boys here who's the better *woman*!'

Once again the audience began to make its sentiments known in no uncertain manner. While Drysdale and some of the men who formed his party at a ringside table adjacent to Agnes' corner rose and objected, it was obvious that the majority of those present were in wholehearted agreement with Binnie's suggestion.

Another dissident, strange as it might have struck some people, was Kretzmer. He began a hurried, if *sotto voce*, protest to Warren Gates, with whom he and Albert Booth were sharing a table at the opposite side of the ring to the mayor. However, his objections were less humanitarian and laudible than those from Drysdale's party.

While Kretzmer was aware that Binnie had boxed bare to the waist on other occasions, they had always been private bouts before carefully selected and well-paying audiences. Such a public flaunting of conventions might offend people's susceptibilities and lose badly needed support for his cause. Yet, for all his misgivings, listening to the delighted response from the majority of the spectators he was warned that he would be ill-advised to state his objections openly. A glance informed him that Gates neither shared his concern, nor appeared other than delighted by the brazen behaviour to which many husbands would have taken exception.

For her part, Agnes was giving just as much consideration to the ramifications of the latest development. She was aware of the blonde's motives and realized she might turn one aspect of them to her advantage. There were, however, other points to be taken into account before reaching a decision.

Although Cheyenne was the capital city of Wyoming, wanting to avoid showing open partisanship with either of the factions contesting the election for mayor, the Governor and every other leading member of the Legislature had found reasons to be elsewhere until after it was over. So nobody who was in sufficiently high office to help further the plans Agnes and her husband had for the future were present to be influenced adversely by whatever decision she reached. What was more, having a similar desire to avoid letting it be thought he was using his reputation as a gun fighter to further Drysdale's candidature, Wild Bill had gone on a visit to the gold camp known as Deadwood accompanied by his friend, 'Colorado' Charlie Utter.[8] Knowing him, however, she was certain he would approve of what she meant to do when he was informed of her actions.

'Very well,' the brunette said, after a pause and speaking in tones redolent of reluctance, as she hesitantly began to peel off the form-hugging blue silk bodice. Making a not entirely successful effort to keep a bosom just as well developed and imposing as that of the blonde concealed with her hands instead of flaunting it, she finished, 'If that's how *you* want it, there's nothing I can do but agree.'

*   *   *   *   *

'Round one!' called the timekeeper, jerking at the lanyard of the bell on his table.

Advancing from her corner in the fashion of a competent male boxer, Binnie Gates was delighted by the evidence that she had been correct in her assumption of one benefit to be gained from her suggestion of fighting bare to the waist. It came from watching how Agnes Hickok advanced in a crouching posture and with her hands covering the breasts. By doing so, she was leaving her face entirely unprotected. The blonde promised herself she would make the most of the opportunity being presented and that Wild Bill was not going to find his wife's face anywhere near so pretty when he came home.

Although Wallace Siddons had tried to oppose the women fighting in such a manner, his wishes were over-ruled by the determination of the spectators to witness so novel a spectacle. Nor had his second objections met with any greater success. When the gloves were produced, they had

---

[8] How disastrous the visit proved to be is told in: *Part Seven, Calamity Jane series, 'Deadwood, August 2nd, 1876', J.T.'s HUNDREDTH.* J.T.E.

not been the large and well-padded kind used in the 'exhibition' bouts which frequently formed the entertainment offered by Battling Binnie's Ring Saloon. Instead, they were the four ounce variety employed only by male pugilists on rare occasions such as genuine grudge fights. Once again, claiming that wearing them would really prove who was the better woman, the blonde had had the majority of the crowd's wholehearted support.

In spite of his reluctant concurrence, the referee had felt a growing perturbation as he watched how Agnes was behaving during the preliminaries. From the moment she had removed the bodice, she appeared to be embarrassed by her temerity and sought to shield her naked bosom from the licientious gaze of the spectators. Nor had she seemed any less ill at ease when, after having been subjected to a careful examination by Siddons, Matilda had laced on her gloves and, the introductions carried out, she left her corner on the signal to commence being given.

Grinning in anticipation and supremely confident in the eventual outcome, Binnie shot her left fist in a jab towards the exposed face. It failed to connect. Leaving their position of shielding at least some of her two sizeable mounds of bust, the brunette's right hand deftly knocked up the approaching arm and, showing an equal precision, the left was driven into the identical target on her opponent. As Binnie's head was jolted back, a trickle of blood oozing from her pain-filled nose, Agnes followed up the attack with a right uppercut that dumped her unceremoniously in a sitting position on the floor of the ring.

Shaking her head to clear it, the blonde rubbed her left arm across her face and stared at the red smear it acquired. Then, with the laughter of the spectators and the sound of the referee counting ringing in her ears, she glared up at the brunette. Fury boiled through her as she forced herself upright and rushed forward impetuously, which proved as disastrous as her previous effort. The blow she launched was much wilder than she generally employed, if more powerful, but also failed to connect. Side-stepping in a way that would not have disgraced a good male boxer, Agnes hooked her in the stomach as she blundered by. As she inhaled sharply, another blow caught her on the ear and sent her staggering to be saved from falling by colliding against the ropes.

'You "something-sucking, something"!' Binnie spat out, as she turned and saw her opponent coming forward in the stance of a trained boxer and showing no signs of her earlier apparent concern over allowing her bosom to be visible. 'You've been in a ring before!'

'In the same place I learned to shoot,' Agnes confirmed. 'The circus. And, before I'm through, you're going to be begging to tell me where you've put Calamity Jane!'

'Try and make me!' the blonde challenged, goaded to the point that – in spite of realizing she might be playing into her opponent's hands – she charged away from the ropes with fists flailing.

And, for the third time, Binnie achieved only further punishment for herself!

With her gloves meeting only the empty space vacated an instant earlier by the brunette, another punch took the blonde in her mid-section. Despite the hard muscles beneath a noticeable layer of fat, the blow hurt. So did the uppercut to her chin as she was driven into an involuntary retreat and the right cross to the head which sent her, senses spinning, sprawling to suck the pungent aroma of resin from the canvas through her throbbing and blood emitting nose. Suffering more from the combination of pain and humiliation of her treatment than had ever previously been the case, she forced herself to rise as the referee's count reached seven.

For all a combination of warnings given by her mind and comments from her husband, Binnie could not prevent herself from continuing to pursue similar rash and pain-creating tactics. She was repulsed just as capably as had been the way previously in the bout. Bombarded by a veritable battery of punches, her own gloves did nothing more than miss their sought-for targets. Yet she might have counted herself fortunate in one respect. As she was to discover in the near future, relieved of the necessity of employing evasive tactics to avoid reciprocal punishment, the brunette was capable of inflicting far more telling punishment than had been delivered so far.

'What the hell's wrong with *you*?' Warren Gates demanded angrily, after his wife had been literally dragged to her corner by her seconds – still struggling to go on despite the signal to cease hostilities – when the bell signalled the end of the round. 'You've not so much as laid a glove on her and she's making you look like a "something" idiot.'

'I'll get her in the next round!' Binnie promised and, before submitting herself to the ministrations of her seconds, elaborated. 'I'll pound her tits flat, see if I don't!'

* * * * *

'You've got her on the run, Miz Agnes!' Matilda Boomer enthused, fanning her employer with a towel.

'I've been lucky so far,' the brunette answered, studying her opponent with experienced eyes. 'She's far from finished yet and she *knows* she doesn't have a patsy on her hands now. So she'll be more careful.'

The clang of the bell to start the second round demonstrated how accurately Agnes Hickok had assessed the situation.

Showing none of the over confidence which had caused her so much misfortune and suffering in the first round, Binnie Gates still bore in determinedly rather than sparring for an opening as she and the brunette came together. What was more, although Agnes had refrained from taking opportunities to do so presented by her earlier incautious behaviour, she aimed deliberate punches into the breasts as often as chances were presented. After receiving the fourth to that extremely sensitive region of the feminine anatomy, however, the brunette started to respond in kind and she was equally effective.

The round passed to the accompaniment of great applause and encouragement from the onlookers, all of whom had lost their disappointment over Calamity Jane having failed to put in the promised appearance, but without either woman gaining any noticeable ascendancy. Nor did the pace of the action slacken during the third round. Hard blows were delivered and received, the tendency on each contender's part being to concentrate on attack rather than defensive tactics. It was increasingly obvious, however, that each was determined to win and Agnes was fully as competent as Binnie to indulge in whatever means were employed in an attempt to ensure victory.

During the second minute, the blonde contrived to come out of a clinch with the brunette's head held under her left arm. Before Siddons could extract her from the illegal position, Agnes was subjected to half a dozen hard punches to her face. Staggering away on being released, she took advantage of the referee expostulating with Binnie to retaliate in kind. Moving in, she caught the blonde in the same manner and, counting each loudly as it was landed, rained six equally hard blows on the defenceless features. Then, on releasing her grip, she backed away and did not offer to resume the attack until Binnie was recovered sufficiently to fight back.

Two further rounds went by, hard fought and gruelling, but without either woman gaining more than a brief ascendancy over the other at any time. Certainly the spectators had no reason to complain as they were being treated to a bout of sustained fury and determination to win far in excess of anything they had seen previously. One thing became increasingly apparent as the bout progressed. Despite having given no indication of possessing such knowledge since her arrival in Cheyenne, Agnes was a very skilful boxer. Furthermore, she proved herself well able to cope with the dirty fighting tricks employed by her far from scrupulous opponent.

Early in the fourth round, after landing a blow to the breast which inflicted sufficient pain to allow her to dominate the action and return some of the punishment she had received in the first, the blonde took advantage of the clinch Agnes went into in an attempt to hold off her onslaught. Bringing up her left hand, she jabbed its thumb into the brunette's right eye and, being at the other side, the referee could not see her. Almost immediately, she was subjected to similar treatment and swung around so Siddons could see what she, but not her opponent, was doing. On being ordered to break, each swung a blow which caused them to stagger some distance apart as they obeyed. They returned to the fray almost immediately, but the ascendancy Binnie had acquired was gone.

Knocking the brunette down in the middle of the fifth, not for the first time since the bout commenced, the blonde pretended to stumble and dropped knees first on to her. Although Siddons suspected this was anything except an accident, he could not prove it and had no option but to let the fight go on. The round went to Binnie and Agnes looked very relieved when the timekeeper signified it was at an end. She was sent to the canvas again early in the sixth, landing supine. Deciding to improve upon the effects of the previous 'accident', the blonde faked another slip, falling sideways with the intention of landing full length on her victim. An instant before the contact was made, however, the brunette rolled clear and she hit the floor with a bone jarring thud instead of descending on the comparatively soft and yielding body she had expected to break her fall. She beat the count, but only just and spent the rest of the round suffering for her trickery to such an extent she had to be helped back to her corner by the seconds when the bell sounded.

Watching the two women working desperately on his wife, Warren Gates felt a sense of apprehension which was not caused through sympathy with her bruised, bloody and battered condition. Experienced in such matters, he realised that only a miracle could save her. A study of the almost as badly marked and exhausted brunette as her very skilled maid worked to revive her warned him that one was unlikely to be forthcoming.

'Wait until they start again,' the saloonkeeper said *sotto voce*, but with such intensity that the two men at his table gave him their immediate attention. 'Then we're getting the hell out of here.'

'Why?' Hubert Kretzmer demanded, having found the sight of the two women fighting bare to the waist a most stimulating experience despite his earlier misgivings.

'Because if Binnie gets licked – and I reckon she's going to real soon,' Gates replied, 'I don't have nowhere near enough money to pay out on all the bets I took.'

'But *I'm* not involved in *that*!' Kretzmer protested, his voice registering alarm.

'Do what you want,' Gates answered coldly. 'But me, I'm getting the hell out of it. I know what they do to folks who welch on bets and it's not going to happen to *me*.'

'I'm with *you*, Warrie!' Booth asserted.

At that moment, the bell sounded and, watching his companions leave their seats as the two women went to the centre of the ring, Kretzmer rose to follow them. Looking back, before the men who had parted to let them through closed in again, Gates cursed himself for having delayed so long. He decided his only hope was that everybody would be so excited at the end of the fight that his absence would not be noticed in time to have measures taken which would prevent him from fleeing as he wanted to do.

Even if Binnie had been aware of her husband's desertion and wanted to help him, she could not have served his purpose better. Sheer guts kept her going, aided by Agnes's greatly weakened condition, for longer than he had anticipated. Stumbling on legs which had lost their earlier bounce and propulsive power, she contrived to keep on her feet in spite of being reduced to the state known as 'following'; whereby her hands repeatedly went to the point at which she had been hit, instead of trying to anticipate and block the blow before it reached her.

Nor, in spite of her desperate desire to terminate the fight and gain relief from her own suffering, was the brunette able to do so for over two minutes. In fact, as the seconds dragged by on leaden feet, she found herself sobbing for breath and almost collapsing from the waves of exhaustion threatening to engulf her. At last, when she felt she could do no more, the memory of why she was engaged in the gruelling fight came to her again. As on the other occasions when she was in dire straits, the thought of what might be happening to Calamity Jane gave her the stimulus she so badly needed. Gathering every last dreg of strength and energy she possessed, she pushed the tottering blonde away from the mauling clinch they were in. Having done so, she threw a punch that had everything she could manage by way of stamina behind it. Her thinly gloved left fist buried itself into the already swollen and bruised left breast. It proved the last straw for the recipient. Giving a croaking gasp, Binnie toppled backwards. For a moment after she landed supine, her body writhed and twitched, then she became still.

Oblivious of the thunderous applause and roars of 'Good for you, Mrs Wild Bill!' which were ringing out on all sides of the ring, Agnes stumbled to and fell against the ropes. It was their support alone which kept her on her feet while Siddons was carrying out the pure formality of making the count and she collapsed as she was being proclaimed the winner.

* * * * *

'Going some place, gents?' inquired a sardonic voice identified as that of Marshal Grover Rymer by the three men who were leaving by the rear entrance of Battling Binnie's Ring Saloon.

Swinging their gaze in the direction from which the words had come, Warren Gates, Hubert Kretzmer and Albert Booth found to their consternation that the local peace officer was not alone It was not the fact that one of the people with him was the solemn faced man they knew only as 'Solomon Wisdom' which created the alarm they experienced. Even discounting the reason why they were quitting the building, carrying all the money from its safe, the sight of Calamity Jane warned them that they were in a very precarious position.

'Get them!' Gates roared, letting fall the bulky saddlebags he was carrying and, instead of reaching for his holstered revolver, he started to raise the walking cane grasped in his right hand, the left going across to take hold of it too.

Knowing the purpose behind the saloonkeeper's apparently pointless action, Booth started to grab for his weapon. However, in spite of having a revolver in a shoulder holster, Kretzmer made no attempt to duplicate the young man's behaviour. Instead, spinning on his heel, he started to flee as fast as his legs would carry him.

Sharing Booth's knowledge that the stick concealed a firearm, its owner's way of handling it precluding the possibility of the weapon being a sword, U.S. Marshal Solly Cole had no hesitation over the manner in which he responded. Dipping his right hand, he demonstrated that his unusual mode of carrying the Roger & Spencer put him at no disadvantage when there was a need to extract it rapidly. Shoving it forward, through the open front of the holster, he thumbed back the hammer while tilting the barrel into alignment and fired all in one single blur of motion.

Swiftly fired though it might have been, the .44 bullet from Cole's gun tore into Gates' head. Jerked backwards by the impact, he pressed the trigger and caused his disguised weapon to be discharged harmlessly into the air. He was dead before his reeling body collided with and bounced from the wall of the saloon.

Slower than Cole, Rymer still proved adequate for the occasion. His revolver was out and barked, sending its lead into Booth's chest before the young man was able to complete the draw and throw down on him.

Nor was Kretzmer any more successful in his bid to escape. Liberating her whip, which she had retrieved along with her property from her abductors at the cabin, Calamity sent out its long lash to snare his right leg and bring him crashing to the ground. Transferring the handle to her left hand, she twisted free the Navy Colt with the right and strolled forward.

'Stay put, feller!' the girl commanded, cocking and lining the weapon. 'I didn't like the look of you from the start. You put me in mind of a city slicker's sold me a watch one time. The son-of-a-bitching thing stopped running afore *he* did.'

* * * * *

'Kretzmer's confirmed all Miss S – your *amigo* told us, Calam,' Solly Cole informed the red-head, as they sat at the table in the dining-room of the owners' quarters of the Hickoks' hotel. The time was half past one in the afternoon on the day after the hectic events which had brought them together. 'He was being backed by that Eastern bunch who're trying to take hold of towns out West.'

Arriving after Calamity Jane's rescue had been effected by

Belle Starr and her two companions, the peace officers had been informed of Warren Gates's reasons for supporting Hubert Kretzmer's candidature for mayor. Leaving Belle and her men to take care of the survivors of the abduction, without offering to ask what had brought her to the vicinity, they had escorted the red-head back to town. Approaching the rear of the saloon with the intention of entering by the back door and arresting its owner for complicity in the kidnapping, they had heard the tumult arising from the end of the fight and were in time to prevent the trio from escaping.

'Something tells me he *won't* be getting elected,' Calamity commented with a grin, but it faded as their hostess hobbled slowly into the room, with every indication that each movement was causing pain. 'Whooee! That must have been one hell of a fight you and her put up!'

There was good cause for the comment. In addition to the way Agnes Hickok was walking, her left eye was reduced to a discoloured slit, her nose badly swollen and top lip puffed to twice its size.

'It's not a thing I'd want to go through again,' the brunette admitted, lowering herself gingerly into the chair Cole drew out for her. After she had heard the story of their adventures, she asked, 'What's going to happen to Mrs Gates? From what Mattie was telling me, she'll have to sell the saloon to pay off the bets her husband took and, on top of everything else, I think that's punishment enough.'

'It's not *my* place to do anything about her,' Cole answered. 'And Grove' Rymer's of the same mind as you-all. He says, so long's she pays off and gets out of Cheyenne, he's satisfied with letting her go.'

'I'm pleased to hear it,' Agnes said sincerely. 'Much as I've always disliked her, I've got to admit she's a dead game fighter.'

'And I know one even gamer,' Calamity Jane declared, looking with open admiration at the brunette and remembering how she had been so confident of attaining victory over the woman who had inflicted the injuries. 'By cracky, I reckon I'll not be sorry to be moving on myself afore somebody wants *me* to lock horns with *you,* Mrs Wild Bill.'

APPENDIX ONE

Deserted by her husband, Charlotte Canary decided the best way she could assure a future for her children was to leave them in a St Louis convent and head west to seek her fortune. However, there had been too much of her lively, reckless spirit in her eldest daughter, Martha Jane, for the scheme to be entirely successful. Rebelling against the strict life being imposed by the nuns, the girl celebrated her sixteenth birthday by running away. Hiding in one of Cecil 'Dobe' Killem's freight wagons, she travelled some twelve miles from the city before being discovered. She might have been sent back to the convent, but the cook had been too drunk to work. One of the things the girl had learned at the convent was good, plain cooking. The meal she had prepared was so good that Killem yielded to her request to be taken to Wichita, Kansas, where she claimed she had an aunt who would give her a home.

Before the outfit had reached its destination, raiding Sioux warriors who wiped out two other outfits failed to locate them. What was more, the goods they were carrying had been sold so advantageously that the whole crew received a bonus and their employer was offered a lucrative contract to deliver goods farther west. Learning that the aunt was a figment of the girl's imagination and regarding her as a good luck charm, the drivers had prevailed upon Killem to let her stay with them. Not that he, having taken a liking to her for her spunk and cheerful nature, had taken much persuading.

At first, Martha had helped the cook and carried out other menial duties, wearing male clothing for convenience. She soon graduated to driving and, learning fast, in a short while there was little she could not do in that line of work. Not only could she harness and drive a Conestoga wagon's six horse team, she carried out its maintenance to Killem's exacting requirements. She was taught to use a long lashed bull whip as an inducement to activity or as a weapon, to handle firearms and generally take care of herself on the open ranges of the West. Nor did her self reliance end there. Visiting saloons with the rest of the outfit, she had frequently been called upon to defend herself against the objections of the female denizens who resented her trespassing upon their domain. Leading a much more active and healthy life than the saloongirls, she had only once been beaten in a fight;[1] although the lady outlaw, Belle Starr, had held her to a hard fought draw when they first met.[2]

Courageous, loyal to her friends, happy go-lucky and generous to such an extent that she deliberately lost a saloon she had inherited jointly with a professional gambler, Frank Derringer,[3] the girl had a penchant for becoming involved in dangerous and precarious situations. Visiting New Orleans, she had acted as a decoy to lure the Strangler, a notorious mass murderer, to his doom.[4] While helping deliver supplies to an Army post, she had fought with a female professional pugilist and rescued an Army officer captured by Indians.[5] In Texas, she had helped wipe out a wave of cattle stealing which was threatening to cause a range war.[6] What started out as a peaceful journey as a passenger on the stagecoach had ended with her driving it and taking part in the capture of the criminals who robbed it.[7] Going to visit a ranch which had been left to her, accompanied by the Ysabel Kid,[8] she was nearly killed when a

[1] The story of how the defeat came about is told in the '*Better Than Calamity*' episode of *THE WILDCATS*. J.T.E.

[2] Told in: '*The Bounty On Belle Starr's Scalp*' Episode of *TROUBLED RANGE, or CALAMITY, MARK AND BELLE*. J.T.E.

[3] Told in: *COLD DECK, HOT LEAD*. J.T.E.

[4] Told in: *THE BULL WHIP BREED*. J.T.E.

[5] Told in: *TROUBLE TRAIL*. J.T.E.

[6] Told in: *THE COW THIEVES*. J.T.E.

[7] Told in: *CALAMITY SPELLS TROUBLE*. J.T.E.

[8] Details of the Ysabel Kid's career are given in the author's *Floating Outfit* series. J.T.E.

rival claimant had her fastened on a log which was to be sent through a circular saw.[9] She had also played a major part in averting an Indian uprising in Canada in the company of Belle 'the Rebel Spy', Boyd, q.v., and a British Secret Service agent, Captain Patrick 'the Remittance Kid' Reeder.[10] Later, while on a big game hunt with a visiting British sportsman and his sister, she was kidnapped.[11]

Among her friends, she counted the members of General Jackson Baines 'Ole Devil' Hardin, C.S.A.'s legendary floating outfit; being on particularly intimate terms with the handsome blond giant, Mark Counter.[12] She also, on one memorable occasion, posed as the wife of its leader, Captain Dustine Edward Marsden 'Dusty' Fog, C.S.A. and assisted him in dealing with a band of land grabbers.[13] Another close acquaintance was James Butler 'Wild Bill' Hickok and she captured his murderer on the day he was killed.[14]

Because of her penchant for finding trouble and becoming involved in brawls, the girl soon acquired the sobriquet by which she became famous throughout the West and beyond.

People called her 'Calamity Jane'.

[9] Told in: *WHITE STALLION, RED MARE.* J.T.E.

[10] Told in: *THE WHIP AND THE WAR LANCE.* J.T.E.

[11] Told in: *THE BIG HUNT.* J.T.E.

[12] Calamity Jane's main meetings with Mark Counter are told in the titles referred to in Footnotes One, Two and Eleven. She also appeared with him in: *THE BAD BUNCH, THE FORTUNE HUNTERS, TERROR VALLEY* and *GUNS IN THE NIGHT.* J.T.E.

[13] Told in: '*A Wife for Dusty Fog*' episode of *THE SMALL TEXAN.* J.T.E.

[14] Told in: *Part Seven, 'Deadwood, August 2nd, 1876' of J.T.'s HUNDREDTH.* J.T.E.

APPENDIX TWO

Wanting a son and learning that his wife, Electra, could not have any more children, Vincent Charles Boyd had given his only daughter, Belle,[1] a thorough training in several subjects not normally regarded as being necessary for the upbringing of a wealthy Southron girl. At seventeen, she could ride – astride or side-saddle – as well as any of her male neighbours, men who were to help provide the Confederate States with its superlative cavalry. In addition, she was a skilled performer with an *épée-de-combat* or a sabre,[2] an excellent shot with any kind of firearm and an expert at *savate*, the French sport of foot and fist boxing. All of which accomplishments were soon to become very useful to her.

Shortly before the commencement of the War Between The States, a mob of pro-Union fanatics stormed the Boyd plantation. Before they were driven off by the family's Negro servants, they had murdered Belle's parents and set fire to her home. She was wounded in the fighting and, on recovering, joined her cousin, Rose Greenhow, who was operating a successful spy ring.[3] Wanting to find the leaders of the mob, who had become members of the United States' Secret Service, Belle had not been content to remain in one place. Instead, she had undertaken the dangerous task of

[1] Among other details discovered by the world's foremost fictionist genealogist Philip José Farmer, q.v., it was established that Belle Boyd was the grand-aunt of Jane, Lady Greystoke, née Porter, whose history is recorded in the *TARZAN OF THE APES* series of biographies by Edgar Rice Burroughs. J.T.E.

[2] An *épée-de-combat* is used mainly for thrusting with the point when on foot and a sabre primarily for slashing with the edge from the back of a horse. J.T.E.

[3] Some details of Rose Greenhow's career are given in: *KILL DUSTY FOG!* J.T.E.

delivering other members of the ring's information to the Confederate authorities. Adding an ability for disguise, dialects and lock-picking[4] to her other accomplishments, she had gained such proficiency that she earned the sobriquet, the 'Rebel Spy'. She had also graduated to more important and risky assignments. On two occasions, she had worked with Captain Edward Marsden 'Dusty' Fog, C.S.A., q.v.[5] and a third had brought her into her first contact with the Ysabel Kid, q.v., and his father, Big Sam Ysabel.[6] However, she had not concluded her quest for vengeance upon the murderers of her parents until just after the War Between The States ended.[7]

While the 'Yankees' might have had reason to hate the Rebel Spy when she was engaged upon her duties against them, the majority had had no cause to feel other than gratitude towards her after peace was reached by the meeting in the Appamattox Court House. On signing the oath of allegiance to the Union, she was enrolled in the United States' Secret Service by its new controller, General Philo Handiman. Despite all the trouble she had given that organization during the hostilities, she served it with loyalty and efficiency. Her participation in thwarting a plot to assassinate President Ulysses Simpson Grant had prevented friction and, possibly another war, between the Northern and Southern states.[8] Assisted by Martha 'Calamity Jane' Canary, q.v., Betty Hardin, and the lady outlaw, Belle Starr, she had brought an end to the reign of terror created by a murderous gang of female outlaws.[9] With the aid of General Jackson Baines 'Ole Devil' Hardin, C.S.A.'s floating outfit,[10] she had

[4] An example of Belle Boyd's lock-picking prowess is given in *Part Eight*, '*Affair Of Honour*' of *J.T.'s HUNDREDTH*. J.T.E.

[5] Told in: *THE COLT AND THE SABRE* and *THE REBEL SPY*. J.T.E.

[6] Told in: *THE BLOODY BORDER*. J.T.E.

[7] Told in: *BACK TO THE BLOODY BORDER*. J.T.E.

[8] Told in: *THE HOODED RIDERS*. J.T.E.

[9] Told in: *THE BAD BUNCH*. J.T.E.

[10] 'Floating outfit': a group of from four to six cowhands employed on a large ranch to work its back ranges, the more distant sections of the property. Taking food in a chuck wagon, or 'greasy sack' on the back of a mule, they would be away from the ranch house for long periods and so

broken up the Brotherhood For Southron Freedom and had refused to let her former loyalty to the Confederate States interfere with her actions.[11] After having helped avert diplomatic difficulties with the Republic of Haiti in the same company,[12] she had joined with Captain Patrick 'the Remittance Kid' Reeder[13] and first Lieutenant Edward Ballinger of the Chicago Police Department,[14] then later Calamity Jane, in wrecking two attempts by European anarchists to create hostility between the United States and Great Britain.[15] She had then once more joined forces with Belle Starr and the Ysabel Kid when involved in the efforts of the international criminal Octavius Xavier 'the Ox' Guillemot to gain possession of James Bowie's knife.[16]

---

were always selected from the tophands. Because of General Jackson Baines 'Ole Devil' Hardin's prominence in the affairs of Texas, the floating outfit of his OD Connected ranch were frequently sent to assist friends who found themselves in trouble or endangered. Details of the General's career are given in the author's *Ole Devil Hardin*, *Civil War* and *Floating Outfit* series and his death is recorded in: *DOC LEROY, M.D.* J.T.E.

[11] Told in: *TO ARMS! TO ARMS, IN DIXIE!* and *THE SOUTH WILL RISE AGAIN.* J.T.E.

[12] Told in: *SET A-FOOT.* J.T.E.

[13] The researches of Philip José Farmer have established that Captain (later Major General Sir) Patrick Reeder (K.C.B., V.C., D.S.O., M.C. and Bar) was the uncle of the celebrated British detective, Mr J. G. Reeder, whose biography is recorded in: *ROOM 13, THE MIND OF MR J. G. REEDER, RED ACES, MR J. G. REEDER RETURNS* and *TERROR KEEP* by Edgar Wallace and whose organisation played a prominent part in the events described in the author's *'CAP' FOG, TEXAS RANGER, MEET MR J. G. REEDER.* J.T.E.

[14] The researches of Philip José Farmer suggest that Lieutenant Edward Ballinger's grandson Frank held a similar rank in the Chicago Police Department at a later date and his exploits formed the basis of the 1957 television series *M SQUAD* starring Lee Marvin. J.T.E.

[15] Told in: *THE REMITTANCE KID* and *THE WHIP AND THE WAR LANCE.* J.T.E.

[16] Told in: *THE QUEST FOR BOWIE'S BLADE.* J.T.E.

APPENDIX THREE

Unlike her partner, Deputy Sheriff Bradford Counter,[1] Woman Deputy Alice Fayde entered the Rockabye County Sheriff's office by conventional means. Prior to her appointment, she had served seven years in the Gusher City Police Department's Bureau of Women Officers, rising through the ranks from walking a beat to becoming a sergeant in the Detective Bureau. She had served in such diverse divisions as Evans Park – the slum area known as the 'Bad Bit' – and the high-rent Upton Heights. In addition, she had worked in various specialist divisions as Traffic, Juvenile and Narcotics. All of which had combined to give her a very thorough knowledge of law enforcement duties. Furthermore, she was an excellent shot with a handgun and skilled in unarmed combat. As a deputy, she had a rank equivalent to a lieutenant in the G.C.P.D.'s Patrol Bureau, or a detective sergeant.

In addition to their other duties, the Sheriff's Office were responsible for the investigation of homicides and twenty-two other legal infractions – such as wife-beating, bigamy, train wrecking, assault – which might end in murder throughout Rockabye County. The idea of handling the latter crimes was so that, if death should result from their commission, the officers in charge would have knowledge of the facts leading up to it.

The Sheriff's Office based in the Gusher Department of Public Safety Building worked a two-watch rota. The Day

[1] Details regarding the career of Deputy Sheriff Bradford Counter are given in the author's *Rockabye County* series. He is the great-grandson of Mark Counter, q.v., and the look-alike cousin of James Allenvale 'Bunduki' Gunn, q.v. J.T.E.

Watch commenced at eight in the morning and ended at four in the afternoon and the Night Watch continued from four until midnight. If deputies were required between midnight and eight in the morning, they would be called from their homes by the G.C.P.D.'s Business Office which was manned for twenty-four hours a day.

APPENDIX FOUR

Always something of a tomboy, Dawn Drummond-Clayton had – with her parents' full approval – duplicated the lessons in martial arts and wilderness survival that her inseparable companion, James Allenvale 'Bunduki' Gunn,[1] was receiving. Even during her formal and conventional education, which had not been neglected, she had contrived to keep up her training and did not forget what she had been taught. In addition, while attending Roedean,[2] she had taken part in every permissible form of sporting and athletic activity, excelling in them all. However, like Bunduki, she had become completely disenchanted by the blatantly one-sided political bias and hypocrisy of the international sporting bodies and authorities, who banned some countries and yet allowed other, more viciously restrictive regimes to compete. So, in spite of being a world class athlete, gymnast, swimmer and fencer with sabre or épée, she refused to compete in their events. For all that, she invariably kept herself at the peak of physical condition.

As was the case with Bunduki, much of Dawn's perfect physical health stemmed from being allowed to share in the longevity pills obtained by his adoptive parents.[3] Specimens

[1] Further details regarding James Allenvale 'Bunduki' Gunn are given in the author's *Bunduki* series. J.T.E.

[2] Although, as is told in the first Footnote of this volume's *Part One*, Dawn Drummond-Clayton's parents served with Miss Amelia Penelope Diana Benkinsop in 'Group Thirteen', for reasons explained in *BLONDE GENIUS*, their family background did not meet the special qualifications for her to be allowed to attend Benkinsop's Academy For The Daughters Of Gentlefolk. J.T.E.

[3] For the reasons explained in *Part Twelve* '*The* Mchawi's *Powers* of *J.T.'s HUNDREDTH*, we can no longer disclose the identities of Bunduki's adoptive parents. J.T.E.

had been given to Dr Clark Savage, Jr,[4] for analysis and reproduction. He discovered that, in addition to slowing down the ageing process in human beings – granting those who took them what amounted to immortality, barring accidental death, suicide, or murder – they also gave immunity from practically every tropical disease and destroyed all such harmful internal parasites as the various nematode worms – commonly called 'hookworms' – of the genera *Necator* which might be ingested while eating the raw flesh of wild animals.[5] This was to become a matter of some importance when, shortly after the events recorded in this volume, she and Bunduki were transported by the 'Suppliers' to the primitive planet of Zillikian. There, too, she was to require all her training and skill in order to survive.

[4] Details of Clark Savage Jr.'s life and adventures are recorded in Kenneth Robeson's extensive series of *Doc Savage* biographies and in: *DOC SAVAGE, His Apocalyptic Life* by Philip José Farmer. The latter elaborates upon the source of the longevity pills. J.T.E.

[5] Unfortunately, Doc Savage was unable to isolate the immunity element so that it could be reproduced without the added effect of increasing the recipient's life expectancy. The latter factor, taken with the human race's ever multiplying birthrate, would have led to Earth becoming over-populated. So it was considered the pills were unsuitable for general use and they were never released to the public. J.T.E.

DOC LEROY, M.D. by J. T. EDSON

Marvin Eldridge Leroy had been on the point of leaving home
to attend medical college when bushwhack lead cut down his
parents. Although he was forced to abandon his plans and take
a job as a cowhand, he never forgot his ambition of following
in his father's footsteps and becoming a qualified doctor.
Working on ranches, or driving cattle over the northbound
trails to the Kansas railheads, he took every opportunity to
continue his medical studies – and gradually he earned a
reputation as a doctor . . . people even called him 'Doc'. There
were men, women and children alive who would have been
dead without his assistance. There were also men who had
died at his hands – experience had made him lightning fast with
a Colt . . .

0 552 10406 X – 50p

OLE DEVIL AT SAN JACINTO by J. T. EDSON

In 1835, the oppressions of Presidente Antonio Lopez de Santa
Anna had driven the colonists in Texas to rebellion. Major
General Sam Houston, realizing that his small force could only
hope to face the vast Mexican army when conditions were
favourable, had ordered a tactical withdrawal to the east.

At last, on Thursday, April 21st, 1836, Houston decided that
the time had come to make a stand. The Mexican Army, fifteen
hundred strong, was on the banks of the San Jacinto river:
Houston, with half that number, launched the attack that would
decide the future of Texas.

0 552 10505 8 – 60p

A SELECTED LIST OF CORGI WESTERNS
FOR YOUR READING PLEASURE

WHILE EVERY EFFORT IS MADE TO KEEP PRICES LOW, IT IS SOME-
TIMES NECESSARY TO INCREASE PRICES AT SHORT NOTICE.
CORGI BOOKS RESERVE THE RIGHT TO SHOW AND CHARGE NEW
RETAIL PRICES ON COVERS WHICH MAY DIFFER FROM THOSE
ADVERTISED IN THE TEXT OR ELSEWHERE.

THE PRICES SHOWN BELOW WERE CORRECT AT THE TIME OF
GOING TO PRESS (DECEMBER '79).

J. T. EDSON
- ☐ 07840 9   THE REBEL SPY NO. 1   65p
- ☐ 07841 7   THE BAD BUNCH NO. 2   65p
- ☐ 07844 1   THE TEXAN NO. 3   65p
- ☐ 10880 4   BEGUINAGE IS DEAD NO. 84   65p
- ☐ 10925 8   THE REMITTANCE KID NO. 85   65p
- ☐ 10964 9   THE WHIP AND THE WARLANCE NO. 86   65p

LOUIS L'AMOUR
- ☐ 09058 1   RIDE THE DARK TRAIL   65p
- ☐ 10084 6   MAN FROM BROKEN HILLS   65p
- ☐ 09027 1   SACKETT   65p
- ☐ 10853 7   THE MOUNTAIN VALLEY WAR   65p

OLIVER STRANGE
- ☐ 08810 2   SUDDEN – OUTLAWED   60p
- ☐ 09063 8   SUDDEN – GOLDSEEKER   60p
- ☐ 08811 0   SUDDEN   60p

JOHN J. McLAGLEN
- ☐ 10788 3   HERNE THE HUNTER 8: CROSS–DRAW   60p
- ☐ 10834 0   HERNE THE HUNTER 9: MASSACRE!   65p
- ☐ 11080 9   HERNE THE HUNTER 10: VIGILANTE!   65p

JAMES W. MARVIN
- ☐ 11099 X   CROW 1: THE RED HILLS   75p

All these books are available at your bookshop or newsagent ; or can be ordered direct from the publisher. Just tick the titles you want and fill in the form below.

CORGI BOOKS, Cash Sales Department, P.O. Box 11, Falmouth, Cornwall.

Please send cheque or postal order, no currency.

U.K. send 25p for first book plus 10p per copy for each additional book ordered to a maximum charge of £1.05p to cover the cost of postage and packing.

B.F.P.O. and Eire allow 25p for first book plus 10p per copy for the next 8 books, thereafter 5p per book.

Overseas customers please allow 40p for the first book and 12p per copy for each additional book.

NAME (block letters) ....

ADDRESS ....

(DECEMBER 1979) ....